A MOMENT TO LOVE

Books by Tracie Peterson

The Hope of Cheyenne
A Constant Love
Designed with Love
A Moment to Love

The Heart of Cheyenne
A Love Discovered
A Choice Considered
A Truth Revealed

Pictures of the Heart
Remember Me
Finding Us
Knowing You

The Jewels of Kalispell*
The Heart's Choice
With Each Tomorrow
An Unexpected Grace

Love on the Santa Fe
Along the Rio Grande
Beyond the Desert Sands
Under the Starry Skies

Ladies of the Lake
Destined for You
Forever My Own
Waiting on Love

Willamette Brides
Secrets of My Heart
The Way of Love
Forever by Your Side

The Treasures of Nome*
Forever Hidden
Endless Mercy
Ever Constant

Brookstone Brides
When You Are Near
Wherever You Go
What Comes My Way

Golden Gate Secrets
In Places Hidden
In Dreams Forgotten
In Times Gone By

Heart of the Frontier
Treasured Grace
Beloved Hope
Cherished Mercy

The Heart of Alaska*
In the Shadow of Denali
Out of the Ashes
Under the Midnight Sun

Sapphire Brides
A Treasure Concealed
A Beauty Refined
A Love Transformed

Brides of Seattle
Steadfast Heart
Refining Fire
Love Everlasting

For a complete list of Tracie's books, visit TraciePeterson.com.

*with Kimberley Woodhouse

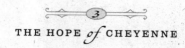

THE HOPE *of* CHEYENNE

TRACIE PETERSON

a division of Baker Publishing Group
Minneapolis, Minnesota

© 2025 by Peterson Ink, Inc.

Published by Bethany House Publishers
Minneapolis, Minnesota
BethanyHouse.com

Bethany House Publishers is a division of
Baker Publishing Group, Grand Rapids, Michigan

Printed in the United States of America

All rights reserved. No part of this publication may be reproduced, stored in a retrieval system, or transmitted in any form or by any means—for example, electronic, photocopy, recording—without the prior written permission of the publisher. The only exception is brief quotations in printed reviews.

Library of Congress Cataloging-in-Publication Data
Names: Peterson, Tracie, author.
Title: A moment to love / Tracie Peterson.
Description: Minneapolis, Minnesota : Bethany House, a division of Baker Publishing Group, 2025. | Series: The Hope of Cheyenne ; 3
Identifiers: LCCN 2025002673 | ISBN 9780764241123 (paper) | ISBN 9780764245701 (cloth) | ISBN 9780764245718 (large print) | ISBN 9781493451319 (ebook)
Subjects: LCSH: Christian fiction. | LCGFT: Romance fiction. | Novels.
Classification: LCC PS3566.E7717 M66 2025 | DDC 813/.54—dc23/eng/20250221
LC record available at https://lccn.loc.gov/2025002673

Scripture quotations are from the King James Version of the Bible.

This book is a work of fiction. Names, characters, places, and incidents are the product of the author's imagination or are used fictitiously. Any resemblance to actual events, locales, or persons, living or dead, is coincidental.

Cover design by LOOK Design Group, Peter Glöege

Baker Publishing Group publications use paper produced from sustainable forestry practices and postconsumer waste whenever possible.

25 26 27 28 29 30 31   7 6 5 4 3 2 1

Prologue

APRIL 10, 1865
PHILADELPHIA, PA

After four years of conflict and bitterness between the North and the South, General Robert E. Lee had surrendered the day before to Ulysses S. Grant at a place called Appomattox Court House. For all his ten years, Spencer Duval could only remember the country at war, and he really had no idea of what surrender might mean for the country.

His father, Harrison Duval, had been gone much of the time during the conflict, working for the Pinkerton Agency, hunting down deserters, profiteers, and other criminal types who sought to benefit from the country's condition. Spencer and his mother, meanwhile, kept the home fires burning in Philadelphia while they prayed for Pa's safety as he performed his job. They prayed, too, for the war to stay far away from the city of "Brotherly Love." Nothing was more terrifying to Spencer's mother than the thought of a war being fought in their hometown. It was frightening enough to both when the Battles of Gettysburg and Hanover had taken place just two years earlier. But now, Spencer knew a sense of victory and elation, as most of the celebratory crowd did. His father, however, said there was still a lot to do. That gave Spencer's mother very little to celebrate. She worried that his job with the Pinkertons was even more dangerous than fighting in the war.

"It's good that this war has finally come to an end," Spencer's father said as the people around them continued to celebrate. He'd only been home a few days, and even then, it was only because the man he was hunting had been seen in town. Spencer had been intrigued by his father's stories of Eugene Astor, a bounty jumper, who pretended to sign up to fight in the war only to take the bonuses offered and flee. Astor and his brothers had made a career over the last four years of robbing the government this way. Theirs was a treasonable act, and Astor's two younger brothers had already been killed, having refused to surrender when caught by the Pinkertons. Only Astor remained, and he had proven nearly impossible to locate, much less to capture.

Pa tightened his hold on Spencer's shoulder. Spencer looked up to see his father's jaw clench. It was a sure sign that he'd spotted something.

"Do you see him, Pa?"

Spencer had been instructed to not gawk around while looking for the man. Not that he knew what Eugene Astor looked like. Pa had explained to Spencer what they were doing and why. He figured a man in the crowd with a boy at his side wouldn't be seen as a threat—definitely not thought of as a Pinkerton.

The idea of being a part of his father's covert operation had excited Spencer to no end. He longed to grow up and follow in his father's footsteps. He wanted so much to be a Pinkerton and root out criminals. When his father was able to be home, Spencer had listened to his stories for hours while Pa worked to show Spencer tricks of the trade. Now

Spencer got to see him working up close. It was the proudest day of his life.

"No, I thought I did, but it wasn't him."

A man took the podium atop the outdoor stage and began. "Friends, we have come here today to give thanks to God for putting an end to this horrific and abominable war. Let us pray."

Spencer noted most everyone bowed their head in reverence, but Pa took the opportunity to sweep the crowd. He didn't miss a thing, and Spencer tried to be just as astute. Pa always told him to look for the thing that was out of the ordinary—the person or object that didn't belong.

Every man in attendance had removed his hat, including Pa, with exception to one. That man now eased across the farthest gathering of people. He wasn't at all remarkable in appearance, but the fact that he wasn't praying with the others struck Spencer as odd. It struck his father as infinitely more. He took off, weaving his way through the audience. Spencer had his instructions for just such an occasion. He was to move closer to the stage and stay there until his father returned for him. But something in Spencer refused to be obedient. He followed his father instead.

The man who'd been moving through the back of the crowd disappeared down the alley. Pa gave pursuit, and Spencer did as well. Somewhere among the people was Pa's best friend, Aloysius Gable, another Pinkerton. Spencer glanced around, wondering if Al had already maneuvered around to corner Astor.

The prayer was finished, and the speaker introduced someone to great applause. Spencer didn't care. He was struggling to keep up with his father. It dawned on him more than once that he needed to stop and return to the stage. His father had made it clear that he wasn't to follow him. It was far too dangerous. Astor hadn't been known to kill, but now that he knew his brothers were dead, there was no telling what he might be compelled to do. He just might be of a mind to seek revenge. Pa and Al had even discussed the possibility that Astor would seek to shoot down some of the men speaking that day. One of the men had been among Harrison Duval's team searching for Astor's brothers. When they had been fired upon by Calvin Astor, it was this man who had claimed the death shot. He was also a war hero and slated to speak to the crowd since he was home recovering from a wound that had taken his left arm.

Pa disappeared momentarily, and Spencer strained to see where he'd gone. They were headed for the alley, so Spencer kept moving toward it, hoping that once he cleared the mass of people, he'd once again see his father.

He broke through a group of older women, who chided him for his rudeness. He tipped his cap and pressed on. There would be time to apologize later. Right now, he had to find Pa. He stepped into the alley, seeing nothing. The applause erupting behind him made it difficult to listen for telltale signs of activity, but Spencer finally heard what sounded like boot steps running. He sprang forward, hoping he might reach his father and Al just as they caught their man.

The sound of gunfire slowed his pace only momentarily. Spencer knew his father was armed. Al, too, carried a gun. But it was a single shot he heard. No exchange. Whoever had fired had either hit his mark or was prevented from firing again.

Something came barreling around the corner. Spencer pressed himself against the brick wall and watched as a couple of stray cats yowled and a large wooly dog came bounding down the alley. The stench of trash assaulted Spencer's nose as the cats ripped through some unmentionable slop and dashed across the toes of Spencer's boots. The dog followed, not giving Spencer a second glance.

There was shouting around the next corner, and Spencer

refocused on why he'd come in the first place. He crept down the alley, doing his best to be silent and invisible. The alley came to a T at the end, and Spencer knew he'd have to go right or left. The voices were coming from the right, and so he figured that was where he'd find his father. He hugged the wall with his cheek flat against the brick. In complete silence, he stretched his neck just far enough to peek around the corner.

"You're done for, Astor. Give up like a man and accept your consequences." Pa stood facing a man matching the description of Astor he had shared prior to their outing. The man was of medium build with brown hair combed straight back, and a scar edged the left side of his lower jaw. He was dressed like many of the politicians and businessmen who'd amassed around the stage. Three-piece brown suit with a frock coat that hit mid-thigh. White shirt, black tie, and scuffed black boots. He also held a revolver, not so unlike the one Spencer's father held.

"We are at a standoff, Pinkerton, but I will end that momentarily. If I'm not mistaken, you are one of the men who helped corner my brothers. Poor Calvin and Amos." He gave a tsking sound. "Cut down in their prime, and for what?"

"For lying to the government. For signing up to fight, taking the bonuses offered, and then deserting. Last count I had, you and your brothers pulled that scheme nearly two hundred times in as many towns."

Astor smiled. "And that was worthy of death? We did what we had to in order to keep our mother fed and housed. If we'd left to fight in that senseless war, she'd have been alone. What did we do that harmed anyone? What did they do that was worthy of death?"

Spencer watched his father. His gaze never left Astor. He stood completely still, gun leveled at the man's heart. Astor did likewise. Neither seemed to so much as blink.

"You broke the law and deceived the government. You weren't the only bounty jumpers, but you were the busiest."

"You can hardly fault a man for being good at what he does," Astor said with a slight shrug. "But that still isn't call to kill two young men who'd never harmed a single soul in their lives."

"They were the first to draw their guns and fire. They refused to surrender and meant to kill us."

"Out of desperation to remain alive."

"We wouldn't have shot them if they'd surrendered." Spencer noted the tone of his father's voice. He wanted an end to this matter . . . a peaceful solution. His father hated taking a life and would much rather take Astor in alive. At least he hadn't dropped to one knee. His father routinely knelt when certain he would have to fire his weapon. The fact that he hadn't yet gave Spencer hope that maybe Astor would give up.

"No, you would have hanged them for treason."

"This is at an end, Astor. You're under arrest. Drop the gun."

For just a moment, Spencer thought the man was going to comply—then everything seemed to happen at once. Pa went down on his knee as Astor's eyes narrowed, and a single shot rang out.

Spencer watched his father's head lurch. The revolver fell from his hands. Without thinking, Spencer screamed and ran to him. "Pa!" He grabbed hold of his father's shoulders and pulled him back. The life had gone out of his eyes. He was dead.

"No, Pa. Don't die. Pa!" Spencer cradled his father's bloody head and rocked back and forth, mindless of Astor.

To his surprise, the man came and knelt beside them. "The score has been settled. This is a day to end all wars."

Spencer stared at him from tear-blurred eyes and memorized everything about Astor. His score might have been settled, but not Spencer's. One day he would find Eugene Astor and make him pay for what he'd done.

A shout and several voices sounded from somewhere behind Spencer. Astor got to his feet and fled down the alley. Spencer could still hear the man's voice. Still see his blue eyes search Spencer's face as if looking for an answer to a question he'd not posed.

The score hasn't been settled, Mr. Astor. This war isn't over.

January 23, 1875
Cheyenne, Wyoming Territory

"What did Mrs. Ostrander mean that you're my mama-sister?" Carrie Vogel asked her mother.

"Carrie, we've talked about this before." Her mother kept ironing the shirt she was working on. "Remember we talked about how my mama died when I was young, and yours died when you were born. Her name was Sarah, and she was my stepmother. She married our father. When she died, I promised her I would take care of you."

"I don't understand. How can you be my mama and my sister?" Carrie struggled to comprehend it all. She had never really paid much attention to what was being said about the origins of her birth. Marybeth Vogel was the only mother she had ever known. Edward Vogel was her father.

Her mother stopped the ironing and fixed Carrie with a loving gaze. "Come sit with me, and we'll go over everything one more time." She put the iron on the stove and then headed for the door.

Carrie followed her mother to the living room and took a seat in the chair her father usually sat in. A warming fire blazed in the hearth as Mama took to her rocking chair. Carrie glanced to the window to see snow was falling once again. It was beautiful, and she usually loved to watch it, but today she felt such a jumble of feelings. Ever since Mrs. Ostrander had said what she had, Carrie had the sensation that she was about to lose something important. Mama began to speak, and Carrie forced her attention away from the snow.

"Sarah Murphy was your mother—the woman who gave birth to you. She married our father, Klaus Kruger, in 1864. You were born in December of 1865. I was eighteen years old, and Sarah and I had become close friends. I loved her very much. I loved you too. I always wanted brothers and sisters.

"You were so tiny and sweet. A head of blond wavy hair just as you have now. And those blue eyes—eyes with a color unlike any other."

Carrie had often had complete strangers talk about her eyes. They were powerful and a shade very unlike most. They seemed almost illuminated, her mama had once said. As if a light were shining within them to draw everyone's attention to their intense blue color.

"From the moment I first saw you, I fell in love with you." Mama smiled in her reassuring way. "I was so proud to be your big sister. But then your mama got sicker, and the doctor said he couldn't save her. She knew she was going to die and made me promise to take care of you—to be your mama. I gave my word that I would, and she died. From that moment on, I became your mama. I've taken care of you as a mama would. I've loved you and raised you. Our father died when you were not quite two years old, but he, too, loved you very much. He often said that his girls reminded him of happier times. Then I married Edward Vogel—the man you know as your papa. He gave you his name, just as he did me. He loves you dearly, just as he loves your brothers and sister."

"So nobody is my real mama and papa?"

"Oh, Carrie, come here." Mama held her arms open, and Carrie climbed up on her lap. Mama's arms wrapped around her. "Carrie, sometimes real mamas and papas are people who come along to do the job when others couldn't. I'm no less your mother just because I was your sister first. We're just doubly blessed with a bond that can never be broken. Your papa feels the same way. We are your real parents and always will be."

Carrie placed her head on Mama's shoulder. "It just feels sad. I wish I could have known my mama Sarah and papa Klaus."

"I wish you could have too. I tell you what. I can tell you stories about them so that you'll get to know them that way. I can tell you how much they loved you and how happy they were to know they had a beautiful baby girl. Your mama was so excited for you to be born. She and I made all sorts of little clothes for you. I saved some of the ones she made because I wanted you to have them one day. Would you like to see them now?"

Carrie jumped up. "Yes! Where are they?"

Mama laughed and headed for her bedroom. "They're in my hope chest. Come along."

They went into her parents' bedroom, and at the foot of the bed was a large cedar chest. Mama opened it and began going through some of the contents. She set aside an assortment of things and finally pulled up a paper-wrapped bundle.

Untying the twine, Mama glanced at Carrie. "Your mama could make the most beautiful clothes. Her embroidery was absolute perfection. She made these little gowns for you while you grew inside of her. She made a lot of other things, too, but these were special."

She pulled open the paper, and inside there were three tiny gowns in a soft white material. Mama held up one and pointed to the tiny rosebuds embroidered across the bodice.

"I didn't bring a lot with us when we moved here from Indiana, but these were important to keep. I wanted to make sure you had something to remember your—" She paused and then smiled. "To remember Mama-Sarah. She was sure that you were going to be a girl. She said she just felt confident of that. Still, she wanted to be prudent, so she only made these three special gowns."

Carrie touched the edge of the lace that graced the tiny collar. Mama-Sarah had made this specially for her.

"Why did she die?" Carrie traced the rosebuds, trying hard to understand a loss that she couldn't explain.

"She was just too weak to pull through."

"Did me getting born kill her?"

Mama shook her head and reached out to touch Carrie's cheek. "She was never all that strong, but she was so excited about having a baby. There was only good about you." Mama smiled and put the rosebud gown aside to show Carrie the next.

It was hard to concentrate on the gowns, however. Carrie's heart broke at the thought of the woman who'd given her life. It was hard for her to understand why God had allowed her to die. Still, she loved her mama and papa, even if they weren't the ones who had been there first.

"You can keep these with your special things, if you like," Mama said, refolding the gowns when Carrie got up and moved to the edge of the bed.

"Is Mama-Sarah with Jesus?"

"Absolutely. Papa-Klaus too. You know the Bible says when we are absent from our earthly bodies, we are present with the Lord. Your mother and our father loved Jesus very much. They would be so proud that you decided to accept Jesus as your Savior. You'll see them again one day, Carrie. They both loved God and served Him faithfully. Until then, I hope you'll know how much your papa and I love you."

Mama finished rewrapping the baby gowns, then came to where Carrie sat. She handed her the bundle, then put a finger under her chin to raise her face.

"No matter what else has happened in your life, you have been dearly loved by many people and always will be."

Although Mama's words were comforting, Carrie couldn't help but feel that there was still something missing. Something that left a hole in her heart that couldn't be filled.

1

Chicago, Illinois
January 1890

Dr. Carrie Vogel read through the *American Journal of Insanity* for the latest articles and information on brain conditions and disorders. When she reached page six, she froze, unable to believe what she was seeing. She scanned the article not once but twice, flipping the page back and forth as if the words might change.

All her life, Carrie had been fascinated with medicine and healing. About the age of twelve, she started reading everything she could get her hands on about medicine, and she helped Mama tend wounds and deliver babies. She advanced through school quickly, and by the time she'd reached sixteen, she was ready for college, just as her younger brother Daniel was now. It had taken some doing to talk her parents into allowing her to leave home and attend a women's college. It was an even harder time getting the college to accept her at such a young age, but after testing her both on paper and orally, everyone acquiesced. Carrie was something of a prodigy, and the college was suddenly excited to welcome her.

Carrie had wondered if her birth mother might have lived had there been a better doctor. But as she studied more and received intense training, she found her interests led her away from women's birthing needs and instead sent her to the brain. Few understood her passion for neuroscience and brain trauma, but since first hearing about Phineas Gage, Carrie had known this would be her field of interest.

In 1848, Gage had been a twenty-five-year-old railroad foreman when a large tamping bar ripped through his head. It entered just below his left cheek, flew up behind his eye and out the top of his skull, destroying much of his left frontal lobe. Even more amazing, he lived to tell about it for a dozen years after that fateful day. The great "American Crowbar Case," as it was often referenced, was a topic doctors discussed at length had they any interest whatsoever in the brain.

Carrie had been a second-year student at the Women's Medical College in Chicago not so many years ago. The doctor speaking had been one of her favorite professors. He was an older man in his sixties with a passion for the brain and the medical conditions that involved it. Dr. Ambrose Willaby had been his name, and his reputation was known far and wide. He had worked with the very team of doctors who had treated Gage. When he taught about Gage, he was intricate in his information, explaining everything and drawing out the details.

"*Mr. Gage was working with black powder, and the tamping bar sparked an explosion. Mr. Gage had his mouth open to speak when the bar, some one and a quarter inches in diameter and three feet-seven inches long ripped through the left side of his face at a point just forward of the mandible and outside the maxilla. It proceeded behind the left occipital orbit in an upward trajectory and into the left frontal lobe of the brain. It exited out of the cranium, flying approximately eighty feet away. When retrieved, the tamp bar showed both blood and brain matter.*"

Carrie remembered Phineas Gage had suffered only momentary unconsciousness and a brief seizure. He had quickly settled and begun talking to the men around him. On his way to the doctor, he even wrote notes in his foreman's ledger. His resilience had baffled and drawn interest from people far and wide.

Carrie knew it was difficult enough to be a woman physician. People seemed tolerant of a female doctor tending to women and their complaints, but one who wanted to work in brain research was an object of scorn or amusement.

Thankfully, Carrie had found Dr. Oswald Nelson felt differently. Oswald was a gentle soul whose work and studies of the brain had been going on for a lot longer than Carrie's. In fact, he was fifteen years her senior and had, like her, gone to college at a young age. Both were superb in their studies, making perfect marks, and both had a great passion for medicine. The most troublesome difference was that Carrie was a woman and Oswald, a man. His interest was applauded and hailed as brilliant, while Carrie was often condemned for her unnatural fascination with the sciences. She tolerated people's attitudes toward her interest but had never stopped longing for a day when her work as a doctor could be as equally respected as Oswald's.

Now, however, it didn't look like that was ever going to happen. She looked back at the article in the journal and felt a surge of bitter anger. Betrayal! Oswald had taken her work and published it as his own. Again.

How could he do such an abominable thing? They were engaged to be married. They worked side by side at his research clinic. He constantly sought her opinion and had convinced her that he respected her as an equal.

Carrie had worked for over a year with a thirteen-year-old girl who had received horrific brain damage after a carriage accident. Her skull had been crushed on one side, but the impact had shifted the brain, causing damage on the other side as well. Once the patient stabilized and it became clear she would live, most of her doctors gave up believing she would ever be able to do anything. She had lost her ability to speak, didn't seem to recognize her family, and reverted in many ways to an infantile-like state. But Carrie worked with her, keeping meticulous notes and experimenting with various therapies to help the child reclaim her skills. Little by little, her recovery was remarkable.

Carrie had shared the details with Oswald. She was convinced that because of the girl's youth, the brain had been able to redirect impulses and heal itself. Her speculation on how this was managed had been of great interest to other doctors, and Oswald had taken credit for all of her work.

Letting out a primal grunt of disgust, Carrie threw the journal across her office, slamming it against the open door. Her rage didn't stop there. She'd had it. She was done with Oswald and his lies. He'd taken credit for her research on at least four other occasions. Enough was enough.

She reached for a stack of books and papers, uncertain what to do. For the moment, she figured to go home to her little apartment, which unfortunately happened to be in the same building as Oswald's. No doubt as soon as he learned she was gone, he'd seek her out, and she had no desire to ever see him again. Not even to denounce his actions.

She glanced at the top of her desk and swept most of the contents into the right top drawer and locked it. With her anger still mounting, Carrie knew she needed to leave before she took it out on the other workers.

But it was too late. The noise had already attracted attention, and someone had obviously gone to the lab to tell Oswald because he now stood in her doorway.

"Whatever is wrong, my love?"

Carrie stopped and pointed at him. "You! You are what's wrong. How dare you?"

He gave her a confused expression and drew his hand to his chest. "What have I done to upset you like this?" He moved to close the door and noted the journal on the floor. Without a word, he picked it up.

"You stole my work. You took credit for my research and my insight. You took my discoveries from the months I've spent with patients and claimed it for your own."

He closed the door and turned to face her. His soft expression was gone, and instead, it was replaced by the determined look Carrie knew all too well.

"My dear, we've spoken of this before. You are a woman and new to this field. I am a longtime veteran, and the industry knows my name well. No one is going to listen to you as a researcher. I'm really doing you a favor."

"Well, your favor has changed my mind about everything." She reached for a carpet bag that she often used to transport books back and forth from her home to the office. There wasn't a great deal of research done on the type of things she hoped to learn, but through the years she'd managed to accumulate some helpful material, and she wasn't about to leave it for Oswald Nelson to use or dispose of.

"You're obviously upset, and I understand. Why don't we go enjoy a sumptuous dinner and talk about this in a calmer environment."

Carrie stopped again and looked at him. "I am a good doctor. I was the top of my class."

"A class for women."

"It's a highly regarded college. You've said so yourself on many occasions."

He smirked. It was the one thing he knew better than to do, and Carrie found the last bit of respect she had for him dwindle away.

"Carrie, you're upset, and in time you'll see that this was all for the best."

"What I see is a man who has clearly come to the end of his ability to find his own discoveries. Therefore, I quit. Not only this job, I quit you. There is no love where there is no trust."

"Now, stop being a child and think about this. We make an incredible team. Your research and my fame will take us far. People will give credence to what you believe, and the discoveries you make will be placed in the archives of education for the future. You cannot accomplish that on your own. No one is going to listen to you, and if you leave me, I'll make sure they don't."

"Do your worst, Oswald." His threats had the strange result of calming her. She shook her head. "I'm not in the least bit concerned. My reputation precedes me, and my research and discoveries will speak for themselves. You aren't the only doctor searching for answers. There are a great many other people working toward a better understanding of the brain. And, if you'll recall, I've been invited by several of those brilliant doctors to come and work with them."

"But with a letter from me, you will no longer be wanted. I can make it so that you can never practice medicine, much less be taken seriously in research."

"So great is your love, Oswald." Despite his threats, she suddenly felt sorry for him. She had been providing him with a phase of research that had taken them in a completely different direction. A direction that had taken other scientific teams by surprise. She hadn't argued when he'd gone to lecture and speak one-on-one with numerous doctors and researchers. He had assured her that he would give her equal credit. Over the past year, however, it was becoming more and more obvious that this wasn't the case, and in the article, he hadn't mentioned her at all. He'd taken full credit for all the information.

"Don't give me that look of pity, Carrie. I can and will do just fine without you."

"Yes, perhaps you'll find another adoring student to take under your wing. Someone who is innovative and thinks in ways that go outside the normal parameters set by science. But you'll never really understand how my mind works." She turned to load several books in her bag. "I'd rather be a librarian and never read another medical journal than live with your deceit."

As if he finally understood her sincerity, Oswald took another direction. He moved closer and held out his hands.

"I'm sorry. I didn't mean to go off like that. It's just that . . . well, it reminded me of my father. He is always so insulting, as you know."

Oswald's father was also a doctor, but his field of expertise was the heart. Carrie had seen the man cut Oswald down to size on more than one occasion.

"Perhaps I can see now that he had good reason for his lack of tolerance where you are concerned."

"You can't mean that. You know how I've suffered because of him. And you know that my love for you is undying. I didn't mean to upset you so. I will send a letter immediately to the journal and tell them that you were the one who discovered our findings. We can take equal credit, and though we might not receive the attention and esteem that could have come otherwise, I'm sure we can work beyond this upset."

Carrie could hardly believe that he was still insisting she stay. "No, Oswald. I'm done with you. Finished. I have no feelings left for you whatsoever except bitterness and remorse for having ever allowed you in my life."

He came around the desk and took hold of her arm. "Please let your anger go. You'll see in the long run that this will all work out. You'll one day make a name for yourself."

"Yes. Yes, I will. But the name I make will be as Vogel, not

Nelson. I'm not sorry to end this, Oswald. I thought I might be, but I'm not. Now release me. I want to finish collecting my things and go."

"Those things belong to our clinic."

"No, they don't. I have a great many personal texts I've brought in from home, and they're coming with me. If you don't like it, bring in the police. I have receipts to show for everything." She gave him a sad smile. "Keeping files and papers on purchases as well as my research findings was something you taught me. I practice it faithfully."

She turned and pulled a stack of books from the shelf behind her desk. "If you have any honor left, you'll forward the money owed me." She finished with the books and picked up a pen. Writing out her father and mother's address, she wondered for a moment if she could really return home. She'd been gone for so long. She had tried to remain on everyone's good side, and her parents had come to see her just last year. They'd no doubt welcome her with open arms, but could she stay there without her work? Her life would have little meaning without it.

"Here, this is the address of my parents in Cheyenne. Forward a bank draft there." She pushed the paper toward his side of the desk, then closed the carpet bag. For a moment, she wished it could be different. She didn't care about the engagement, but they had been doing such great research here in Chicago. She would miss her patients and the people she had worked with.

"I know this isn't what you want to do. I can read you like a book."

His comment brought her out of her thoughts. "No, you can't. I'm written in a language you can't even begin to comprehend." With that, she took up the carpet bag. It was much too heavy, but she wasn't about to show that to Oswald.

Instead, she moved across the office, back straight and gaze fixed on the door.

"You'll come back. You can't leave like this. You will miss it too much."

Carrie kept walking, knowing that if she stopped, she might change her mind. She would miss the work. More than she wanted to admit.

"What a horrible thing to do to someone," Rebecca Broadstreet declared as she shared a cup of tea with Carrie.

Rebecca lived with her elderly aunt and mother in the apartment next to Carrie's. She had heard Carrie come home, and since it was the middle of the day, she felt it her duty to investigate. Carrie had no reason to keep the truth from Rebecca and so shared every detail, including the broken engagement.

"He's wicked to have stolen your work."

Carrie nursed her tea and nodded. "I should have expected it. He's done it so many times before. Still, I thought we'd talked it through, and he was going to stop and start giving me full credit for that which was mine."

"I suppose as a man he doesn't feel the need to acknowledge your work. It's probably easy to steal your thoughts and print them as his own. After all, who is going to believe a lady could be smarter than a man?"

"It's never even been about being smarter. I love what I do. I want to keep researching the brain so that we can fix the problems that come from disease and injury. There are all sorts of issues that affect the brain, and if we can do research and study them out, we can find cures. We can better understand how the brain works. Right now, it's still such a mystery."

"Goodness, but you are so far above me in those kinds of things." Rebecca put her cup down and shook her head. "I can't imagine finding such things important, but I'm so glad that you do. Since my mama has gotten old, she doesn't reason at all like she did when she was younger. Sometimes she doesn't even know where she's at or who I am. If you were to figure out what caused her to forget, well, I know there are a great many people in the world who would be grateful for a cure."

Carrie gave her friend a smile. "There's just so much to learn, and I know God has put me here to work in this field. I guess I just don't know what He has in mind for me to do next."

"Give Him time, deary. He'll show you. He's faithful to us that way. Trust in Him. That's what gets me through each day. Sometimes, when my mama doesn't know me, I wonder how I can possibly go on. How can a mother forget her child? I ask myself. But then I remind myself, she might have forgotten, but I haven't. She was the best of mothers and deserves the best of care."

"You're a good woman, Rebecca. Your mother and her sister are blessed to have you."

Rebecca blushed and lowered her head. "I hope you'll find a way to help them someday."

Carrie reached out and patted her hand. "I hope so too."

For several long moments neither woman spoke, then at the sound of a whistle blowing from somewhere in the city, Rebecca's head popped up, and she jumped to her feet. "Oh goodness. It's five o'clock. I must get supper on. Thanks for the tea." She moved to the door and opened it. She paused, however, and looked back.

"You're better off without him. I'll miss you, but going home is a good idea. I just feel it here," she said, putting her hand over her heart. Then she left, closing the door behind her.

Carrie hoped she was right. It wasn't that there were any real problems between her and her folks. They all got along well enough. Carrie and her siblings were quite close. She couldn't really explain why she'd moved away . . . stayed away. She supposed, in part, her reasonings had to do with the scars of the past. She loved her parents, but for all the love they'd given, Carrie still had an empty place in her heart. How could she ever admit to that? They'd been good to her. They had loved her as much as anyone could love another person. Carrie had always felt safe and protected by her father and mother. So how could she be so ungracious as to mourn the loss of something she'd never had in the first place?

At times she hated herself for feeling that way. Yet, there was always that emptiness. Always that sense of something missing that should have been there. She found herself unable to stop wondering about her birth father and mother. What might her life have been had they lived?

She heaved a sigh. "You've got to let it go. You are never going to know the answers to those questions. No one can possibly tell you what might have been."

She chided herself with the same words she always used when these feelings came about. Mama would have told her to pray about it and ask God for His guidance, but God had been the one to orchestrate it all. He was the one with power over life and death. He could have left her parents to raise her, but He hadn't. He'd taken them. He'd taken them both away from a baby, and that was something Carrie simply could not understand.

The very idea seemed cruel and unfeeling. And frankly, for all her prayers, there never seemed any comfort being offered. Of course, she would never denounce God. She believed completely in the salvation offered her through Jesus and did her best to honor the commandments He'd given.

"But I fail miserably at loving God with all my heart and soul and mind, and loving others as myself." The whispered confession seemed to echo off the walls.

She glanced at the clock and began to gather up the tea things. She had theater rehearsal tonight at six. Long ago, when faced with needing to do something to take her mind off research and patient cases, Carrie had signed up for the local theater group of amateurs. They were a fun bunch and performed for free to entertain poor children in a wide variety of plays and musicals that seemed to bring unlimited happiness.

Carrie knew she'd have to let them know she was leaving. She had no desire to stick around Chicago for any longer than she needed to. She would explain to her landlord in the morning and pack up her belongings. By this time next week, she'd be back in Cheyenne.

If only that thought would bring comfort.

2

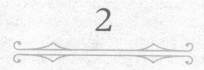

Play practice had gone well, but Spencer's heart wasn't in it. He was grateful just to be the understudy for the handsome prince rather than hold the starring role. Acting had been a wonderful release for him over the years. After particularly stressful days seeking to bring criminals to justice with the Pinkertons, Spencer felt the theater was an escape. Not only that, but many of the men and women employed by the Pinkerton Agency were encouraged to take on acting lessons in order to better play roles in which they might stop illegal activities.

Spencer hadn't really intended to stay with the amateur theater for as long as he had, but his attraction to Dr. Carrie Vogel had kept him interested enough to remain. Carrie was unlike most of the young women he'd met. She was brilliant and more than a little talented in a wide variety of things. Spencer had done some research into her background and education, as well as the job she currently held. She wasn't sitting around hosting tea parties or seeking to better herself in marriage. She was engaged, but Spencer could tell that the biggest attraction Carrie held for the man was their common interest in medical research. In fact, he'd done some investigating on Oswald Nelson. The man didn't come across as someone who could be trusted but, as far as Spencer knew, had done nothing illegal. Upon meeting the man, Spencer was even less impressed. But Carrie was an entirely different story.

Spencer could listen to Carrie talk about her studies for hours. She was fascinated by her patients and their needs, whereas her fiancé was fascinated with himself.

Spying Carrie, Spencer made his way to her. She seemed no more interested in playing her role as the beautiful princess than he did the role of prince's understudy. Before he could ask her what was wrong, the director approached the group.

"As you know, we have one more week before we open the play," the man began. "I need all of you to make sure you have been fitted for your costumes. We will meet every night and all day Saturday to make certain that we are ready. If you have any concerns, please voice them now."

Carrie stepped forward. "I'm afraid I am giving my notice. I learned today that I will be returning to Cheyenne in a matter of days. I know that Lydia can handle the role perfectly." She glanced at the young woman who was her backup. "I do apologize that I couldn't give you more warning."

There was a buzz of comments among the actors and actresses while the director did his best to consider the situation. Finally, he gave a nod and motioned to Lydia. "Come to my office. Mary, you come as well. Carrie, I can only imagine this has something to do with either your work or family and therefore will not pry; however, we are heartily sorry to lose you. It has been a pleasure to have you working with us this last year."

"Thank you." She turned away and headed to her dressing room.

Spencer followed at a distance. He wasn't at all sure what

was going on, but it at least gave him an answer as to why she'd seemed distracted, even troubled, that evening.

Carrie was pulling on her fitted jacket when Spencer reached the doorway. He stood silently watching . . . waiting for her to notice him. When she did, he could only offer her a smile.

"What was that all about?"

"It's a long story."

"Good, then you can tell me over a late supper. I haven't eaten yet, and you have a look that suggests you probably haven't either."

"I haven't." She picked up her purse and wool hooded cloak. "Where did you have in mind to go?"

Their friendship over the last year had given them a familiarity with each other that Spencer would have liked to have moved toward something more intimate, had Dr. Vogel not been engaged.

"I was thinking perhaps O'Malley's. They have the best Irish stew and soda bread."

Carrie actually smiled. "I should have expected that from an Irishman."

"I'm only part Irish. I could have suggested French, English, or German food just as easily," he teased.

"O'Malley's is fine. Let's go." She brushed past him, heading for the back exit. She paused only long enough to put on her gloves and pull her cloak around her shoulders, then she raised the hood to cover her lovely blond hair.

Spencer followed after her, taking hold of her arm as they stepped into the alley. "You've a taste for danger tonight. Dark alleys aren't exactly the safest place to be."

"But I'm with a Pinkerton and have no fears. I know you're armed and alert. You've already noticed the drunk at the end of the alley and the policeman who's about to roust him. I'm fairly certain you've even seen the little boy and his dog who are hiding behind that stack of pallets at the opposite end."

"What about the shirtless old man on the fire escape up three stories?"

She laughed as they continued to move in the direction of the police officer. "I saw him."

"You're getting better at observation."

"I had a good teacher." Carrie looped her arm through his. "All of your suggestions have made me a better researcher. I never imagined that Pinkerton training would help in medical findings, but careful observation is needed in both. And just as with criminal investigations, medical situations are often not what they seem."

Spencer was surprised by how carefree she suddenly seemed. He was even more surprised by the way she clung to his arm. Usually, she allowed very little physical touch.

"So tell me what's happened. Something has changed."

"Your observation skills are as good as ever." Carrie gave him a quick glance and waited until they reached the street.

The policeman was far too concerned with the drunk to give them much attention, but Spencer gave him a nod as he looked up. The man seemed to recognize Spencer as safe and nodded in return.

The streets were crowded tonight. Chicago was always alive with masses of people moving quickly from one place to another. Spencer spied several he figured to be up to no good. No doubt at least a dozen pickpockets were working the block. He'd already picked out six who were wreaking havoc.

"Keep your purse close," he whispered against Carrie's ear.

He maneuvered her through the people and past the dangers until they safely entered O'Malley's. Here, Spencer relaxed a bit. He knew the people and the layout. The folks were good, honest souls who kept the rowdies under control. And unlike most of the pubs around the neighborhood, Sean O'Malley believed in limiting his customers' drinks. When they started showing signs of becoming disorderly, he vacated them from the premises in quick order. Given Sean was six-foot-six and weighed two hundred and fifty pounds of solid muscle, few questioned his decisions. If they did choose to protest, they didn't do it more than once.

Spencer found them a table in the corner and motioned the serving girl over. She fixed him with a smile. He knew she fancied him. She'd done her best to sweet-talk him on more than one occasion.

"Spencer, for sure I've missed yar company. Yar lookin' mighty fine tonight."

"Thanks, Eileen." Spencer looked to Carrie. "Do you know what you want to eat?"

"Not really. Why don't you order for the both of us."

Spencer sensed Carrie was overwhelmed with all that she had on her mind. "We'll have the special and coffee."

"Ah, now luv, wouldn't ya want to be havin' a fine pint with yar food? And what about the lady?" Eileen winked at Spencer. "A bit of ale would thaw that ice."

"Coffee will be just fine, Eileen."

She shrugged and walked away, avoiding the customers who seemed inclined to draw her attention by being a bit too familiar.

"She's rather forward, isn't she?" Carrie said, pulling off her gloves.

"She is, but she knows I'm not interested. Now, tell me what's happened." Spencer wasted no time.

Carrie drew a deep breath and settled back against the back of the booth. "I put an end to most of my life today."

He frowned. "What do you mean by that?"

"I ended my engagement and my position at the Nelson Research Laboratory."

"Start at the beginning and tell me everything." Spencer wanted to say he was particularly interested in the part where she ended her engagement, but he said nothing.

Carrie unbuttoned her cloak and shrugged out of it. "Well, if you're really sure you want to hear it."

He laughed. "I want to know it all."

Just then Eileen returned with two coffees. It was exactly what was needed to ward off the cold. "I'll be right back with yar stew and bread."

"The coffee smells nutty," Carrie commented, bringing the cup to her nose. "I much prefer the coffee here to almost anywhere else."

"I do too. They make a good lamb stew as well."

Eileen came with their stew, as well as a plate of soda bread and butter. "Ya might wanna save room for dessert." She leaned a little closer to Spencer. "We've got a fine bread pudding and a vanilla sauce that will make you weep. There's even fresh cream if yar preferrin'."

"Eileen! Come bring me a beer!" a man yelled from across the room.

She rolled her gaze upward. "For the sake of all the saints." She shook her head and made her way back to the bar.

"Honestly, I'm not sure you're safe here," Carrie said with the hint of a smile.

Spencer laughed and tore off a piece of the soda bread. "Forget her. I want to know what's happened to you."

Over their meal, Carrie explained Nelson stealing her research and publishing it as his own. Her hurt over the betrayal left Spencer with a strong desire to pummel Nelson, but of course he wouldn't. However, he was quite happy to hear she'd ended her relationship with the man. He'd never liked him and felt he was always up to something underhanded, not that Carrie had ever spoken against him until today. Now Spencer knew why the man made him feel that way.

"I really thought we had something special," she said, pulling apart a piece of bread to dunk in her stew. "I thought he believed in me."

"He did, but only so far as it helped him get ahead. That's not your fault. He's a trickster and a thief. Men like that think only about what will make their own lives easier. Stealing your research was a simple matter for him. He knew the public would be far more accepting of new insight coming from a man. If you dared to say anything about it, he could merely point to you being a woman to have you disbelieved. He could even say you're just jealous of his brilliance and ability."

"I know. I thought of hiring a lawyer to go to the journal and explain my situation but figured no one would care. They'd think me simply a scorned woman because I'm sure Oswald will tell the world he ended our engagement. He threatened me. Told me he'd make certain to ruin my career. I don't know what to think or do. Well, I do in part. I'm going back to Cheyenne and my family. At least for a time. I need to be away from this place."

Spencer didn't like hearing her plans to leave. "I wish you wouldn't go."

"I live in the very building where Oswald lives. I'm sure to run into him and have no desire to do so. I feel certain that he believes once I calm down, I'll come crawling back. Or that I'll be at ease enough that he can come to me and beg my forgiveness. He'll promise me equality and assure me that he will never again steal my findings. But I know better. He's already done it more times than I care to admit." She shook her head. "I have no feelings left for him but anger and frustration." She paused and lowered her gaze to the table. "I don't believe it. He's here."

Spencer looked behind him and saw Dr. Nelson approaching their table. "Don't worry, Carrie. I'll keep you safe."

"I can't believe you'd be seen in a dump like this," Nelson said as he stopped at the table. "I've been searching for you everywhere. I even went to that ridiculous theater where you playact. Someone mentioned you might be here."

"There's absolutely no reason that you should have been looking for me," Carrie replied, looking up to meet his gaze. "I have nothing to say to you, Oswald."

"I think we have a great deal to say. All of this is just a misunderstanding. You need to put aside your pride and come back to the clinic in the morning. We'll forget all about this, including your indiscretion with this . . . man."

"Spencer is a good friend to me. He's never played me false, unlike you. So please just go. I have nothing more to say to you."

Carrie's blue eyes narrowed. Spencer wasn't sure what a rage of anger from this woman might look like, but there was no sense in letting her be the one to make a scene. That would only give Nelson a sense of power over her.

Spencer got to his feet and gave Oswald Nelson a small push. It was just enough to put his body between Carrie and Nelson. "I'm afraid you are interrupting our dinner. I'm going to ask you nicely to leave now. If you choose to go, then nothing further will be said or done. If, however, you desire to fight, then I can guarantee you a beating that you'll always remember."

Nelson's eyes widened, and even in the dim lighting, Spencer could see him pale. Nelson seemed to consider the matter, then backed away another step.

"Carrie, this isn't over. Letters are rolling in regarding the article. Several universities back east would like to hold a symposium on our findings. You must give me—us—another chance."

Standing beside Spencer, Carrie shook her head. "I gave you several already. I'm not fool enough to keep giving you my findings. Those were my findings—not ours, not yours. I'll be interested to see what you come up with on your own, Oswald. I think your colleagues will be as well."

"We can change the world together, Carrie. This man can't give you what I can."

"I don't want what you have to give. Spencer gives me honesty and kindness. I trust him far more than I trust you. He has never stolen from me. Never sought to undermine me or lie to me."

"All men lie, my dear. If he tells you otherwise, that proves my point." Nelson's expression turned smug, but Spencer held his temper in check. He had dealt with a hundred Nelsons over his career. Men who thought they knew more than everyone else. Men who thrived on deception.

Carrie shook her head. "I'm done with you, Oswald. Go now and leave me be."

She reclaimed her seat, and Spencer straightened, hoping the six inches he had over the shorter man would add just enough intimidation to send him on his way. For added measure he squared his shoulders and moved his arms away from his body as if to prepare for throwing a punch.

Nelson hesitated a moment, then left. Only after he'd exited O'Malley's altogether did Spencer return to his side of the table.

"I'm sorry about that," Carrie said, obviously unhappy at the situation.

"Forget about it and him."

"I just know he'll be waiting at my apartment."

"Then I'll walk you home and see you safely inside." Spencer smiled. "Don't let him ruin the evening for you. He already took the day."

She nodded. "You're right, of course. I'm not sorry to have ended the engagement, but I will miss my patients. They're good people, and helping them has been so fulfilling. I plan to continue studying on my own, but it won't be the same. Cheyenne has nothing like this going on."

"Then why return there?"

"My family is there. I haven't made myself very available to them over the last few years. My research has taken all of my attention. I know they miss me. My folks came just last year to see me. When they left, I thought my mother would never stop crying."

"I lost my mother when I was fifteen. I'd give anything for more time with her, so I can understand how you might feel."

Carrie reached out and put her hand atop his. "I will regret losing you as a friend."

"You'll never lose me, Carrie. I'll always be your friend."

"Oh, I know, but I mean leaving here and not working with you at the theater. Not being able to talk to you. I've really enjoyed our evening together, despite Oswald's interference. I always find it easy to talk to you."

"Would you two be wantin' anything else?" an older woman asked, interrupting the tender moment. Apparently Eileen was busy elsewhere.

Spencer looked to Carrie, who was already gathering her cloak and purse. He fished money out of his pocket and handed it to the woman. "No, I guess we're done here."

He followed Carrie to the door, where he helped her on with her cloak. "How soon do you plan to leave Chicago?"

Carrie handed Spencer her small purse, then did up the frogs on the cloak. She pulled on her gloves as they stepped outside. "I'm not sure. I have to pack up my apartment. Of course, most of the furnishings belong to the landlord. There are a few things I'll give to my friend Rebecca because I certainly don't want to have to ship everything home. I suppose the end of the week will be soon enough. I should probably say good-bye to a few folks I know."

"Good. Then we'll have time to get together again." He

handed her back the purse and was glad to see her tuck it under her mantle.

"You'll be busy with rehearsals. Don't forget the play is soon to open."

"I know my part well enough. Promise me you'll go out with me again. Maybe lunch on Wednesday or supper tomorrow?"

She laughed. "You sound like a desperate man. Of course we can meet again. I won't leave without saying good-bye."

Spencer offered her his arm. He didn't want her to say good-bye at all, but he knew he could hardly beg her to stay. She had to heal over all that had happened. Besides, Spencer was in no position to get serious about a woman. What was he thinking? There was still Eugene Astor to capture. Until he was able to bring that man to justice for his father's death, Spencer wasn't going to be worthy of any woman's love.

He glanced over at Carrie as they made their way to her apartment. He cared about her. He had from their first encounter. How could he just let her go? Leave for Cheyenne and never see her again?

His mind wrestled against him. He wanted Carrie in his life, but his life was devoted to hunting down Eugene Astor. That search had taken him from the East Coast to Texas and then to New York. After two years in New York, he went to St. Louis and now Chicago. He was always just a few steps behind Astor. The man was good at being hidden away. He knew what he was doing—knew, too, that the Pinkertons were on his trail.

He saw Carrie to her front door, then tipped his hat and bid her good night. Thankfully, Oswald Nelson was nowhere in sight. Spencer headed for his own apartment, anxious to figure out what he should do. He could hardly ask Carrie to remain in Chicago. Her mind was set on going home. Maybe he could tell her what he was doing and why it mattered so much. If he explained how his father had died, maybe she'd be willing to wait for him.

The Pinkertons had already spent twenty-five years on their pursuit of Astor. It could take another twenty to actually capture him. If it did, Spencer would be fifty-five by that time. His entire life would have been devoted to chasing a ghost in order to avenge his father's death. Was it worth giving up everything? It wouldn't bring his father back. Astor had to be in his sixties by now. He probably wouldn't live another twenty years.

But then Spencer remembered the look on the man's face. He didn't seem at all sorry for what he'd done. He'd left a ten-year-old boy with his dead father. No concern. No remorse. Someone had to bring Astor to justice, and Spencer had promised his dying mother that one day he would be that man.

3

"How could we have been so wrong?" Spencer paced his supervisor's office. Aloysius Gable's information regarding Eugene Astor had completely turned the investigation on its ear.

"I know this isn't what you want to hear. It's not what I wanted either, but at least now we have some certainty in where he's gone."

Spencer went to the window and watched snow fall on the buildings outside. "We've thought for years we had that certainty. Now you're telling me it was all a hoax—something Astor made up to keep us guessing for twenty-five years."

"I'm no happier about it than you. When your father and I were working this case together, we thought it a simple thing to catch Astor. We caught his brothers, after all. We thought we had him in Philadelphia, knowing that was his hometown."

"But instead, he killed my father." Spencer ran his hand through his hair and turned to face his friend. "Al, you've been good to me. You stepped up to be a father to me after mine died. You took me in to live with you when my mother passed. Finding Eugene Astor has haunted us both, and it's become my main purpose and goal, despite serving other cases for the Pinkertons. Now you're telling me that after all this time, we weren't even close."

The older man sank into his chair. "Astor is a master criminal. He's led us on a merry chase to be sure. If his mother hadn't died, we'd still be no wiser. He's just that good at hiding his whereabouts."

"So tell me what happened." Spencer felt a wave of hopelessness drive him to sit.

"As you know, we've had our best agents on Astor since he killed your father. We had trusted sources and tracked him around the country as he moved from place to place. We were perplexed by the fact that we couldn't ever seem to pin him down. Now we have proof that he didn't move around at all."

"So where's he been? Abroad?"

"No. As far as we can tell, he's been working for the Union Pacific in Wyoming Territory."

"How did you find this out?"

"Astor's mother recently passed away. We've had her under surveillance since he and his brothers first started their bounty jumper game. The postmaster reported to us when Dorcas Astor received mail. Since she lived in a small area outside of Philadelphia, it wasn't hard to keep an eye on it.

"When she died two weeks ago, someone cleaned out her house, and we took the letters from Astor as evidence. One of our staff pored through each one to see if we'd missed anything over the years. It turns out we'd missed everything of importance. Astor has been sending letters from Cheyenne to various conspirators of his. Some were located in New York, Texas, and all the other locations we thought Astor had lived. In those letters, he included one for his mother. His cohort would mail it from their town, and when it arrived to be delivered to Astor's mother, our people noted where it had come from, and you went on the hunt."

"I know that well enough. I followed those letters around for all these years."

"Exactly. Now, reading through the contents of the letters his mother had saved, we learned that Astor decided to go west with the Union Pacific almost immediately after the decision was made to move the railroad west. The letters indicate that Astor had friends working for the company, and given his background in accounting and bookkeeping, the railroad found him to be a great asset and hired him on immediately. It would seem he's lived a quiet life in Cheyenne for the last twenty years."

"If that doesn't beat all." Spencer could hardly believe what he was hearing. He had followed a long list of locations, figuring that sooner rather than later he'd pinpoint Astor before he could up and move away. When in fact, Astor had been fixed in one place. No doubt it humored the older man to imagine the time and money he'd cost the Pinkertons attempting to follow him around the country. If he hadn't stolen so much money from the government, they probably would have given up the search for him and accepted the loss.

"As far as we know, he's still there. Cheyenne is considerably larger now. However, it was hardly big enough to be considered much of a town when Astor would have settled there. We have no idea what name he's been using or where he actually resides. None of the letters to his mother made any mention of it. They commented on money he was sending her, things that were happening in Cheyenne and the area. He mentioned in several of the letters that he longed to see her and wished he could sneak her out west, but he admonished her not to try to come. Apparently, she was never healthy enough to attempt the trip. Plus, I'm sure he knew we'd be watching her every move."

"I just don't understand how we could have been so completely duped."

"We didn't expect him to be as good at this as he's been. He apparently has more intelligence than we ever gave him credit for. He's played this out perfectly. It appears in the few years between fleeing your father's murder and taking up a job with the Union Pacific, he was able to put this plan in motion. Of course, the years following the war were ones of great change."

"I can't believe all the time I've wasted. I've accomplished absolutely nothing."

"That's not true, Spence. You've worked hard for the agency on other projects as well as this one. You've received commendations and high praise for your work, in fact. Your father would be proud of you." Al smiled, though for Spencer it was bittersweet.

"But the one thing I vowed to do, the only thing that really mattered, I've failed at. My father's killer is no closer to being caught."

"Look, we know he's been living in Cheyenne somewhere. You'll go there and settle in and find him. I've already cleared things up here for you. You can leave right away. I've sent word to the Union Pacific explaining what we need. When I get that information, I'll forward it on to you."

"I need a plan. Cheyenne can't be all that big yet. Certainly not the size of Chicago or even Denver. If Astor has lived there since it was just a small town, he's bound to have made friends—folks who would hide him and even lie for him."

"It's possible. I'm not suggesting you just storm into the Union Pacific offices and demand to know where they put Eugene Astor to work. Leave that to me."

"He won't be using his real name." Spencer knew the man wasn't that stupid.

"No, I'm sure he put that aside. Look, he's gone to a lot

of trouble to stay hidden, but the letters gave us a location and even the company he works for. Cheyenne is where we need you and where you can finally arrest Eugene Astor. The man is as old as me. Nobody lives forever."

"What was the date of the last letter he sent his mother?"

"Christmas last year. As far as we know, Astor doesn't realize his mother is dead. He'll probably write her again. We have someone in Philadelphia keeping a watch. Meanwhile, we'll have you in Cheyenne."

At this, a thought came to Spencer. Carrie was going home to Cheyenne. He could travel with her. A plan began to take shape. "I have a friend who used to live in Cheyenne. She is planning to head home in a few days. Maybe I can travel with her. Her family has been there from the beginning of Cheyenne, or nearly so. They'll know most everybody from the early days, maybe even know Astor himself. Her father is the chief of police."

"That's perfect. As a fellow lawman, you could go to him and confide what you're doing."

"It might be best to keep it a secret for a time. Astor could be a dear friend of the family for all I know."

"Good point."

"I wouldn't want to give myself away. I could trust Carrie to keep my identity a secret, however. I know she'd do this for me. She'll vouch for me too. Maybe I could ask her father for a job."

"Maybe you could pretend to be married to her. Would she go that far? It would be a perfect cover. No one would question the chief of police's son-in-law."

Spencer shrugged. "I don't know, but it would be worth asking. Give me a day or two. I'll let you know."

He got to his feet and grabbed his hat. The sense of frustration and loss was replaced with the hope of a new plan. Carrie could help him to maintain cover and get him an inside view of the townspeople and the legal system there. And if she agreed to the things he had in mind, he wouldn't have to say good-bye to her. At least not yet.

Eugene Astor contemplated the days to come. Having just returned from Denver, he had hoped to be in a better frame of mind. Instead, the doctors there confirmed his worst fears. They believed a tumor was growing in his brain. A tumor that couldn't be surgically removed or treated in any way to reverse the damage it had already done. Nothing would stop it from killing him, and the time left to him was short. It was a sad ending to contemplate.

The first person who came to mind was his aging mother. She was in her eighties now and no doubt had few years left. But he had only weeks, maybe months. He would need to put his affairs in order. He picked up a pen and began to write a list of what he needed to accomplish in whatever time was left to him.

At the top of the page, he wrote a single word: *Mother*.

Under this he began to write the various things he needed to do to ensure she had what was needed. He would speak to a lawyer tomorrow. Over his years of working for the Union Pacific as Rowland Knowles, Eugene had amassed quite a large amount of money. He had found a way early on to skim a steady portion of money from the railroad using various accounting tricks he'd learned over the years. There was more than one scheme in operation at any given time, just as there was more than one bank where he placed his savings. All along the Union Pacific line, he had found places to set up his accounts and hide his money. Now he would need to arrange for that money to go to his mother. There was more than enough to take care of her until her death, even if she lived another twenty years. That's all he and his brothers had ever really cared about. Seeing to their widowed mother's needs and best interests had turned them into criminals and had cost his brothers their lives.

Their mother had been widowed at a young age with three rambunctious boys to care for. She had no other family to help her, and Eugene had watched her grow old before her time. She made only one demand on them: They must finish school. She wouldn't brook any conversation about leaving early to work full-time and ease her burden. They honored her wishes, and upon graduating, Eugene had even taken some additional courses in bookkeeping and found he excelled at the task. He soon took on a job and continued his training until he was placed in charge of accounting at a large factory. That job was where he first experimented with ways to manipulate the books and keep extra portions of money for himself. As soon as his brothers were old enough, Eugene got them hired on at the same factory, and together they were able to set their mother up comfortably so that she didn't have to work anymore.

He paused in his writing to remember his two younger brothers. Calvin and Amos had been all for the plan when he had figured out a way to make money during the war and avoid military service. Neither he nor his brothers desired to fight. Who would care for their widowed mother and make sure she had enough money to live if they were killed in battle? Who would be there to comfort her in her grief? The Astor brothers were adamant that she come first. After all, she'd put them first after their father died.

Their father had taught them to avoid the law and the public record. *"The less the government knows about you,"* their father always said, *"the better time you'll have of it."* He hadn't really approved of his sons being in public school, but it was one battle he couldn't win with their mother. Still, they never lived in one place long, moving around to avoid complications. So when the draft went out in the early years of the war, the Astor brothers weren't on anyone's list. This only served to benefit them all the more as time passed, and the idea of bounty jumping became more and more appealing.

Bounties were given to sign up to fight. At first, they were only issued after service was completed. Unfortunately, too many men died and the appeal for enlistment came to a halt. The government finally switched things around and issued payment up front in order to help families who would bid their husbands, sons, and fathers farewell. This was when bounty jumping became popular. A man could sign up for service, receive his bounty, and then desert. In big cities this was a fairly simple arrangement. After all, many a man was unknown to all save God.

Amos gave it a try first. He and Calvin had heard about it from their friends. By the time Eugene had a chance to further investigate the matter, Amos had already done the deed. Several times, in fact. He'd gone into New York City and joined a recruitment celebration going on in the five boroughs. He'd come home with hundreds in bounty money. It was impossible for any of them to ignore such a haul.

Eugene had figured they'd do it for a short time, then stop. And they had rules. They wouldn't enlist in Philadelphia. They'd never use their own names, and there was to be no drinking or celebrating. They would go and enlist, claim their bounties, then silently slip away and put as many miles between them and the city as possible. They would also keep meticulous lists of where and when they enlisted. Eugene felt certain this would prevent any possibility of getting caught. However, a great many other men had the same idea, and the government became aware of the situation and hired the Pinkertons to chase down the thieves. Many of the bounty jumpers were caught. They hadn't been as cautious as Eugene demanded.

But even with all their careful planning, the Pinkertons soon caught up with the Astor boys. First Calvin and then Amos. Both resisted and fought against incarceration and died for their efforts. Eugene was livid. They'd done nothing worthy of death. By the time the Pinkerton agent caught up to him, Eugene's anger had taken charge.

Eugene could still see the face of that child as he cradled his father and wept. Eugene hadn't meant to kill the man. He was only going to wound him, but now he was dead, and his son was a witness. He could identify Eugene. The thought of murdering the boy in cold blood was an abomination, and he quickly put it aside. He wasn't a killer, and yet he'd just killed.

Eugene could still remember the feel of the gun in his hand. Still smell the blood of the Pinkerton. Hear the sobs of his son. He was haunted by his actions that day. It was the only regret he had in life.

Killing hadn't been on their agenda, and even though Eugene held the government and the Pinkertons responsible for his brothers' deaths, he knew they, too, were as much to blame. Had they simply given up and gone quietly, there might have been a chance of escape at a later time. Eugene could have helped them. Guards could have been bribed. They didn't have to die.

A sigh escaped his lips. They had chosen their end, and he had chosen his. Well, in part. He certainly hadn't chosen a brain tumor. But at sixty, he'd had a good long life. His intelligence had allowed him to amass a tidy amount of money. He wasn't wealthy by robber baron standards, but he was comfortable. At least he had been. Now the dizziness and blurred vision came regularly and made it impossible to keep figures straight and perform his job. He'd retired his position just three weeks earlier, receiving a lifetime pass on the

Union Pacific and a plaque for his twenty years of service. And of course the money he'd embezzled over the years. Money they would never find no matter how many audits took place. Of this, Eugene was absolutely certain.

He looked at the paper once again. He had to make sure that his mother would have everything she needed. She would be heartbroken to know he was dying, but perhaps with the help of some of his friends, she'd need never know. He made himself a note to contact one of the men who'd helped him over the years. He would write a series of letters and get cash to send with each one. He could package these up and send them to his friend with the request that the letters go out once a month.

Of course, it would be nice to know how his mother was doing. He had explained to her in the letters why they couldn't communicate, but in his heart he knew how it must have devastated her. No amount of financial support could ease her loneliness.

Guilt heaped on top of guilt. Eugene had never wanted life to turn out this way. Never. He hadn't wanted to be a criminal. The bounties seemed like a harmless way to get extra money. No one person suffered for their thievery. Only the government came up short.

But he had killed Harrison Duval, and he could never make that right.

4

Carrie sorted through her clothes, deciding what to keep and what to discard. She'd been meaning to do this since first moving into the apartment after graduating from the medical college. She had a certain image to preserve, and so most of her outfits were drab little suits in tones of grays, browns, and navy blue. With these were several high-necked white blouses, equally simple and plain. In the winter, she generally added a vest for extra warmth, but otherwise the outfit was the same no matter the season.

Still, she had quite a few dresses that were more feminine in nature. She had kept these for special occasions but rarely had a chance to wear them. Now she feared they were a bit girlish for her age and position.

"Goodness, I'm only twenty-four," she murmured to her reflection in the mirror. She held a peach-colored muslin up under her chin. Mama had sent her the dress as a Christmas gift two years ago. Carrie had loved the style and fit, but she'd hardly ever worn it.

A knock on the apartment door interrupted her consideration. She left the gown on the bed and hurried to see who had come. The place was in such a disarray with crates being packed that she hoped it wasn't Rebecca looking to visit.

She opened the door to find Oswald, hat in hand. He held up his hand as if knowing she was considering slamming the door shut. "Please, give me a moment."

"What do you want?"

"I've come to apologize. I'm sorry for the way I acted at the tavern. I'm afraid seeing you there with someone else was a bit unnerving for me. Carrie, I want you back. Whatever your terms. Whatever I must do to convince you of my sincerity. I never meant to hurt you this way."

"What's done is done, Oswald. I am going home." She stepped back so he could see the packing crates.

"But you can't, Carrie. I love you. I need you. My life wouldn't matter without you."

She put her hands on her hips. "We both know that isn't true, Oswald. I suggest you stop this here and now. You forget that I've known you for four years, and in that time I've learned just about all there is to know about you. You are smug and arrogant, conceited and self-serving. You need no one and love only yourself."

"That isn't true." He stepped into the apartment, moving toward her.

Carrie took several steps back. "I've given you my answer, and now you should go. I'm leaving town for good. I have no desire to work here, especially since you threatened my professional well-being."

"It was just words. I didn't mean a thing I said."

"Which is my point exactly." She shook her head. "You've never meant anything you said to me. I don't think you're even capable of the truth."

"That's a cruel thing to say. You know that I love you."

Carrie heaved a sigh and shook her head. "Please just go. We're finished, Oswald. There's nothing left. I have other interests now."

"Like that actor? I suppose you fancy yourself in love with him."

"If I did, I wouldn't speak of it to you." She pointed to the door. "Now go. I have a lot of work to do."

But to her surprise, instead of leaving, he charged toward her, slamming her up against the wall. Carrie let out a scream, causing Oswald to drop his hat and cover her mouth with his hand.

"Shut up, you fool. Do you want to bring the building down around us?"

"Let her go, Nelson!"

Carrie watched in stunned surprise as Spencer rushed across the room and took hold of Oswald. He threw the man aside as if he'd been no more than a sack of potatoes. Oswald landed in a heap on the floor, trapped between two crates. He struggled almost humorously to remove himself from the situation.

"How dare you?" he declared, struggling to his feet.

"I might ask you the same thing." Spencer looked to Carrie. "Are you all right?"

She nodded, surprised by the way Spencer's dark eyes seemed to blaze. He turned back immediately to Oswald.

"I think you've caused more than enough trouble here, Nelson. Unless you want me to call the police, I suggest you leave."

"I only came to apologize to Carrie." He bent to retrieve his hat.

"Apologies include throwing her against the wall and smothering her with your hand?"

"I only wanted her to stop screaming. I didn't mean to scare her."

"Just go, Oswald. I don't need to hear anything more," Carrie said, coming forward. "This is good-bye. I'm sure if you go back to the Women's College of Medicine to offer one of your wonderful lectures on my discoveries, you're bound to find another female naïve enough to believe your lies."

For a moment, Oswald held his ground, but when Spencer moved toward him, he backed up all the way to the door.

"We were a good team, Carrie. Now I fear you'll never accomplish what you've set out to do."

Whether he meant it as a veiled threat or not, that was how Carrie took it. She thought to upbraid him, but then remained silent. He wasn't worth the effort.

"It's time to go, Nelson," Spencer said, taking a step in his direction.

Oswald scurried out the door. It reminded Carrie of a rat she'd chased out on New Year's Day. That thought made her smile.

"You are a strange woman, Carrie Vogel. Most would be in tears, but instead, I find you smiling." Spencer closed the door.

"Well, if you'd seen the resemblance of Oswald to the rat I ran out of my apartment a few weeks back, it would make you smile too."

"Be honest with me," Spencer said, crossing the room. "He didn't hurt you, did he?"

"No, I'm fine. He hadn't been here all that long when you showed up. I hadn't meant to scream, but his actions took me completely by surprise. Oswald has never been physical in any way. Goodness, he never even allowed for hand-holding or putting his arm around me." She laughed. "I suppose I've been a complete ninny where he's concerned. His biggest attraction for me was his research clinic. What a fool I was."

"No, you were pursuing your passion. Which is what brings me here today."

Her brow furrowed as she narrowed her eyes. "Do tell."

"You look as if you are examining a specimen. Relax, I

just need to ask a favor. But first I want to explain why it's important."

"All right. Let me put on the tea, and we can sit down like civilized folks. The place may look a complete mess, but I can still act the proper hostess."

"It's not really proper for us to be here alone," he replied, looking rather sheepish.

His appearance of discomfort endeared him all the more to Carrie. "You're right, of course. Let me get my coat, and we can go down to the café on the corner. They serve a wonderful selection of pastries. I was just thinking I'd like to sample their wares once more before leaving town."

She went to the coat-tree and took up her heavy gray tweed. Spencer helped her into the coat, then waited while she did up the buttons.

"I have to admit, you have me quite mystified as to what you wish to tell me." Carrie grabbed her black wool bonnet and gloves. "I'm ready." She secured her bonnet as she exited the apartment, then pulled on her gloves.

"Do you have your key?" Spencer asked, closing the door behind them.

"Oh, I suppose I should grab my purse." He reopened the door, and Carrie went back inside to find her bag.

It was where she'd left it on the kitchen counter. She snapped it up and hurried back out. Pulling the key from her purse, she found herself eager to hear what Spencer had to say. "So tell me what this is all about."

Spencer took the key from her and locked the door before handing it back to her safekeeping. Carrie could feel his excitement and knew that whatever he'd come to say would be quite the announcement.

They walked from the building and out into the icy air. Chicago in the wintertime was bone-chillingly cold. The dampness from the lake only served to intensify the effects.

"So you know that I'm a Pinkerton."

"Of course. We've talked about that many times."

Spencer nodded. "But I haven't talked about a longtime project of mine for the agency . . . more so for myself."

"And now you need to do so?"

Spencer took a protective hold of her arm as they came to a snowy spot that hadn't been cleared from the sidewalk.

"Yes. You see, my father was a Pinkerton, and I was with him the day he was killed. I've been after the man who did it ever since. Well, of course, not at first. I was only ten. But when I was accepted into the agency after college, I began my pursuit of him."

"I didn't know your father was murdered. How terrible, and for you to be with him when it happened . . . how awful."

"It was the worst day of my life. Even losing my mother five years later to sickness wasn't as bad, though it hurt, to be sure." He fell momentarily silent, then shrugged. "The man who is my supervisor now took me in. He was my father's best friend, and he has helped me to pursue Eugene Astor all these years."

"Astor is the man who killed your father?"

"Yes."

They reached the café and waited until they were settled inside with their orders on the way before Spencer continued.

Carrie was grateful the host had seated them by the fireplace. She was chilled through and through even though the walk was brief.

"We thought Astor was in Chicago these last few years. Letters home to his mother were postmarked as such, but now she has died, and we learned otherwise. For nearly two decades he has been working for the Union Pacific in Cheyenne."

Carrie's eyes widened. "My Cheyenne?"

"Yes!" Spencer's excitement was evident in his expression as well as his tone. "That's why I came to talk to you—to ask for your help."

"How can I possibly help you catch a murderer?"

The waitress arrived with a pot of tea and platter of tiny pastries. She placed the dish in the middle of the table. "Would you like for me to pour?" she asked.

Carrie shook her head and motioned her away. "No, no, I'll manage it, thank you."

The girl could see she was clearly not needed and left them to their discussion. Carrie lost no time and lifted the pot.

"So what is it you need from me?"

She poured the tea while Spencer began to explain. "I'd like you to pose as my wife. We'll go to Cheyenne on the train, and no one will suspect I'm there for any reason other than accompanying my wife back to her hometown. Your family is well established there, and with your father being the chief of police, I will probably be able to pass unnoticed. Perhaps even work for him since my background is law enforcement."

"I assure you, young men show up alone in Cheyenne every single day. They aren't suspect in the least. This is the frontier west we're talking about, and even though it's not that far away in miles, it's a world away in culture and behavior. There are far more single men there than women. I doubt anyone would even give you a second glance."

"I understand that. However, being associated with your family will allow me to forgo months of introductions and gaining people's trust. I know that might seem unimportant, but I assure you it's critical that I move fast. Being associated as the son-in-law of the chief of police will allow me to travel in circles that I wouldn't otherwise be allowed into, at least not until after some time proving myself. With you vouching for me and your folks in turn standing up for me, people won't question my presence."

Carrie added cream to her tea and stirred while thinking of what Spencer had said. "I suppose that does make sense. But what happens after we arrive? We can hardly live together. My parents would never allow that."

"They wouldn't need to know that we aren't actually married."

"Believe me, they would know. My mother and father have the most incredible sense for knowing when something isn't quite right. They call it spiritual discernment. Besides, after you capture your father's killer, then what? We just announce that we were never married and go on our merry ways? My reputation would be ruined."

"So then we marry."

Carrie didn't even try to hide her surprise. "What are you saying?"

He chuckled. "Carrie, we're good friends. You know and trust me. We could marry platonically and annul the marriage once Astor is caught. That way we could get a place together and your parents would be none the wiser."

"Oh my." Carrie had the cup midway to her lips and stopped. "Marry you?"

"We like each other well enough to pretend to be in love. You know me, Carrie. I would never impose myself on you, nor take liberties. You could work on your research, and I wouldn't interfere. I'm completely supportive of your interests. The things you've told me about the brain are quite fascinating. Even helpful at times."

"I'll need my brain examined if I agreed to do this." She finally sampled the tea to steady her nerves. The idea of pretending to be married to Spencer caused her stomach to quiver a bit. She'd always found him to be handsome and exceptional company. She had even thought at one time what a marvelous husband he would make some woman. Never dreaming it might be her.

"It's important I move quickly. The Pinkertons are sending me right away. Astor is notorious for finding out when a new agent is in a town. He would flee at the first chance, so it's important my arrival not be threatening in any way. It would put everyone's minds at ease regarding our appearance in Cheyenne. I have no way of knowing who might count Eugene Astor among their friends. He probably doesn't even go by that name, but we believe he's been there since 1870, and Cheyenne wasn't very big then."

"Don't I know it. I was a little girl growing up there. It was like living in the middle of nowhere at all." Carrie remembered those early years well. She had wondered even now if she could go back to the small-town life after living in Chicago.

"Do you remember knowing a man called Eugene Astor?"

Carrie considered that a moment and sipped the tea some more. The warmth did much to clear her thoughts. "No, I can't say I ever heard that name mentioned. Papa knew most everyone because of his law work. When he first arrived in Cheyenne, he was a deputy city marshal. He worked at that for several years and got to know the bad ones and the good. But I can't say that I recall ever hearing the name Eugene Astor. In fact, I don't think we even had any Astors in town." She frowned and put down her cup. "But you did say that you didn't think he would have continued to use his own name."

"Right. I think he probably took an alias. Most criminals do that to keep their identities a secret, especially if they intend to stick around and make a new life for themselves. Astor knew he was wanted not just by the law, but by the government. He knows the Pinkertons would never stop looking for him."

Carrie selected a delectable-looking cherry tart. It was a little bigger than a silver dollar, the perfect mouthful. She popped it in, hoping Spencer wouldn't think her too unladylike.

Instead of condemnation, however, Spencer did likewise with a lemon custard tart that was half again as big as the cherry. He smiled and gave her a nod. After he swallowed, he reached for another kind.

"Those really are incredible."

"I know. I don't allow myself to come here but once a month. It's too much of a temptation." She picked a couple of other treats for herself and placed them on her plate.

"You haven't said anything about the idea of marrying platonically."

"I know." Carrie toyed with the flaky dessert on her plate. "I'm trying to reconcile in my mind what that would be like. We would have to be somewhat intimate." She glanced up, afraid that she might have embarrassed Spencer. She lowered her voice. "I am a doctor, so please forgive me if I'm uncharacteristically bold about speaking the truth. I am not suggesting we share a bed, of course, but my parents are rather affectionate. They will expect us to be affectionate as well."

"Your boldness doesn't offend me, but I am curious as to what you're proposing." He grinned.

Carrie found his reaction a little intimidating. He was, after all, a very compelling man. He was self-confident and yet quite open about trusting in God for direction. His looks drew the attention of more than one woman, and his easygoing manner made him a delight to be near. Could she truly marry him and only pretend to enjoy his affection? This caused a wave of doubt to wash over her. Did she have feelings for Spencer Duval that went beyond friendship? For the past year she hadn't allowed any inappropriate thought to cross her mind because of her engagement to Oswald. But now he was no longer in the picture, and Carrie had to admit there was something about Spencer that held her attention.

"I, uh, well . . ." She could hardly believe he had her stammering. She took a drink and cleared her throat. "Sorry. I just mean that my parents will expect us to act like newlyweds. The sweet glances, the gentle touches, the spontaneous kisses. Those are the kinds of things I'm talking about."

"I think we can manage those. We've been in acting classes together and played roles where we did those kind of things."

She took another drink. "This will be different. My parents, as I said, seem to know things that others miss. It won't be easy to fool them."

"So you'll do it?"

Carrie looked down at her plate for a long moment. "I'll consider it. Let me pray on it and think it through. I want to help you."

"Well, think it through quickly. I'll need to know by tomorrow. Like I said, we need to move fast."

She looked up and met his gaze. Carrie couldn't explain what was happening to her, but even in this moment, she knew it was something that could very well change her entire future.

"Come by the apartment tomorrow, and I'll have your answer."

5

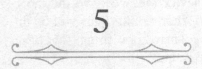

Spencer set out for Carrie's the next morning, whistling as he went. The temperature had warmed some twenty degrees and melted a good portion of the snow, making a slushy mess of the roads and sidewalks. It didn't matter, however. He felt good about the day and confident that Carrie would see the sense of his proposal.

Of course, she might say no. Somehow Spencer didn't think that would be her decision. Carrie was a logical woman. She weighed matters out in precise order. It was part of the way her brain reasoned, and he loved that about her.

As he approached her apartment building, Spencer considered how things might be, married to Carrie. In fact, he'd thought of little else since suggesting they wed to afford him the perfect cover. Carrie was an astonishing young woman. Where most women were happy to pose as inferior in intelligence, Carrie was proud of her abilities. Yet for all the awards she'd been given in school and high praise of her teachers, she was humble. She never made a fuss about getting the glory or standing out in the crowd. Not only that, but her studies in the sciences had not caused her faith in God to waver. If anything, she had told Spencer, it had strengthened her beliefs. Nothing as intricate and complicated as the human body could have just happened into existence. There had to be a divine Creator.

Spencer wiped his boots, then entered Carrie's building. He whispered a prayer as he made his way to her door. God alone knew if this was the right path, and Spencer wanted to be certain. He knocked and held his breath. Carrie was there in a moment. She had dressed simply in a skirt and blouse, as she usually did. The one surprising thing was that her long wavy hair hung loose down her back.

"I wasn't expecting you so early. I haven't even managed to pin up my hair."

"Looks beautiful down." He found himself wanting so much to touch the long strands.

"Perhaps, but that's hardly the acceptable fashion." She turned away from him and wove her way through the crates. "Give me a moment."

She disappeared into her bedroom and was gone only a few minutes. When she returned, she had braided her hair into a single plait down the back and tied it off with a piece of ribbon.

"I had just finished my Bible studies when you knocked. The time got away from me."

"What have you been studying?" Spencer glanced to the table where her Bible still lay open.

"I was reading in First John, chapter four."

"A chapter all about love," Spencer replied, remembering it well. "'Beloved, let us love one another: for love is of God; and every one that loveth is born of God, and knoweth God.'"

She smiled and went over to the open book and closed it. "'He that loveth not knoweth not God; for God is love.'"

Spencer continued. "'In this was manifested the love of God toward us, because that God sent his only begotten Son into the world, that we might live through him. Herein is love, not that we loved God, but that he loved us, and sent his Son to be the propitiation for our sins.'"

"You've memorized it well."

"I can quote the entirety of First, Second, and Third John. In fact, I have a good portion of the New Testament memorized and parts of the Old Testament as well. My mother and father were both big on Scripture memorization."

Carrie gave a bow of her head. "That's quite remarkable. I was encouraged to memorize Scripture as well, but never accomplished all that you have. My goodness, what a blessing. You can just sit and recite the verses in your head and linger on God's Word without anyone around you being the wiser."

"It's served me well on many occasions."

"Something my parents will definitely admire."

He looked at her for a long moment. "So you've decided to marry me?"

She nodded. "After a very restless night. I probably only slept an hour at the most, and that was fitful. I just kept praying and wondering if I could marry you in the manner we discussed and not betray God. Marriage is, after all, a commitment not only to each other, but to God as well."

"And what conclusion did you reach?" She'd already said she would marry him, so Spencer hesitated to even ask lest she change her mind.

"I can't marry you in a church ceremony. Not with the anticipation that as soon as you catch your man, we would annul our marriage and go our separate ways. I will, however, marry you in a civil ceremony. I will not pledge until death do us part, nor any of the other traditional promises. It would be a lie to say that I will stay with you for better or worse, in sickness and in health, for richer or poorer."

"What do you suggest then?"

"We get a justice of the peace, or if you have a judge who works with the Pinkertons that would be acceptable. So long as it's all legal, we can explain to him ahead of time that we will simply agree to be husband and wife without any extra fanfare. Then I won't feel that I'm betraying God in the matter."

Spencer was once again impressed with her simple logic. She wasn't wrapped up in emotions and rhetoric, nor did she have any false expectations about what their marriage would mean.

"I believe we can do that without any problem. I'll set things in motion immediately. I'm sure my supervisor can arrange it all. Are you free this afternoon?"

"To marry? Seems even you would have trouble getting that accomplished." She smiled, and her blue eyes seemed to twinkle. Spencer was momentarily mesmerized.

"But perhaps not," she added, seeming to study him.

Spencer pulled himself together. "No, I figure Monday will probably be the earliest, however, we should make our plans for travel and arrival in Cheyenne."

"It's certainly not what I thought I'd be doing today, but there is no reason we can't get together. However, before you go, I must ask a favor."

"Anything. You're certainly doing a huge favor for me. What do you need?"

"I need those four crates delivered to my friend's apartment. It's here in the same building. Just down the hall."

"That won't be a problem. I'll do it right now and then go take care of business. Later today, say around four, I'll come pick you up, and we'll have dinner and make our plans."

"I'll be ready and waiting."

He wanted to give a shout but wasn't really sure why. It wasn't as if they were in love and planning a great future. They would no doubt get along just fine and perhaps even enjoy their time together, but it wasn't a real marriage. Yet it felt like something wonderful had just happened. He felt even happier now than when he'd first come to see Carrie. Maybe it was just for the fact that the matter was settled, and he would hopefully soon have Astor in jail.

"Show me where to deliver them," he said, going to pick up the first wooden box.

Carrie moved to the already open door. "Just follow me."

Carrie could see in Spencer's reaction that he was quite pleased with her agreement to marry him. He didn't even seem to mind that she wanted nothing more than a civil service with no false pledges of love between them. This was a job for him. Nothing more. She had told herself this over and over through the night, and yet something in her heart suggested it could be more. Did she want it to be?

Rebecca opened the door to admit them into the apartment she shared with her mother and aunt. Spencer followed Carrie inside and glanced around.

"Where would you like me to place this crate?"

"Over here," Rebecca said, leading the way to an empty space in the living room. "I hope I've made enough room for all of the boxes."

"I think so," Carrie said, noting the space. "There are three more, and they're about the same size."

Spencer exited to retrieve another crate, while Carrie spoke to Rebecca. "I just want you to know that I plan to leave for home on Monday. I've spoken to the landlord, and he already has a waiting list of people for the apartments here, so he has no trouble in letting me out of my lease early. Plus, I did much to improve the place, so he won't have to do a thing to attract a tenant."

"It's very fortunate for you that it is a furnished apartment. That way you won't have to load up the furniture and ship it home."

Carrie laughed. "Oh, believe me, I would just sell it off or leave it here. It's not in that great of shape. Don't you remember we had to work together to nail the frame of the bed to keep it from separating at the footboard?"

Rebecca chuckled. "I do. Most of the pieces we have here are our own. We never figure to leave this place, and Mama felt so much better having her own things about her."

"Where are your mother and aunt?" Carrie glanced around as Spencer entered with two more crates. He set them down without a word and went back for the last one.

"They are out on early morning visits. In the building, of course."

"Of course." Carrie smiled. The two older women were often seen creeping along the hallway, making their visitations to some of the other elderly residents. "Well, I'm sure to see them before I go."

Spencer brought the final box and placed it with the others. Carrie gave Rebecca a hug. "We can say our good-byes later."

"Why don't you come for tea Sunday afternoon at three?" Rebecca suggested.

"I'd like that very much. Thank you." Carrie made her way back to her apartment with Spencer following close on her heel.

"I'll be going now. Are you sure you don't need me to do anything else?"

"No, I'm quite fine. There are a few things I'm giving away to other people here, but I can manage that myself." She lowered her voice with a quick glance in the direction of Rebecca's apartment. "Thank you for helping me. They struggle to keep their heads above water, and they're quite proud and hate to take charity. I confess that I included a few new things that I bought specifically for them. I figured by stressing to Rebecca that they were doing me a favor taking the stuff off my hands that they wouldn't be hesitant to take it."

"You've a tender heart, Carrie Vogel. I've known that since I first met you." Spencer lifted her hand to his lips and kissed her fingers.

Carrie's breath caught in the back of her throat, and her eyes widened.

"See, looking like that you're going to raise all sorts of suspicions with your folks. You better start practicing for this new role, or no one is ever going to believe you're madly in love with me."

She watched him go, chuckling to himself as if he'd just told a great joke. She pulled her hand to her chin, rather stupefied by what he'd done. Still, he made a good point. She was going to have to work at this or her parents would immediately see that something was wrong.

The pain was blinding, and the only thing Eugene could do was seek the comfort of his darkened bedroom. He buried his head under the pillow and moaned in agony. The mornings were always the worst.

The doctor in Denver had told him to expect the pain to worsen. The dizziness had started causing him some nausea as well, but at least his vision seemed stable today. Of course, with the pain he had little desire to read, which was a monumental disappointment. Reading was one of his few pleasures, and a new crate of books had just arrived from London the day before.

Would he live long enough to read them all?

The doctors in Denver held little hope for him. They had given him suggestions for dealing with the pain and had given him a liquid opium mixture that was deemed stronger than laudanum.

"*Take it sparingly,*" the doctor had warned. "*It's quite powerful and will render you unable to do much but sleep.*"

Sleep wasn't at all what he wanted to do. In death, he would sleep enough. At this moment in time, his desire was to see to his mother's needs and perhaps locate a doctor who had a differing opinion as to what might be done to alter his condition.

Of course, there was still Kansas City and Chicago. He had heard of doctors there who were making great strides in brain-related surgeries. The physician in Denver thought it would be a waste of time for Eugene to travel so far. He stressed that Eugene could suffer any number of problems before the tumor ended his life.

The pain began to subside a bit. Clear thought returned to remind Eugene that there was far too much to accomplish to succumb to the misery just yet. He'd seen the lawyer and made arrangements for his mother, but there was still other work to do.

He rolled to his side and took the pillow away. The small amount of light that filtered into the room from beneath the window shade forced him to look away. It still exacerbated the pain. He closed his eyes, and for reasons beyond his understanding, he thought again of that day in Philadelphia when he'd killed the Pinkerton.

Eugene had known the moment the man appeared that he meant business. It was Duval's intention to take Eugene to trial for his sins. And if he couldn't get his prisoner willingly, he would take him by force, even kill him if necessary. His drawn and cocked revolver made that much clear.

Eugene hadn't ever planned to take a life. Even after his brothers had been killed, he didn't want that kind of retribution. But the man was determined to end his life, and that Eugene could not allow.

As they raced down the alleyway, Eugene had fired a warning shot. He'd hoped it would scare off the agent. Unfortunately, that only caused the man to be more determined to catch him. Eugene had pulled back against the wall behind some piles of trash. It was poor refuge, offering very little protection, but it allowed him to wait for the Pinkerton to catch up.

Why couldn't the man have stopped his pursuit? The war was over. Why not just stop hunting him and let bygones be bygones? Eugene hadn't taken his money, and it wasn't like a few thousand dollars had set the government on its ear.

"It's not what I wanted," he muttered.

Then the terrified and anguished face of the Pinkerton's son came to mind. The boy couldn't have been more than ten or twelve. He was devastated by his father's death. It was clear to see that the two had been very close. After all, here the boy was with his father on a day of celebration.

Eugene had looked into the eyes of that poor boy and known the agony he felt. For only a moment, he had considered ending the boy's life to spare him years of misery and nightmares. But Eugene wasn't a killer. The death of that man had been a mistake. He had figured to shoot and graze him—just enough that he would have to stop chasing after him. Why had the man moved?

Sitting on the edge of the bed, Eugene did his best to push those memories aside. He needed to make his plans for going to Chicago and Kansas City. He didn't have time to waste. The doctor in Denver said he might well go blind or suffer a stroke at any given time. Memories were useless . . . his regrets even more so.

"Well, will you look at this?" Marybeth Vogel said, showing the telegram to her husband.

"What is it?" He took the paper and read the brief message before looking up at his wife.

"She's coming home?"

"That's what it says." Marybeth looked her husband in the eye. "Carrie is moving back to Cheyenne. I never thought I'd see the day."

"I wonder what's wrong."

"Why does anything have to be wrong?"

Edward put the telegram down and raised a brow. "Do you really want to pretend that you think it otherwise?"

Marybeth shook her head. "No. Something's wrong. I agree."

"We'll just need to pray about it and trust the Lord to guide us," Edward said, getting to his feet. "I'm heading to my men's Bible study, so I'll ask them to pray as well."

"Don't tell them about the surprise Carrie said she's bringing. I can't even begin to imagine what that might be, and I certainly don't want others speculating."

Edward took her in his arms and kissed her soundly. Pulling back, he grinned. "I won't say a word about the surprise."

Marybeth sighed and watched her husband go. Her mind raced with thoughts. Carrie had once said she'd never come back to Cheyenne, that she thrived on the big city life and all the amenities such places offered. When they had visited her, it was easy to see that Chicago agreed with her in every way.

A new thought came to mind, causing Marybeth to bite her lip. What if the surprise had to do with the man Carrie had engaged herself to? What if they had married already? The idea made Marybeth a little queasy. She didn't like Dr. Oswald Nelson. He had been arrogant and far too full of himself for Marybeth's taste. When they'd all gone to dinner together,

Oswald had talked on and on about himself. Marybeth had even asked him why he wanted to marry Carrie, and the answer came in rather vague comments about his own needs and desires.

She glanced upward. "Oh, Lord, please don't let her have married that man."

6

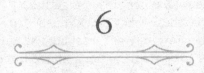

Spencer helped Carrie take off her coat and then took her bonnet as well. He was nervous about the day and what they were about to do. He'd spoken at length with Al. Together they had discussed plans for his finding Eugene Astor. There were numerous departments in which Astor could work. Even if he'd taken on his old job of accounting, there were multiple places where he might be. For all they knew, he could have left the Cheyenne area since the Union Pacific had a lot going on in Laramie and elsewhere along the line. But Cheyenne seemed the logical place to start. It was the last place Astor had mentioned to his mother, and his consequent letters said nothing of leaving. If anything, the bits of information he'd shared about Cheyenne made it clear that Astor must still reside there.

The judge's clerk took their coats and hats, then directed them to the judge's office. "Judge Benson is waiting for you." He smiled at Carrie, seeming momentarily enchanted.

Spencer hadn't taken the time to really look at Carrie until now. He turned and found her a vision in a blue gown that matched her eyes. Oh, those eyes. He studied her from the top of her carefully coiffed blond hair to the toes of her black boots.

"You've forsaken your uniform. That dress suits you very well. You are absolutely beautiful," he said, taking hold of her arm as she removed her gloves.

"Thank you. It is, after all, my wedding day." She grinned and glanced over her shoulder to the departing clerk. "After a fashion." She folded her gloves together.

Spencer noted the way her cheeks flushed. It made him feel a moment of hesitation. Was he asking too much of her? "If you don't want to do this, I'm not going to force your hand."

Carrie's head tilted ever so slightly to the side as she looked into his eyes. "I don't feel forced. I know this will help your cause. And I want to be a part of helping you. I had no idea of all that was going on in your life. In fact, I have very little knowledge of your life."

The clerk reappeared. "Go on in. He's waiting." He shooed at them like they were wayward children off to encounter a reprimanding father.

Spencer chuckled. "I guess we can talk later." He noted the gloves again. "Here, let me put those in my pocket." She handed the gloves over, then squared her shoulders as if readying herself for battle.

Still feeling a little guilty, Spencer opened the door and led Carrie inside, where Judge Benson was seated rather casually by a fireplace. It was a much homier setting than Spencer had figured on. The paneled room had a sofa and chairs up against the far windowed wall. Shelves lined the area beside and above the fireplace, and on these were legal publications that Spencer had seen on many occasions during his years with the Pinkertons.

"Come in, you two. I understand we need to conduct a wedding. Mr. Gable advised me of the details and the purpose of this union. I must say, at first I thought you were making quite the sacrifice, Mr. Duval. However, upon seeing your choice of brides, I can see it's no sacrifice to wed such a beauty."

Carrie lowered her head. "You're much too kind."

"I'm much too curious. Please tell me that Mr. Duval didn't blackmail you or otherwise force you into this marriage."

She laughed and lifted her gaze. "Not at all. Spencer and I have been dear friends for over a year now. He explained the need for this, and I agreed to help."

Spencer stepped forward. "And as Mr. Gable no doubt told you, our only stipulation was that we wanted it to be a civil ceremony without the expected vows that might be exchanged in a church service. We've agreed to a set of conditions which will see this marriage annulled once I've captured my man."

Judge Benson sobered and nodded. "I understand completely. Let's be about it." He got to his feet and crossed the room to his desk. Taking up his glasses, he glanced around as if in search of something. Finally, he picked up a piece of paper.

"Mr. Gable and I have arranged for all the legalities. I believe you are a doctor of medicine, are you not?" He didn't wait for Carrie to reply. "Would you like for me to call you Dr. Carrie Vogel in the ceremony?"

"That isn't necessary. Carrie is sufficient."

Spencer could see she was anxious, perhaps even unsure that they were doing the right thing. He took hold of her hand and gave it squeeze. She met his gaze and nodded again.

"Carrie, it is my understanding that of your own accord you have come here today to be married to Spencer Duval. Is that true?"

"It is, Your Honor."

"And Spencer, it is your uncoerced desire to be married to Carrie Vogel?"

"Yes, Your Honor."

"Do you have a ring for her?" he asked, looking at Spencer.

"I do." Spencer had managed to buy a ring from a jeweler that morning before their appointment with the judge. It wasn't anything special, just a gold band, but it seemed appropriate. He fished it out of his vest pocket and held it up.

"Well, place it on her finger, son."

Carrie held her hand up for him, and Spencer slid the ring on without fuss or ceremony. He was relieved to see it fit perfectly. His skills of observation as a Pinkerton had once again come to his aid.

"By the authority given me, I now declare that you are husband and wife. You may kiss your bride, Mr. Duval. After all, you have a great many people to convince that you're madly in love. You might as well start here."

Spencer drew Carrie a little closer and lowered his lips to hers before she could protest. He had no problem with kissing her. They'd done it before in a play they once acted in. This was just another of those times. At least that's what he told himself, but as the kiss deepened, and Carrie's arms went around his neck, Spencer forgot all about the role he was playing.

She felt right in his arms, and her return kiss was something he had not expected. As they pulled away, it was easy to see that she had been just as affected as he was.

The judge gave a laugh. "You two are better actors than any I've seen on the stage. Either that, or maybe you're hiding the way you feel about each other. Either way, it's too late to turn back now."

Still chuckling, he signed the papers and then instructed Spencer and Carrie to do likewise. Spencer took up the pen and signed. His stomach still felt as if a hundred butterflies had suddenly been set free.

He turned and handed the pen to Carrie. She looked composed and confident. She took the pen and dipped it in the well before scrawling her name on the paper. She paused and looked up at the judge. "Should I add Duval to my name?"

"That is who you now are, Dr. Duval."

Carrie seemed to consider this a moment, then looked at Spencer. It was his turn to nod. He hoped his reassurance would settle any doubts that she might have.

She quickly added the name onto her signature, then placed the pen back in its stand. She stepped back and waited as if there were something more.

"I hope you have an easy go of it, Mr. Duval. From what Mr. Gable told me, this man has eluded capture for some years. I will pray for you." The judge looked at Carrie and smiled. "I'll pray for you both."

"Take these, and I'll get our things," Spencer said, handing over her gloves and picking up their marriage papers.

Carrie pulled her gloves on as Spencer retrieved their coats and hats. She felt almost in a state of shock from all that had taken place. Perhaps shock wasn't the exact feeling, but given her familiarity with the symptoms of such a state, it fit rather well. Her skin felt clammy, her breathing was rapid, and her heartbeat felt irregular. Added to this, she was slightly lightheaded, and her mental state was a mix of anxiety and confusion. There was also an overall sensation of weakness.

"Here you go." Spencer helped her into her coat and then handed her the wool bonnet. "Are you hungry?"

"It is lunchtime. I suppose I am hungry." She added that to her list of symptoms. It didn't really fit with shock, but it certainly could account for her feeling of weakness.

"I thought we might go to Armand's. I know you love his pasta."

"I do. But I'm surprised that you remember that." She secured her bonnet as Spencer opened the door. "We haven't been there in months. Not since the troupe went together after rehearsal that one night."

"I remember a lot of things and know a great deal about you. But right now, I feel we should celebrate."

"I don't feel much like celebrating a wedding intended for deception." She frowned, hoping she hadn't offended him. They were stuck together now whether she liked it or not.

"Then we won't celebrate the wedding. We'll celebrate my birthday. I am thirty-five today."

She looked up in surprise. "I didn't know it was your birthday." She shook her head and felt a rush of despair unleash itself upon her. "I don't know anything about you. I'm completely in the dark. How in the world did I convince myself that we could fool my parents this way?"

He stopped outside the office and took hold of her shoulders. "Stop fretting. We've got time. That's what we'll spend the next few days doing. We'll talk and share information and make certain we know all about each other as we finish packing to leave."

Carrie shook her head. "I couldn't possibly learn enough about you to fool my parents. They'll know, and then your entire investigation will be compromised."

He took hold of her arm and looped it with his. With a little pull, he started them down the street. "It's going to be all right, Carrie. You'll see. We can do this. Starting with my birthday. I was born February third in 1855. I was born at my grandparents' house in Philadelphia while my father was away on business."

Half an hour later, they were enjoying Armand's finest pasta with Bolognese sauce and crispy bread dipped in olive oil. Carrie had to admit it had gone a long way to calming her. So had all the information Spencer shared about his childhood and ambitions. As a medical student, she'd had no trouble memorizing facts and figures and set her mind to consider this to be like any other class. She was learning about a particular topic. Memorizing information. She could do this.

"I've been so determined to catch Astor that I'd allowed myself very little time to really think beyond that moment. Even Al has reprimanded me for my obsession. Still, I feel I owe it to my father to deal with this man once and for all."

"Do you plan to kill him?" Carrie couldn't stop herself from asking the question. After seeing how consumed Spencer was, she wondered if arrest would be enough.

"I don't plan to kill anyone. I've not yet had to, and frankly, I don't want to have that on my conscience. But if he won't surrender any other way, I won't let him kill me or someone I love."

Carrie nodded. "Fair enough. So, what can I tell you about myself?"

He glanced toward the copper tiles on the ceiling. "Well, the truth is, I already know quite a bit about you. I've paid very good attention, and I did some investigating."

"On me? When?" She could hardly believe what he was telling her. He had investigated her? Had he involved the agency?

"Well, when I first met you, I thought you were unlike any woman I'd ever met. You were beautiful, but also intelligent. I was fascinated that you were a medical doctor and that you were interested in research on the brain. You were so serious. But then, there was the playful side of you as well. The fact that you enjoyed acting interested me. I gave serious thought to seeing if you would go out with me to dinner and see where it led. So I looked into who you were."

Carrie was rather stunned by this confession. She considered the fact that Spencer had just declared that he had wanted to court her, or at least pay her attention.

"And what did you learn about me?"

"Well, beyond the obvious interest in medicine and ability to memorize scripts and perform for audiences, I suppose the most important thing I learned was that you were engaged. I have to admit, I was sorely disappointed."

"And yet, here we are, an old married couple."

He laughed rather loudly, causing people at several other tables to glance their way. He controlled his mirth and looked at her with a shrug. "Not so old."

"Nor so married," she added.

He chuckled and nodded. "But at least you didn't waste your time with Nelson. I checked into him as well, you know."

"You didn't!" She gasped and shook her head. "Did he ever find out?"

"Hardly. I'm very good at what I do, Carrie. You didn't find out."

"It's true." She picked up a piece of the bread and dabbed it in the oil. "Go on, please. What's my favorite color? When's my birthday?"

"You are partial to lavender but feel it's too whimsical for a researching physician. And you were born in Indiana on December thirtieth in 1865."

"So you know that my mother died in childbirth."

"Yes, I did learn that. Your sister took over caring for you. I believe her name is Marybeth."

Carrie was amazed at what he had learned. "I suppose you must also know that my father died two years later."

"I do. Your sister then married Edward Vogel, and he adopted you as his own. The three of you then moved to Cheyenne, where he took on a job as a deputy town marshal. You also have three siblings: Robert, Greta, and Daniel. All living in Cheyenne."

"Daniel is gone to college in New York. He was very smart and graduated high school when he was sixteen, like me."

"I knew that." He grinned. "I'm hoping my interest in knowing you better isn't going to put a rift between us."

"Not at all. It's something of relief to learn that you already know a great deal about me and my family."

She sampled the bread as Spencer continued. "What do you want to know about me? I told you about my father and how he died. I was ten at the time. My mother died at the young age of forty, just five years later. Aloysius Gable, who is now my supervisor, took me in. He had already filled the role of father, after mine died. He was very good to my mother and me."

"Did they marry?"

"No." Spencer pushed the pasta around his plate. "My mother was never interested in anyone but my father. They were so in love, so devoted to each other. Al knew that and never tried to pursue my mother. I don't think it was for a lack of interest, however. My mother was a great beauty."

"Do you have photographs?"

"I have a single tintype of my mother and father. That's all. I cherish it."

"And you have no siblings?"

"No. My mother nearly bled to death giving birth to me. She was told she would never be able to have additional children."

"They must have performed a hysterectomy." Carrie grew very thoughtful. "That might have saved my mother's life, but our small Indiana town apparently suffered for experienced doctors."

"She said they left her with a tremendous physical scar, as well as emotional."

"What was your mother like?" Carrie could see Spencer was feeling rather emotional.

"She was kind and generous. Always helping the neighbors and doing what she could to ease people's burdens. Even after losing my father, she never wavered in doing for others. She grieved him deeply, but I think serving other people helped her. It also killed her. She died of consumption after caring for others who also had it. At least that's what the doctor said of her death. Still, my mother would never have done it any other way. She loved to help people."

"Mama always says that when you feel at your lowest, you should get up and do something for someone else. I've known it to help tremendously and get me past sad situations. I'm sorry it claimed your mother's life."

"So you call your sister Mama?" he asked.

The question took Carrie off guard. "I do. She's the only mother I've ever known, just as Edward Vogel is the only father I remember."

"When did you learn the truth?"

"They never really kept it from me. It was something I just sort of knew in the back of my mind, but it was never really something we discussed. When I was ten, someone in the church brought it to my attention, and I remember asking about it. My mama sat me down, and we talked about it, but I found instead of helping, it just sort of opened a bigger hole in my heart. I've never been able to quite understand it.

"My folks were good parents. As my mama tells it, she and I have a unique and doubly bonded relationship that few ever experience. She's my older sister and my mother. She's never failed to be there for me. Even saved me from being raised by strangers by marrying Edward Vogel. They were good friends, nothing more. He was a widower who had lost his wife and child, and she had been best friends with his wife. They needed each other. It wasn't your typical romantic marriage."

"Kind of like us."

She studied his gentle expression. "Yes, rather like us. It was more of a business arrangement in the beginning. But their marriage turned into a real love affair."

An awkward silence fell between them. Spencer cleared his throat. "I hope you won't regret this . . . regret me." He put his fork down. "I enjoy your company, Carrie. Our friendship has gotten me through some rough patches. You might never have known that, but it's true."

Carrie felt a moment of tenderness for him unlike anything she'd ever felt for Oswald. Spencer seemed vulnerable in that moment, and she wanted to reassure him.

"I don't think I'll ever regret you. You've always proven yourself honorable and trustworthy. I want very much for this to all work out for you and will do whatever I can to see it through." She paused, determined to lighten the mood. "But just for the record, while I do enjoy lavender, my favorite color is blue. That's why I wore it for my wedding day. I want to remember this day as something special. I may never have another. Men tend to be intimidated by intelligent women. I thought things would be different with Oswald, but that wasn't the case."

"He was more than intimidated by you. He knew he didn't begin to have your level of understanding. He could only stand by and watch you achieve all that he had dreamed about doing."

Carrie considered that a moment. "I know you're right. Oswald was never really able to go beyond the limits of what he knew to be certain. I, on the other hand, constantly push that limit aside and ask what else might be known . . . what else can I discover? I wasn't afraid of considering strange possibilities. I could see that wasn't a quality that Oswald was capable of grasping. It's sad too. Oswald isn't good with people, so research has always been more to his liking. Now, who knows what direction he'll go. Either he'll find another person willing to let him take credit for their work, or . . . well, who can say?"

"Well, he won't be able to steal your ideas anymore. I'm excited to see what this new freedom does for you."

"I'm not sure it can happen in Cheyenne. Although there is a new sanitarium in town. I believe it's mostly focused on recuperation." She smiled. "Oh, and there's a new asylum in Evansville. I could always take the train back and forth and do some research there on insanity."

"Whatever you need to do, I will support you in every way possible. I know you don't have a lot of money, and while your folks might have done good to put aside some savings, they have your brother's education and sister's wedding to worry about. I've saved up a decent amount of money over the years, plus the money I made when I sold my parents' house. We weren't rich, but we were comfortable. I'm pretty frugal, but it's all yours."

Carrie shook her head. "You are a wonder. I don't know how you managed to learn so much about me. But even if you hadn't, I wouldn't try to hide things from you. That's not my style. I abhor lies."

"Good. I'd rather we be completely open and honest with each other."

"Yes, I'd rather that too."

And she meant it, but in truth she wasn't ready yet to discuss how his kiss had affected her, nor the strange feeling that overcame her in realizing that she was going to spend the next few weeks—maybe months—as wife to this very handsome and charming man.

7

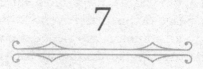

Carrie glanced at her husband sitting across from her on the train. For several nights they shared hotel rooms as the train made its way west to Cheyenne. At first, they had laughed nervously about the arrangement. Then the initial discomfort wore off, and they settled into the routine of being husband and wife for the public and good friends behind closed doors.

Spencer had been a complete gentleman about everything. He generally took to the floor for his bed, but last night there had been a small sofa in their large hotel room. It had come to them completely by surprise, but Al had arranged for them to have a suite in a newer hotel in North Platte. Spencer had started the night on the sofa, but soon made his way to the floor once again, declaring the floor to be softer.

His words still made Carrie smile. She felt bad that he wouldn't allow her to take a turn on the floor but grateful that he hadn't suggested they try to share the small bed. Most of the beds were only wide enough to accommodate two people sleeping side by side in a most intimate fashion. Carrie wasn't at all sure what that arrangement might bring about. She was already confused by her feelings.

She had been Oswald's fiancée when she'd first met Spencer, and her mind and heart had been fixed on that relationship and nothing else. When she became friends with the men and women at the theater, Spencer was just one of the actors. He was quite handsome, and most of the single women were more than a little interested in him. Carrie found him intriguing, as he often told a variety of stories. Usually things based on historical events with strange bits of information, not common knowledge. He was fun to be around, and she loved his enthusiasm for each of their plays. She loved, too, the way he acted with the children who came to see the plays. They adored him. He would do little magic tricks for them at times and seemed completely at ease with them. Even without the benefit of growing up with siblings, Spencer seemed to have a natural ability to relate to the young audience.

Thinking of siblings brought Carrie back to the present. In a few hours, they would reach Cheyenne. She hadn't sent word of her and Spencer's exact arrival. She didn't want a show of family at the depot. Everyone in town knew her father and would have no doubt made a fuss had they known when she was slated to come back to Cheyenne. She had horrifying nightmares of the town turning out to welcome the prodigal daughter home.

Of course, she wasn't really a prodigal. She certainly hadn't left on bad terms nor forsaken the faith of her family. But Carrie knew that there was a kind of disjointed feeling between them, and it was all her fault. She was the one who couldn't seem to find her place. Couldn't seem to embrace a sense of belonging.

Since understanding the truth of her birth and upbringing, she felt like an intruder. Robert, Greta, and Daniel were the true children of Marybeth and Edward Vogel. She was just the orphaned sister who'd made their marriage necessary in the first place. Of course, they found a great love for each other, and her mother and father had an enviable marriage and friendship that everyone believed was ordained by God. They were the perfect couple with the perfect family. If only Carrie could see herself as belonging.

She knew her feelings were ridiculous. Mama and Papa loved her as much as they loved the others. Carrie had never felt that they cast her aside in favor of the children they'd given life. It was only Carrie who had an issue with the situation.

Carrie looked out the window at the passing prairie landscape. With each mile west, she felt the weight of her discomfort sink in. She didn't understand why she felt so at odds with her family. They loved her, and she loved them. She was going to be happy to see everyone. She knew Mama and Papa would welcome her with proud, open arms, and when they heard what Oswald had done, they would be encouraging and urge her on to make more discoveries on her own. They'd always believed in her. Always loved her.

"It seems vast and empty out there, doesn't it?" Spencer asked.

Carrie met Spencer's gaze, then noted the man beside him. Even though he seemed consumed by the newspaper, Carrie could hardly converse that she felt much as Spencer had just described the land. It was far too intimate.

"It does. Although, I know from experience that looks can be very deceiving. There's no doubt a lot of life going on even though it's the dead of winter."

"I figured we would find it all covered with snow," Spencer replied. "It's been an interesting trip to be sure."

"Yes." She looked back out the window. They'd already discussed her mixed feelings about returning to Cheyenne. Spencer had assured her it would do her good in the long run. After being away for so many years, she might see her life through different eyes. Her experiences had certainly changed her. She was now an accomplished doctor, and even if credit for her medical findings hadn't been given her, she was confident in knowing they were hers. She would go on to do great things. He was sure of this.

Carrie appreciated his confidence in her. She could never fault him for lacking in that area, but most of the men and women in Cheyenne would see her as a strange young woman for her interests. She wasn't by any means the first woman doctor, not even the first in Cheyenne, but her area of study had perplexed a great many, according to her mother. It wasn't easy to explain her fascination with the brain and the way that injuries often altered the behavior and personality of the injured person. The correlation had a great many scientists and doctors pursuing answers, but they were nearly all men. She certainly wasn't going to find a woman sharing her research passion in Cheyenne.

God, I don't know why You've given me this life and interest. I don't know why the circumstances of my birth and childhood act more as a stumbling agent than a foundation of assurance. Please help me to understand who I am and why I'm here. My passion to make discoveries that can help people is one I've always felt confident came from You, the Great Physician. Show me the way, Lord. Help me to do whatever I do to bring You glory.

"It's all going to be fine, Carrie." Spencer leaned forward to take hold of her gloved hands. He smiled, and some of her tension faded away. The last few days had proven he had an uncanny capacity to read her mood. Whether it was from the prayer she'd silently offered, or Spencer's efforts to ease her worries, Carrie felt a little better and nodded.

The hired carriage came to a stop in front of a quaint two-story house. Spencer had taken in the details all around him and already approved of Cheyenne. It was a fine town with a distinct order to it. Having lived mostly in big cities, Spencer was actually impressed with the smaller town's efficiency.

He helped Carrie down and then worked with the driver to unload their luggage. Most of Carrie's things had been arranged for at the depot. They would be warehoused until she and Spencer could rent a house. What they'd brought with them were mainly clothes and toiletries.

They made their way up the walkway, and Carrie paused at the porch steps. "They built a bigger porch after I left. Mama wrote to me about it. She had always wanted a wide porch where they could enjoy the evenings in the summer and have friends and family gather with them. My brother has the house across the street." She motioned, and Spencer noted the place.

He followed Carrie up the steps and put the luggage to one side near the door while she knocked. She glanced at him, biting her lower lip as she often did when nervous or deep in thought. When the door opened, an older woman appeared. Her jaw dropped in surprise. This had to be Carrie's mother.

"Carrie! We didn't know you were coming today. Greta! Carrie's here!" She looked Carrie up and down. "Oh, you look so fine. I can't believe you're finally here. It's been so very long since you were home."

"Nearly eight years," Carrie replied.

Spencer could hear a sort of tightness in her voice. He whispered a prayer for his wife and stood ready to support her in whatever way he could.

Her mother embraced her and kissed Carrie's cheek. She pressed her face against Carrie's and continued to hold her. The tenderness of the moment reminded Spencer of his own mother. She always made Spencer feel that he was the most important person in the world.

"Why didn't you let us know you were coming in today? We would have met you at the depot. Come in," she said, pulling on Carrie's arm. "You must be freezing."

Carrie pulled back. "Wait. I want to introduce you to someone very special."

It was only then that Marybeth Vogel seemed to realize Spencer was even there. He smiled and took off his hat.

"I'm so sorry. I didn't mean to ignore you. I was so caught up in having Carrie back with us."

"No problem." He offered her a smile and then looked to Carrie, hoping she would continue with the introduction.

"Mama, this is Spencer Duval . . . my husband."

Again, the older woman's jaw dropped open, and her eyes widened in surprise. "Husband? But I thought you were engaged to Oswald Nelson."

"I was, but he discredited himself and betrayed me, and I ended the engagement some time back."

Spencer knew she was trying to make it sound as if their betrothal had ended months ago instead of a couple of weeks. He smiled and extended his hand.

"I've heard a great deal about you, Mrs. Vogel. I'm excited to get to know the family better."

Marybeth was still in such a state of shock that Spencer wondered if she'd be able to accept the situation. Just then a young woman showed up at the door.

"Carrie! Oh, you've come home at last. You've been gone forever."

"Greta, just look at you. You're all grown up and so pretty." Carrie hugged her sister and turned to Spencer. "This is my husband, Spencer Duval."

"Husband? You got married without the family? But I wanted to be your maid of honor."

"It was a sort of last-minute decision," Carrie offered. "We probably wouldn't have wed quite so soon, but we wanted to be married before moving to Cheyenne."

"Moving here? You've come to stay, then?" Greta's tone was evidence of her pleasure and disbelief. "You've really moved back to Cheyenne?"

"For now. I am still pursuing my research, and if I can't do that here, then I'll have to push on, but for now it seems possible to settle in and remain here."

"Oh, that's wonderful news. Papa will be so happy."

"Let's go inside rather than continuing here," Mrs. Vogel said, seeming to finally recompose herself. She led the way back into the house, with Greta pulling Carrie along inside, and everyone leaving Spencer to follow.

Inside, a petite dark-haired young woman approached them in the foyer as Spencer closed the door behind him.

"Who's come?"

"Oh, Rosie, this is my daughter Carrie and her . . . husband, Spencer." She put an arm around the young woman and drew her closer. "This is Rosie, Robert's wife."

Carrie smiled and reached out to give Rosie a hug. "I wish I could have come to your wedding last fall."

"You gave us crystal glasses." There was something about the young woman that Spencer couldn't yet figure out. She was almost childlike in her mannerisms and speech. "Robert and I love them very much, and we talk about you when we use them." She then looked to Spencer. "You're tall like Robert."

"And you're tiny like a pretty little fairy."

"Fairies aren't real, you know." Her reply surprised him, but Spencer just gave a nod. "And fairies have wings." Her contradiction regarding fairies amused Spencer in a way he thought best to keep to himself.

"Come and sit in the front room. We've a fire going, and

you can warm up," Mrs. Vogel directed. "First, give me your coats. I know that seems rather counterproductive, but I'm sure you'll soon be amply warmed."

Spencer shed his wool coat, then reached to help Carrie with hers. He handed both to Mrs. Vogel while Greta took Carrie's hat and gloves.

"I'll take your hat, Spencer." Greta's cheeks reddened slightly, as if embarrassed. "May I call you Spencer?"

"Of course." He chuckled. "I'm not particular. Call me Spence, Spencer, brother. Whatever you like."

Greta nodded. "I like you already."

Carrie took hold of Spencer's arm and led him without further comment to the fireplace. He noted the room as he always did. Even though he doubted there was any danger in this setting, it was always good to be aware of one's options.

"Rosie, would you and Greta bring us some refreshments and hot coffee?" Mrs. Vogel paused. "Unless you prefer tea? We tend to drink more coffee. There's always a pot on the stove just like there used to be."

"Coffee is fine, Mama. Spencer and I like both." Carrie took up the fireplace poker. "I'll stir up the fire, if you don't mind."

"Throw another log on," her mother instructed.

Spencer took the poker. "Allow me." He took up a log from the woodbox at the edge of the fireplace and worked the fire up into a fine blaze. When he turned back, the ladies had already taken their seats.

"When will Papa be home?" Carrie asked.

"Very soon. I expected him some time ago. He had a meeting with the mayor and some of the other city fathers. You know we're hoping this will be our year for statehood. There's been a great deal of work done behind the scenes to push our agenda. Apparently, Congress is less than eager to act, although no reason has been given except concern over our low population."

"They've been clamoring for statehood here since we were made a territory," Carrie said, looking to Spencer as if to explain. "Becoming a state has been of the utmost importance."

"It does offer certain benefits, to be sure." Spencer went to sit beside his wife.

"Yes," Mrs. Vogel agreed.

Greta and Rosie appeared with a serving cart and immediately began pouring the coffee. Spencer wasn't sure what to say as the room fell silent. He could feel Carrie stiffen at his side and reached over to take hold of her hand. She looked at him, and he gave her what he hoped was a reassuring smile.

"It's obvious you two are very much in love," Greta said, handing a cup and saucer to Spencer. "I'm so glad you found each other. I can tell you now that from the things you wrote about Dr. Nelson, I found it difficult to like him."

"Well, you certainly don't need to worry about that anymore," Mrs. Vogel declared. "I hope that I don't sound too critical, but didn't this marriage take place rather fast?"

"We've been friends for over a year, Mama. Spencer and I just have a great friendship and . . . love for each other. You and Papa always maintained that when a thing is right, you should hurry to do it."

"Well, that was mostly in speaking of God directing us."

"I felt directed," Spencer chimed in. "I think we both did. We prayed a great deal about it, and I can say for myself, it was exactly what I felt led to do. Carrie is an amazing woman, and we fit very well together. We're both college educated and intellectually minded. We enjoy reading and theater and a great many other things. I believe God put us together for a very special reason."

The front door opened and closed with a bit of a bang.

Everyone straightened and looked toward the foyer at the same time.

The man who entered was tall with brown hair that was graying at the temples. He turned to the group in the front room and seemed momentarily surprised. Then his lips broke into a grin.

"Carrie, when did you get here?"

"Just a short time ago. Came on the afternoon train." She got up and went to her father. Spencer watched as they embraced and the older man whispered something in her ear. Carrie gave him a hug and kissed his cheek. She took him by the hand and drew him into the room. Spencer got to his feet and waited for her introduction.

"Papa, this is Spencer Duval. He's my . . . we're, uh, married."

Edward Vogel sobered and fixed Spencer with a hard look. "Married?"

"Yes, sir." Spencer extended his hand.

Mr. Vogel ignored it and turned. "Come with me."

8

Spencer wasn't surprised by Edward Vogel's reaction to him. In fact, had he done otherwise, Spencer would have wondered at his handling of the matter. Carrie had told him how extra cautious her father was when it came to strangers. That along with his own research regarding Chief Vogel had given Spencer a pretty good understanding of what he might expect.

They passed out the back of the house and across the yard to a small wooden-framed building at the back of the yard. Vogel unlocked the door and entered, leaving it open for Spencer to follow. By the time Spencer entered and closed the door, Vogel was already making a fire in the stove.

Spencer stood, watching and waiting. With the light from the windows streaming in, he could see this was a woodworking shop. There were a variety of projects in various stages of development. Even if Carrie hadn't already told Spencer all about it, it was clear this was Edward Vogel's domain.

Vogel worked in silence to get the fire going, then when he seemed satisfied, he closed the door to the stove and turned with a narrow-eyed gaze.

"What in the world makes you think you can just marry my daughter without discussing it with me first?"

Spencer gave a slight nod. "That would have been my preference as well, sir. I suppose we did rush things a bit, but Carrie was eager to move back to Cheyenne."

Vogel kept watching him. It reminded Spencer of times he'd stared down a suspect he'd just apprehended. Well, the man was entitled to wonder about his new son-in-law. Spencer would patiently endure whatever questions or scrutiny the man had in mind.

"Grab a chair and come sit over here." Vogel sat in a chair already positioned near the stove.

Spencer did as instructed. The wooden chair felt something like the seats he'd encountered in witness boxes at court. It seemed appropriate.

"Who are you, Spencer Duval?"

Spencer smiled. "I'm a man of God, sir. Well, not to say I'm a preacher, because I'm not. I've spent most of my adult years in law enforcement like you. I graduated college in Philadelphia and have done what I could to keep the peace ever since."

"I suppose yours is more detective work than walking the streets?"

"I've always done a mix of jobs. I'm not afraid to get my hands dirty, nor to study the procedures of other officers."

"You mentioned Philadelphia. Is that where you're from?"

"Yes, sir. Born and raised there. Some time in New York as well. Lately, however, it's been Chicago. For the last five years, I've called it home."

"Where's your family?"

"All dead, except for a gracious man who took me under his wing after my mother passed on. I was fifteen at the time."

"I'm sorry to hear that. Family is important."

"They are. I think about my folks often. They were good people who raised me to know God and fear Him."

"I'm glad to hear that you're walking with the Lord."

"I find it impossible to consider doing otherwise. My faith has gotten me through a great many things. On her deathbed, my mother made me swear to never forsake God. I assured her she didn't need to worry about that. I couldn't begin to imagine life without Him at the center."

"I feel the same way," Vogel replied. "I'm part of a men's Bible study on Saturday mornings. Maybe you'd like to join us?"

Spencer didn't hide his smile. "That would be wonderful. Thank you."

"So how did you meet my daughter?"

"At the theater. We had both signed up as volunteers in a local children's theater. It was a much-needed change from the intensity of our jobs. Carrie with her research and me with my law enforcement duties . . . well, we found playacting for children to be refreshing. We were introduced and became fast friends. I mentioned having trouble finding a church that I felt was strongly focused on the Bible rather than man's teachings, and Carrie recommended her church. So then we had yet another place where we saw each other and had a chance to speak. Over the last year, we have had an opportunity to discuss many fascinating topics, and our friendship deepened."

"But she was engaged to marry Dr. Nelson."

"Yes. We didn't allow for anything but friendship in our relationship until Carrie ended the engagement. I suppose she told you that Nelson stole the credit for some of her medical findings?"

"She did write to us about some of that. Seems like it was quite a long time ago."

"Yes, well, it wasn't that long ago he did it again, this time with a major find that Carrie was responsible for. She was devastated by the betrayal."

"And you offered her comfort and reassurance."

"I certainly hope I did. I know her pain ran deep. Carrie has a brilliant mind and wants to make a difference in medicine. I don't pretend to understand the things she does, but I do admire her." He grinned. "Beautiful and astute."

"Her intellect would scare off most men. When she was in school here, she was always ahead of everyone else. When she graduated at sixteen and announced her desire to go to Chicago to the medical college, I have to admit her mother and I were hard-pressed to allow for it. Thankfully, a good friend had trustworthy relatives in Chicago who were willing to oversee Carrie's move and attendance."

"I'm sure it was hard to let her go."

"It was. It still is. I hope you know that I won't brook any harsh treatment of my daughter. If you're cruel to her in any way, you'll answer to me."

Spencer nodded. "I would expect no less."

"What are your plans? I'm sure she intends to continue her research, maybe even open her own doctor's office, but what about you?"

"I intend to pursue what I'm good at, law enforcement. I know you're the chief of police, and I don't expect any favors. However, I would like to know if there are positions available."

Vogel smiled. "I'm sure we can find something for you, Detective."

Spencer laughed. "I can walk a beat as well as deduce a criminal's pattern of operation."

"I think I'm starting to like you, Spencer."

The door to the shop opened, and Carrie hurried inside. "That wind is getting colder."

"Well, the sun is setting," her father countered.

"That's why I've come. Mama says it's time to wash up for supper. Robert is home, and the food is on the table."

"Then we'd best get to it," Vogel said, getting to his feet.

"I hope Papa didn't intimidate you too much." Carrie came to Spencer's side and gave him an apologetic shrug. "It's his way."

"Especially with men who intend to marry or have married my daughters." Vogel put his arm around Carrie. "But never fear, I like your young man well enough. I even intend to give him a job."

Carrie smiled up at her father. "Thank you, Papa. Spencer is a hard worker in every way. I know you're going to enjoy having him around."

They gathered around the large oak table that Carrie remembered from childhood. Back then it had seemed so massive, but now, with the addition of Spencer and Rosie as well as Greta's fiancé, Michael Decker, the space looked much smaller.

Carrie had helped to get the table set, while her mother put the finishing touches on a large pork roast. Given the time of year, pork products were the main source of meat most families were eating.

The roast was accompanied by a brimming bowl of roasted potatoes and another of green beans. Papa had always enjoyed peas, so there was a bowl of creamed peas as well. Greta placed a basket of dinner rolls on the table and took her seat. Everyone looked to Papa for the blessing.

"We are doubly blessed tonight because Carrie and Spencer are here to join us. Let's give thanks." Papa bowed his head and asked a blessing on the food and all who were about to partake of the meal.

"And Lord, we ask that You would bless the marriage of Carrie and Spencer. Let them draw closer to You as they draw closer to each other. Amen."

"Amen," everyone around the table murmured.

Carrie said nothing but grabbed her glass of water and took a long drink. How could she ask God to bless their marriage when she knew it was a sham?

"I love that you can be here, Carrie. Spencer too." Greta smiled at them both and offered them the rolls. "I was hoping you'd be my maid . . . well, matron of honor when Michael and I marry in May."

Carrie wasn't surprised by her sister's request. "I'd love to stand with you, Greta." Carrie took a roll. Her mother made delicious breads. "You'll definitely want at least one of these," she told Spencer, handing him the basket.

"I just wish you would have waited to marry here," Greta continued. "I wanted so much to be with you. You're my only sister, and that's so special."

Carrie appreciated Greta's comment. It touched her heart. Greta was really her niece, but they'd grown up together as sisters. The bond they shared was very special, even though they didn't share the same mother and father by blood. They shared them in love and their day-to-day living. Wasn't that what really mattered? Carrie sighed. She needed a change of heart and mind.

"Where are you two staying?" Robert asked as he took the platter of roast and helped his wife.

"We're going to rent a house, once we can find one," Carrie said. "I'll set up an office there, and Papa is giving Spencer a job."

"That's right," her father interjected. "Rob's been after me to hire more men."

She smiled. "I know you won't be sorry. Spencer is a talented . . ." She hesitated, knowing that Spencer wasn't yet ready to announce himself an agent of the Pinkertons. She forced a laugh. "Well, you know how I feel."

No one seemed the wiser and chuckled with her. Carrie looked at Spencer and smiled. "For the time being," she continued, hoping no one would question her further, "we're going to stay at the Inter Ocean Hotel."

"No," her mother said, looking to Papa. "I won't hear of you staying in a hotel. Carrie, your room is available. After you took your things and moved, we got a bigger bed and made it our guest room. You two can stay there."

"We already have a reservation." Carrie was uncomfortable with the thought of sharing a room with Spencer in her family home.

"I'll cancel it for you," Robert said. "I have to go back to work right after supper and can swing by there on the way. Besides, I brought your things in from the porch."

"That settles it," Mama said, smiling.

Carrie accepted the decision with a smile as Spencer squeezed her hand under the table. It would no doubt work out just fine. The rest of the meal went well, with each person sharing something about their day. Spencer spoke of the seemingly endless prairie and how Cheyenne was the farthest west he had ever lived. After that Greta brought up the wedding and all the plans she had for the day.

"We've rented one of the big halls at the opera house for the reception. We're going to have dancing and food and lots of people."

"What say you to all that fuss, Michael?" Papa asked.

"I told her I'd be just as happy to elope, but a big wedding seems important to her," Michael Decker replied. He grinned and nudged Greta in the side. "So I told her just this once she could run things like she wanted." Everyone laughed.

By the time they were ready to retire to bed later that night, Carrie was more than a little spent. The day had been long, and the emotions of seeing her family again left her feeling like a wrung-out cloth.

"Well, I have to say that I really love your family. They're wonderful," Spencer said, closing the bedroom door.

"They are. They've always been that way. That's why I don't understand why I should feel the way I do about not fitting in." She sighed and sat on the edge of the bed and began unbuttoning her boots. Thankfully, part of Mama's arrangements for the dressing table included a button hook because she wasn't sure where she'd packed hers.

Spencer began undressing. This had been their routine since their first night together. Neither paid much attention to the other. Usually, they just turned away to give each other privacy.

"Looks like someone has already put the clothes away." Spencer held up an empty suitcase.

"That's probably where Rosie and Greta disappeared to after supper." Carrie removed her second boot and went to the armoire. Opening the door, she found their things arranged inside. "Goodness, they even pressed them. How in the world did they manage such a feat?"

Spencer shrugged. "I've never been good at things like that and always paid my landlady extra to iron my clothes."

Carrie nodded. "I paid Rebecca to do mine. She needed the money, and I was always so busy. Mama taught me how to do all the household chores, but we're gonna need help. I have no way of knowing what I'll be able to keep up with as I do my research. Of course, I may not have any patients at all and will be grateful to revisit my skills as a seamstress and cook."

Spencer shook his head. "Don't worry about it. I'm sure it will all work out. We'll figure it out bit by bit. First, we have to find our own place. We can go looking tomorrow. This is Monday, after all. We can buy a paper and see what might be available. If that doesn't work, then perhaps your folks will know. Now, would you like me to unbutton your blouse?"

"Yes, please." She brought her nightgown and robe with her and came to stand with her back to Spencer. This, too, was their routine. He undid the buttons, then turned away. This time, however, Carrie clutched her things and headed for the door. "The bathroom is next door. I'm going to go clean up a bit. It will give you some privacy to finish changing."

She was impressed with the new bathroom. The copper tub encased in an oak frame that her father and brother had created was difficult to pass up. Maybe there'd be time for a long soak tomorrow. The rest of the room was just as nice, and Mama had seen to it that every comfort was available, from towels and washcloths to bars of homemade soap that had a distinct scent of roses.

Carrie quickly removed her clothes, doing her best not to be nervous about being home, nor the days to come. Everyone had been so welcoming and supportive. Even the news of her marriage to Spencer hadn't gone over too badly. Carrie looked into the mirror that hung just over the sink. She could well imagine the ease with which this might allow her father to shave in the morning. It was certainly better than the life they'd had when Mama and Papa had first arrived in Cheyenne. Carrie couldn't remember their tenting days, but Mama always told stories about it when they were young. After living in a tent during the cold winter months, the Vogel family had progressed to the small building in back of the house, where the original owners planned to make a woodshop similar to the one Papa had there now. Carrie didn't remember that time or place either, but then they'd taken over this house, and her memories were plentiful.

Coming home had brought to mind a great many things. She'd had a good life here even if she didn't feel that she fit in or belonged. One way or another, she had to overcome her doubts about her family's love and acceptance. There was no benefit in continuing to feel the way she did. Besides that, things had changed in the last eight years. And she was certain that it didn't just extend to the house alone, although those changes were quite impressive and even unexpected.

Mama had written about some of them, but Carrie hadn't really given it much thought. Having the huge porch created for visiting and a big upstairs bathing room with indoor toilet had been a longtime desire of her mother's. Carrie had left home knowing that one day her father would see to it that the changes were made. He loved Mama and wanted to give her all the worldly comforts.

And he had. The house was hooked up to plumbing, sewer, electricity, a furnace system, and telephone service. The latter was especially fascinating and annoying, Mama had told her. The officers at the jail thought nothing of calling Papa day and night.

Carrie washed up and changed into her nightgown and robe, then made her way back to the bedroom. She found her husband already changed and ready for bed upon her return. That was when she finally allowed herself to think about their arrangements. She glanced around the room. There wasn't really decent space to set up a comfortable pallet on the floor. Not only that, but while the house had come up to date in many ways, there were still no locks on the bedroom doors. In her family, there was always a sort of unspoken rule about not keeping people out. She bit her lip and pondered the matter. There wasn't really a choice.

"What's wrong?" Spencer came toward her.

He wore a loose-fitting nightshirt and had no idea how handsome he was. Carrie tried to ignore her thoughts. "We've got no choice but to share the bed."

"I can sleep on the floor."

She shook her head. "No, you really can't. There's not space to begin with, but you might as well know that my parents or siblings are likely to come barging in. I mean, they usually knock first and make sure it's all right, but there would be no time to get you up off the floor and into bed." Her voice was barely a whisper. She gave a sigh and looked at the bed. It was larger than any of those they'd had at the hotel.

"It'll be all right." She looked at Spencer. "I'm sure we can make do for a night or two."

"Are you sure?" He took hold of her shoulders and waited until Carrie lifted her gaze to meet his. "I don't want you uncomfortable. I will be a perfect gentleman. I promise."

"I know." She forced a nervous smile. "I trust you, Spencer. I'm sure we'll be just fine. Besides, my folks keep it cold at night. We'll appreciate each other's body heat, I'm sure."

He laughed and waved his arm toward the bed. "Which side do you want?"

She swallowed the lump in her throat. It would be all right. They were on a mission here, and the end results were far more important than her discomfort for the moment. She truly wasn't worried about Spencer breaking his vow.

She was, however, starting to question her own resolve.

9

February was cold, and despite the new furnace heat in the house, it seemed the Vogels kept the temperature low, and inevitably each morning Spencer found Carrie snuggled up close to him for warmth.

For five days now, he had awakened before her, momentarily mesmerized by her presence. She was the most beautiful and desirable woman he'd ever met. But like every other morning, he slipped quietly out of the bed, hoping not to awaken her. He wanted to save her from any embarrassment from having slept so close to him. He also needed the time to set his own mind straight. Carrie Vogel Duval was starting to rearrange his thinking—his focus. He was in Cheyenne to do a job, and so far, he'd not even started.

He dressed and tried not to think about the woman he left sleeping in his bed. He had agreed to work for Chief Vogel, taking on an early morning shift that put him out of the house by a quarter of four. He had to rotate working Saturdays with some of the other men, and today was his day to work. He honestly didn't mind the early hours, nor the extra days. Chief Vogel was a good man and a competent city marshal. The deputies he worked with were men Spencer considered solid, sensible officers who cared deeply about their town. That made a difference in any law enforcement worker.

Spencer pulled on his uniform coat and made his way downstairs, buttoning the jacket as he went. He'd never been one for a uniform, but given his plan of working only a short time for the city of Cheyenne, Spencer wasn't going to take issue with their manner of dress. The important thing was to keep his eyes open for Astor. He needed to remember the real reason he'd come west.

Spencer headed to the kitchen and straight for the icebox. Mrs. Vogel always left him something for breakfast. Sometimes she made him a sandwich from leftovers from the night before. He had to smile at the way she had embraced him as family. It had been a very long time since he'd had a motherly figure in his life, and Marybeth Vogel played the role quite well. In the icebox he found a covered plate. He took this out and uncovered it to find a thick slice of ham sandwiched between some of her homemade bread. Cold breakfast was better than no breakfast. He took up the sandwich and put the plate in the sink. Before he walked out the back door, he donned his regulation hat and headed to the jail.

After checking in, Spencer began his job walking the streets of Cheyenne, checking doors and storefronts to make sure all was locked up tight. He made one trip along the street front and then walked the next in the alleyway. If anything looked at all suspicious, he'd pause and give it an extra look over.

For the most part, downtown Cheyenne was pretty quiet. Chief Vogel had already warned him about certain trouble spots where heavy drinkers liked to settle in until daybreak, playing cards and causing trouble. For the time being, Spencer didn't have to patrol those areas. His patrol did, however, include the train depot, repair shops, and warehouses. He was getting to know the men who worked the rail line and handled freight. Most seemed to be good, solid citizens.

There were a few who were less than cordial, but Spencer didn't mind. So long as they obeyed the law, he could respect their privacy.

"You stayin' warm, Deputy?" a man asked as Spencer left the yards and came up to the back side of the train station.

"Doing my best. I have to say the drier climate helps with that. The air was a whole lot damper in Chicago."

The man nodded. "I used to live in Duluth, so I know how that can be. Some of the snows and storms up there were not for the faint of heart."

"Agreed." Spencer glanced around. "Had any trouble?"

"Not a bit."

"Good. I hope it stays that way." Spencer kept moving, knowing that neither of them had much time for conversation.

He came back around to the front of the stately depot just as the sun's rays hit the building. The red sandstone exterior was designed with Romanesque arches and dormers, giving it a grand appearance. Overhead a steeply pitched roof would discourage the buildup of snow. The large clock tower was the crowning jewel for the building. Spencer knew the town of Cheyenne was more than a little pleased with how the magnificent building turned out.

Having seen to the depot, Spencer began walking up Capitol Avenue. It was a quarter after seven, but since it was Saturday, he presumed there would be far fewer people on the streets than the weekdays might have brought. He liked the quiet moments to study the layout of the town. Soon enough some of the businesses would open for their Saturday shoppers, and the streets would fill with activity.

Spencer considered his real purpose in Cheyenne. He wondered if he might encounter Astor on one of his patrols. What would he do if he did? He knew Astor wouldn't know him by looks. He might shy away from a lawman, but given he'd lived in Cheyenne for more than a decade, he had probably learned how to fade into the crowd and be unassuming. Astor was seeking to remain anonymous these days, and so Spencer had no doubt the older man would avoid breaking the law.

But just as Astor wouldn't know what he looked like, Spencer wasn't sure he'd recognize Astor. The man would be in his sixties by now. Spencer could remember the face of the younger man who'd killed his father, but time and circumstances could have completely altered that image.

"Morning, Spencer. How's it going?"

He turned to find Robert Vogel trailing his steps. He gave his brother-in-law a smile. "Really well. Thanks." He pushed aside thoughts of Astor. "I find that I do like your town."

"It has a lot of good to offer." Robert pulled even with Spencer, and they kept walking. "We're pushing for statehood, as you probably already heard. Hope to get it this year. I don't imagine, though, that you and Carrie will stay."

Spencer glanced at the younger man. "Why do you say that?"

"Well, I know Carrie wants to pursue her research. I don't expect she'll find what she needs here."

"We did talk about it. She feels there is some research she can do on her own or working with a local physician. You know her former fiancé stole her work and claimed it for himself. She's going to have a hard time proving her value to a research team."

"I heard a little about what happened but no real details. I mean, at least not for the latest episode. I know Ma said something happened last year."

"Apparently Nelson made a habit of it. I told Carrie that she has to go wherever her work takes her. I fully support her research. She's a brilliant woman."

"It's good of you to be so encouraging. A lot of men

wouldn't bother to consider what their wife needed, especially as it pertained to working a job."

"Carrie's special," Spencer said, stopping to check a door.

"She is special. I want to see her be able to work at what she loves. How about you? Does this job satisfy you?"

"Keeping law and order? I've been about that most of my life. Always had an interest in it since I was quite young. My father was a lawman, and I guess it just felt natural to pursue it." He gave Robert a smile. "Seems like it fell naturally on you as well."

"It did, to be sure. I never had any desire to go off to college like Daniel and Carrie. I do have some other ideas in mind for the future, but college isn't one of them."

"I went to college and even graduated, but I think the day-to-day experiences have served me better than book learning. Of course, the things I learned from books benefit me in other ways, so I'm not against the additional schooling."

They reached the end of the block, and Spencer stopped and added, "But college isn't for everyone."

"No, it isn't. Frankly, I'm planning to become a gunsmith. I've been working with a local fellow who's going to retire in another year or so. He can't afford to have me work for him full-time, but he's been training me and has already had his lawyer draw up paperwork that will sell me the business. Some of the work I'm doing for him now is being counted against the cost of buying the business. It's a really good deal."

"And a much-needed business. Guns are important, especially here on the frontier."

"Yeah, just about everyone carries them. Not in town so much. At least they're not supposed to, although I hear there are plans to change that."

"I read something in the newspaper about that." Spencer thought it interesting that the territory wanted to again make it legal for open carrying of firearms and other weapons within city limits.

"Yeah, I think it was stirred up by folks coming into town and not wanting to have to check their weapons or leave them at the livery stable. I understand why folks traveling would want to be armed. Snakes can be bad, two-legged as well as the slithering kind."

"Speaking of the two-legged kind, your pa gave me insight into some of the rougher areas of town, but I wondered if there are any particular men who have caused more problems than others?"

Robert shrugged. "There are a few. I'm sure you're bound to meet them soon enough. I wouldn't go looking for them. Most stay on the Chicago side of town."

"Chicago?"

Robert laughed. "That's an old nickname for the west end of town. That among other choice names."

"Having just come from Chicago, I suppose I can understand. We had some very tough neighborhoods to contend with. A lot of evil folks trying to ruin the place for everyone else."

"My father always said it's best not to go looking for trouble. It'll come to you in time, so be on your guard."

"I've got no plans for seeking it out. For now, I'm just getting the lay of the land. Your father is keeping me on the good side of town to break me in."

"Well, I'd better get on my way. Bible study with the men is at eight. Sorry you couldn't be there today. We meet at the Deckers' school, and Mrs. Decker makes the most delicious breakfast for us."

"I'll be there next week. In fact, I'm looking forward to it. Never been involved in a men's Bible study. Should be quite interesting." Spencer gave him a nod, then parted company, heading to the left when Robert went right. He seemed to be a likable fellow. Carrie spoke of him as a reasonable, smart, and loving brother.

In fact, the entire family could be described that way. Spencer couldn't say that any of them gave him a sense of foreboding or trouble. Not that he'd expected they would. That made it all the harder to imagine how they might react once they learned the real reason he was here and found out he and Carrie weren't intending to stay married after he caught Astor.

Carrie came down to breakfast only to find everyone gone with exception to her mother. Mama sat reading the newspaper and sipping a cup of coffee that had been heavily creamed.

"Good morning. Where is everyone?"

"Well, Spencer had street duty, as you probably know. Your father and Robert are at the men's Bible study. Greta has a cold, and I told her to stay in bed and sweat it out. I told Rosie to stay home since we have sickness here. No sense in her coming down with the cold as well."

"She's already been in close contact with Greta, so if it's something contagious, she's already been exposed." Carrie reached for a biscuit, then noted her mother had also made sausage gravy. "I haven't had biscuits and gravy since I left home. What a treat. I remember how much I looked forward to this on cold mornings." She broke up the biscuit on her plate as her mother put the paper aside.

"We have it at least once a week, during the winter especially. Sometimes more often than that."

"I remember Papa was always quite fond of it." Carrie ladled gravy onto her biscuit and smiled at the memory. She bowed her head for a brief, silent prayer, then went to work on the treat.

From the first mouthful, Carrie couldn't help sending her thoughts back in time. She remembered Mama teaching her how to make the gravy with sausage drippings. After a little salt and flour, she would pour cream into the pan, and once it thickened up, they would put the cut-up sausage back into the pan and add pepper. It was always so rich and delicious.

"With everyone else gone, I thought you might explain to me what's really going on with you," Mama said, wasting no time. "This is the first chance we've had to be alone, so you have no reason to remain silent."

Carrie paused and looked at her mother. "I haven't been silent. I told you about Oswald's duplicity."

"Yes, but that doesn't explain the rush to marriage with a man you never even mentioned in your few letters home."

"I never wrote you about much of anyone in Chicago. Not even Oswald. I didn't see the need. You met Rebecca and her mother and aunt when you visited last year."

"And spent time with Oswald rather than Spencer. You can't fool me. This marriage to Spencer is much more sudden than you want to let on. Was there a need for it?"

Carrie stiffened. "Are you asking if I'm with child? The answer is no, so stop worrying that your reputation will be ruined."

"I'm not worried about my reputation, Carrie. What a thing to say. I just want to know the truth of why you married so quickly without even giving yourself time to recover from your engagement to Oswald Nelson."

Carrie felt bad for her response. She hadn't meant to be abrasive. Her mother and father had probably already discussed the matter at length, and while Carrie couldn't give away all that was going on, she needed to say something to put her mother's mind at ease.

She smiled. "Spencer has been in my life for over a year. I

didn't pay him much attention because I was already committed to Oswald. However, upon reflection, Spencer was the one I was always talking to. At least about things other than those pertaining to my research and work. Spencer and I had such an easy friendship. We worked together at the theater and often went out with others after rehearsals. Inevitably, we ended up being together."

"But you were engaged to Oswald. Didn't he object to you keeping time with another man?"

"Oswald never paid much attention to anything but my medical findings. His focus was the work we were doing. He would take me out to dinner from time to time and occasionally to the opera or a wealthy donor's party, but for the most part our relationship revolved solely around our work. You even noted that when you came to visit. It did give me pause to consider whether we were suited to each other in a married capacity, rather than just a working relationship."

"I didn't think you paid me much mind on what I said back then."

"Just because I didn't react about something doesn't mean I didn't hear you and take the matter under advisement."

Mama studied her for a moment, and Carrie quickly took another bite of the biscuits and gravy. She knew her mother sensed she was leaving something out, but Carrie could hardly tell her about Spencer's job. Not until he was ready to reveal the details himself.

"Still, it hasn't been that long, and you up and marry another."

"You married Papa without much consideration."

"To save you, in part."

"Yes, but also because you knew it was the right thing to do. You told me you felt certain God had led you to do so. I feel certain God has led me to do the same. If you can't have any faith in me, at least have it in God."

"Carrie! I never said I didn't have faith in you." Her mother looked hurt. "I have always believed in your abilities to use good sense and reason. You're probably the most logical of all my children."

"Maybe because I'm not really your child."

"Meaning what?"

"You're very reasonable and logical, and I am as well. Maybe we got it from the father we shared." Carrie shrugged. "There are studies that such things are transferred to the children from their parents. They're just starting to really explore this, so there's nothing fixed on the research. Of course, environment also plays a strong role in the way children think and act."

"You and your studies." Mama shook her head. "Sometimes things come about because of the heart as well as the head."

Carrie smiled. Her mother would never really understand her research, but she did understand love. "I just don't want you to worry, Mama. God has brought me to this place, and I don't believe He'll abandon me now. I don't know if I can continue in the research I love and remain in Cheyenne, but for now, I'm exactly where I'm supposed to be. Spencer believes this as well. He's very solid in his faith, whereas Oswald had none at all. The man revealed to me not long ago that he truly believed there was no Divine Creator. That alone caused a cavernous separation between us. I know I could never have overcome that, although I kept praying God would prove Himself to Oswald."

"What a strange train of thought. That God should have to prove Himself to anyone is absurd."

"I agree, Mama, but Oswald was one of those people who thought the world owed him. Had he believed in God, he would no doubt have thought He owed him as well. I'm quite glad to be rid of him. His disbelief in God should have caused me to end the relationship first thing. Instead, it took Oswald betraying me. God forgive me."

"He does. Given all that you've related, I'm glad you put an end to your engagement as well as your working relationship. A husband should be someone you can trust with your heart."

"And your soul," Carrie added. "A husband should be someone who strengthens your faith and encourages its growth in the Lord. You taught me that. And as I've matured in my faith, I've come to believe that it's imperative that a husband and wife be in complete agreement regarding who God is and what it means to serve Him."

"I could not have said it better." Mama gave her a look of approval and a nod. "You'd better eat, your food will get cold."

Carrie was relieved that she had successfully steered the conversation away from why she'd married Spencer so quickly. At least for now, Mama was satisfied with thoughts of Carrie and Spencer's shared spiritual beliefs.

Of course, there was still Papa to deal with.

10

Carrie looked over the local news board at the Armstrong Emporium. Cynthia Armstrong kept a board in her store from their early days when folks needed to find places to live or other things available to buy or trade. Those early days in Cheyenne made such boards necessary, and now they just gave a bit of convenience. There were several houses listed for sale, but only a few very small apartments for rent. Nothing seemed overly suited for Carrie's ambitions. Her thoughts were to get a three-bedroom house, maybe something close to town where she could receive patients. She and Spencer could each have their own bedroom, and the third could be her office and examination room.

"Why, if it isn't Carrie Vogel," an older man declared. "Your mother and father tell me you consider yourself a doctor."

Carrie turned to find old Dr. Lyons, a longtime physician in Cheyenne. Another man stood beside him and gave her a nod. "I remember when I removed your tonsils."

"Dr. Lyons, how nice to see you again."

The older man tipped his hat, then turned to his companion. "Dr. Bruce Compton, meet Carrie Vogel."

"Actually it's Dr. Vogel . . . Duval. I married recently, and we've decided to settle here for a time."

"Bruce is interested in the brain, as I hear you are," Dr. Lyons proclaimed. "I still think women are better suited to keeping house and raising children, but this modern age has distorted the thinking of our youth." He laughed and slapped his thigh. "Now, there's a disorder to study."

Dr. Compton extended his hand. "Dr. Vogel-Duval, I'm pleased to meet you. I am interested in studies on the brain myself. Quite fascinated with the research that's being done."

"My particular interest is not only injury or disease of the brain, but the correlation between those things and the personality changes and mental conditions the patient often endures because of them."

"Oh, grief!" Dr. Lyons said, sounding most vexed. "Psychiatry hoodoo and all that. A waste of time."

"I hardly think so," Carrie countered. "There have been great strides in that area. Look at the work of Dorothea Dix, for example. Her efforts have given great insight into the mentally ill and why they should not be housed with dangerous criminals when jailed for their actions. We can learn from her work that many people are not capable of reasoning right and wrong due to deficiencies in the brain. A great many of those patients started out with specific brain injuries."

Dr. Compton's expression betrayed excitement. "Exactly so. I've been quite fascinated regarding patients who develop tumors in the brain and how that affects their behavior, memory, and ability to reason."

"I have a few good articles on those very topics if you'd like to borrow them sometime." Carrie was more than pleased to find a fellow doctor who shared her passions.

Dr. Lyons had had more than enough. He waved them both off and shook his head. "This is just a passing fancy.

Doctors will find out soon enough that the brain is no different than any other part of the body. It gets injured and heals or doesn't."

"But unlike other parts of the body that don't heal and must be excised, one can hardly remove the brain and still have a living patient." Carrie had heard these kinds of protests since first entering college. Dr. Lyons was simply an older doctor without insight into the future of medicine.

"Exactly," Dr. Compton replied. "Which is why we must study in detail every aspect of the human brain."

"Bah!" Dr. Lyons started to go, then stopped. "Carrie Vogel—Duval—you would do much better to stay home and take care of your husband rather than worry about his brain." With that, he left her and Dr. Compton and trudged across the store to the front counter.

"Sorry about his obvious dislike of female physicians and brain disorders. He's spoken his feelings on both many times, especially given we have two female physicians here in town. I've always tried to assure him that women could bring much-needed insight into the sciences, but of course he is from another age."

"Yes, as are so many men. You seem not to mind my field of interest, however."

"Not at all. In fact, I remember reading a short article you published in the *American Journal of Insanity*. You spoke of the various affects you were discovering when introducing experimental medications to patients with severe melancholia."

"I wrote that shortly after graduating medical college. I was working with a research team at the college, but this was something I'd done on my own." She remembered how furious Oswald had been that she hadn't consulted him before agreeing to publish the article. It was one of the last times she got credit for her own work.

"I found it quite interesting. Did you continue with that research?"

"No, my partner . . . fiancé took me in a different direction. Now, however, I'd like to get back to it. There is still so much to learn."

"But you've married?"

"Not to the same man. I was engaged to Dr. Oswald Nelson at one time."

"I know that name well. He just published a major finding on the brain repairing itself and recovering various skills."

"You may not believe this, Dr. Compton, but the finding was mine, and he stole it. Which is why I broke off the engagement and married another." She wasn't sure why she felt the need to mention this. Now that she'd offered the information, Carrie felt embarrassed. She hadn't meant to sound like a braggart.

"I do believe you. In fact, I would love to discuss this at length. Would you have time to come to my office sometime next week? I live just north of the capitol. My office is there, and my wife manages my appointments for me." He handed her a card. "Come by any time."

"I would be happy to." Carrie glanced at the card for the man's address and then smiled. "I see you have a telephone number. I will call you to let you know what day might work best. Would that be all right?"

"Absolutely. It was a great pleasure to meet you, Doctor." Carrie shook his hand. "And you as well, Dr. Compton."

She watched him go, then turned back to the board. Just then, someone else approached and called her name. What a day.

"Carrie, it's me. Katie Combes."

Carrie turned to find her childhood friend. "Katie? Goodness, how long has it been?"

"You know very well. It's been eight years, and in all that time you only wrote me six letters."

"I do apologize, my friend. It was a terrible show of friendship on my part." Carrie hated that she'd lost touch with the vivacious woman. They had been friends since they were little, and Carrie had always anticipated that they would remain so for life.

"Are you back now to visit or stay?"

"For the time being, I plan to stay. I'm married and a doctor, so it will all depend on my work and my husband."

"Where are you planning to live?"

"That's why I'm here today. I came to look at the board to find a place to rent."

Katie's mouth dropped open, and she gave a squeal of delight. "You're in such luck. My grandmother moved back to Missouri to live with my uncle. We have her house to rent out. It's completely furnished, but I'm sure we could move some things to storage if you've brought your own."

"No, we haven't anything. I remember your grandmother lived off of Sixteenth, didn't she?"

"Yes! It's just a few blocks from your folks and close to town."

Carrie nodded. "How many rooms?"

"There are two large bedrooms, a kitchen and dining room, a parlor and separate music room. Grandmother used to give piano lessons there, if you remember."

"I was hoping for three bedrooms. I want to set up my research and perhaps see patients, but it seems the music room might work out well for that."

"Why don't you come with me and see it now? The rent is very reasonable, and Mama might even want to lower it once she knows it's you renting the place. She was always very fond of you and your family."

"I'd be happy to come see it."

"Then I won't even post the information on the board. I am almost certain you'll love it."

Carrie followed her friend from the emporium and out into the cold morning air. They made their way from downtown along Sixteenth with Katie filling Carrie in on all the news of who had married and who had children.

"I think you were the only young lady who went off to college. At least from among our friends. Most married or moved away when their families left the area. So many people left here in '87 after the big blizzard."

"Yes, Mama told me all about it," Carrie admitted. "It sounded very bad."

"It was." Katie's eyes darkened. "There was so much death. So many cattle were lost and people too. It was just tragic for everyone. Even the wealthy big ranches suffered, and some completely folded. We're just now seeing folks get back on their feet. At least the ones who stuck it out."

Katie turned at the corner, and Carrie kept pace with her rapid strides. The cold air seemed unimportant as the quick pace kept them quite warm.

"So, you have mentioned others in our class marrying and having children, but what of you, Katie?"

She glanced at Carrie. "I have a beau, but we haven't yet gotten quite that serious. You wouldn't know him since he just moved here around Christmas. However, he attends our church, and if you're there tomorrow, I can introduce you."

"That sounds perfect. I'll introduce you to my husband, Spencer Duval. He's one of Papa's law officers, so you might even run across him on the street. In fact, he's working now."

"Here we are." Katie stopped abruptly and waved her hand. "If you like it and decide to rent it, we can go from here to see Mother. It's just a block away, if you remember."

"I remember it well, but not so much this place." She gazed across the yard. "I love the picket fence."

"My grandmother was very fond of white picket. She said it reminded her of the place she grew up in Missouri. Do you remember the time we came here to learn how to crochet doilies?"

Carrie vaguely remembered the small white house and the challenge of crocheting. "I remember your grandmother loved lemon verbena. The house always smelled of it." Glancing up and down the street, Carrie felt certain it would be an easily accessible address for her patients to find.

"She loved that scent as well as lilies of the valley. Oh, I'm going to miss her so much." Katie motioned Carrie to follow. "Let me show you the place."

Once inside the house, Carrie was even more convinced that the house would work well for them. The music room would be perfect to set up an examination table and laboratory. Since she planned for them to have separate bedrooms, she was particularly interested in what that arrangement might look like. When Katie showed her the first bedroom, Carrie immediately thought it would be perfect for Spencer. It wasn't all that large, but it would suit him. There was a large chest of drawers and a bedding box at the foot of the double bed. The single window was not only shaded but had heavy blue curtains as well.

The next bedroom was much brighter. It had been papered in a rose-print pattern. There was a smaller bed here, as well as a writing desk and bookshelf. On the far side of the room was a small closet, a rarity to be sure.

Carrie was already thinking about the future and how the little house would suit her quite well as a practicing doctor living on her own. If the rent was right, then she could imagine herself living here quite comfortably. As long as she could get patients.

"I think this room would make a pretty nursery, don't you?" Katie moved to the double window and pushed back the rose-colored curtains. "There is a lot of light to be let in since the room is on the south side."

"I see that." Carrie hoped the conversation wouldn't linger on children. She didn't want to have to answer questions about whether she and Spencer planned to have offspring right away.

"Did you know that Charlotte Aldrich—well, she's a Hamilton now. She married Micah Hamilton. Anyway, they're expecting a baby almost any day now. Their first."

"I'm sure they're very happy about that." Carrie moved toward the door. "Can we see the kitchen now?"

Katie closed the curtains and joined Carrie in the hall. "I used to bake cookies with Grandmother in this kitchen. We spruced it up a bit when Mama arranged for her to have electricity and a telephone, but it still brings happy memories."

Carrie was glad to hear that the place had a telephone. She would have arranged for one even if it hadn't, but to have it already in place was a nice benefit that she hadn't counted on.

She looked the kitchen over and nodded. "It would work very well for us. I think we'll take it."

Katie looked delighted and then sobered. "What about your husband? Shouldn't you discuss it with him first?"

"We have already talked about it. He told me if I found something today to go ahead and agree to the rental." Carrie smiled. "Let's go speak to your mother."

Eugene Astor was none too happy to hear what the doctor had to say. As he left the hospital in Kansas City, he barely found the strength to keep walking. He was exhausted from the examinations, explanations, and lack of solutions. All he wanted now was to return to his hotel and seek comfort in a bottle of whiskey and a warm bed.

There was no hope. No help for him, and perhaps that's what he deserved. He had lived a selfish life. He had never concerned himself with helping to better the lives of others, with exception to his mother. Never sought to have a religious experience that might propel him into thoughts of eternity in the presence of God. Surely murderers weren't allowed in heaven, even if sins could be forgiven.

He hailed a cab and gave the driver the address of his hotel before settling back against the cold leather. It was snowing again, and noting the color of the skies, Eugene was convinced a heavier storm was moving in. Perhaps it was just as well. He would need several days to restore his energy before moving on to Chicago, where he was supposed to see a specialty clinic. One that focused solely on the brain.

"But why bother with Chicago?" he murmured aloud. "The doctors have made it clear there is no help to be had."

He tried not to become maudlin about his condition. He was, after all, an old man who had lived a good life. It hadn't been ideal by any means, and he still regretted the fact that he'd never allowed for a woman to mean more to him than a passing fancy. What a difference it might have made had he known the right partner with whom to face life's woes.

He shook his head at this thought. No, if he'd married and had children, then they, too, would be facing his demise. There would be all sorts of sentimentality. Bad and good. It was better to face this alone. There was no one he needed to comfort or convince that he was doing well enough . . . that he wasn't in any pain.

But he was in pain. A great deal of pain. It wasn't constant, for which he was quite grateful. However, it was often enough and bad enough that he had no desire to share that part of his life with anyone.

The cab halted in front of the multistory brick building, and a hotel doorman helped Eugene down from the carriage.

He handed the man money to pay the driver and headed toward the door of the hotel. The doorman quickly caught up and reached out to hand Eugene the change.

"Keep it. You've more than earned it."

"Thank you, sir."

The man opened the hotel door and ushered Eugene inside just as the wind began to pick up. "Welcome back, Mr. Knowles. Would you care to have dinner brought up?" the front desk clerk asked.

Eugene nodded. He wasn't really hungry, but it seemed the right thing to do. "Yes, send me the same thing I had last night."

The man nodded. "The evening papers have been delivered to your room, along with the whiskey you ordered."

"Thank you." Eugene handed the man his gratuity and headed for the elevator. His body was breaking down with each step. He needed very much to be in his room . . . alone.

It seemed to take forever, but Eugene finally closed his door and shut out the rest of the world. He made his way to an overstuffed chair and sank down. Closing his eyes, he mourned the news he'd received. The same hopeless news he'd been told before. There was no doubt a tumor pressing against several important nerves and parts of his brain. The tumor was inoperable and growing. His time was limited. Weeks, possibly months, but definitely not any real length of time or quality of life. He would most likely go blind, given the way his vision was already blurring. The dizziness would increase, as would the pain, and leave him unable to rise from his bed. Eventually he would fail to awaken, and from this state of coma, he would pass from the earth to whatever existence awaited him.

Facing the truth was hard. Ignoring it, however, was impossible.

Eugene reached over for the awaiting bottle of whiskey. It

was a fine brand and age. He'd spent extra money to purchase it and have it delivered to the hotel. What was the sense of having money if he couldn't enjoy some of it himself?

He opened the bottle and poured a bit into a glass that the hotel staff had thoughtfully left. The aroma brought back memories of happier times. Times he spent in his brothers' company before the war. They had been young and carefree. The world awaited them, and their dreams were limitless.

Eugene gazed across the room, imagining Calvin and Amos joining him there. He lifted the glass in salute.

"I shall see you both soon."

11

"You chose well. This little house is more than adequate for our needs," Spencer told Carrie. Their short time in the house had proven the accommodations to be more than acceptable. Spencer still had trouble accepting their separate sleeping quarters, yet knew it was the right thing to do. He supposed he had gotten used to having Carrie near him, and the loss was surprisingly hard for him.

Still, he could hardly expect her to live as a wife when their agreement was to separate after he found Astor. Her reputation would be compromised enough. Of course, Carrie was used to people questioning her standards and practices. He had even heard some rather negative comments about her at church. Of all the places he expected to find love and acceptance, church hadn't proven to be one.

He still recalled the Sunday before when he'd overheard two women exchanging their disapproval of Carrie becoming a physician. *The Cheyenne Leader* had come out with an article on Carrie's return to town, explaining how she had set up shop as a doctor specializing in head injuries and disease. They thought it all rather scandalous, and their questions were plentiful. Would she see male patients as well as female?

Would she treat only the head or other parts of the body? They thought it completely unacceptable that she might be called upon to treat any condition particular to a man's needs.

Spencer had smiled at their concerns, but at the same time he was troubled to consider that Carrie would probably face women like this all her life. Even Oswald Nelson had convinced her that no one would ever take her research seriously. Such attitudes made him even more determined to help Carrie in any way possible. He wanted her to succeed. Wanted her to see all of her dreams come true. The only problem was, he was starting to hope he might find a way to be included in those dreams.

"I put away the food Mama sent home with us. I suppose I should be grateful they have us over to dinner almost every night. Neither of us are great cooks," Carrie said, coming to the front parlor.

Spencer had settled down in front of the fire on the sofa and patted the seat beside him. "That's what restaurants are for."

She smiled and sat down at his side. "I agree. However, Mama is a great cook, and she loves having the entire family around. She misses Daniel something fierce, and even though he's been good to write, it's not the same."

"Of course it's not. So what is that brother of yours hoping to do with his life?"

"Who can say. He changes his mind all the time. He went through a stage when he wanted to engineer and design bridges. Then he was sure he wanted to be an architect. After that I believe he wanted to build ships. It's always been about creating things. He has such a brilliant mind. Probably even more capable than mine."

"I find that hard to imagine." Spencer gave her a smile.

"Tell me how things are going in your pursuits. Have you any new leads on Mr. Astor?"

"None. I spoke to someone with the Union Pacific, a man who handles initial interviews for new positions. I told him I was looking for a distant family member and told him the name Eugene Astor. He'd never heard of him, and he's been with the UP for over twenty years. Said they never employed anyone by that name in Cheyenne. I told him he might have changed his name since there had been some problems when he lived back east. I asked if perhaps he remembered a comptroller or accountant who looked like Astor, and then I described the man I remembered."

"And what did he say to that?"

"That the description pretty much fit half of the men they'd hired for the UP and that they had dozens of comptrollers." Spencer shook his head. "I've asked around to some of the other men, but no one seems helpful at all. I've been hesitant to push too hard for fear of Astor catching wind of my search and making a run for it."

"So what will you do to further investigate?"

Spencer heaved a sigh and stared into the blazing hearth. "That's what I keep asking myself. I'll probably have to go to the offices at night and search through their files. I don't know that it will reveal the information I need, but I have to start somewhere."

"You say this man came here perhaps twenty years ago or so. Is that right?" Carrie looked to him for confirmation.

"Yes. One of the earliest letters Eugene sent his mother stated that he was moving to Cheyenne. That letter was sent in the early part of 1870. It might be possible, however, that he didn't stay here. The Union Pacific could have hired him to work anywhere along the line as a sort of traveling employee."

"What do you mean?"

"Apparently, some workers went back and forth between various towns on the line. As an accountant or comptroller, they might have had him doing that. Maybe taking inventory and making payrolls to the smaller towns where the UP had no offices. Of course, he might just as well have been headquartered here in one place. The Union Pacific employed a great many men here in Cheyenne."

"The town was still very small back in 1870. You might want to talk to the folks who were in charge of selling town lots, although I know the railroad did that as well. You could also talk to boardinghouse owners and get a list of folks who rented out properties back then. Papa would probably know who you'd want to talk to."

"I can't involve him. At least not yet. I want to, mainly because he deserves to know what I'm up to. But if I explain that much, there'd really be no excuse not to be honest about our marriage."

"And we can't tell them that because they would insist we stop the charade, and that would create problems for you," Carrie said, shaking her head.

"And even more troublesome, he could be good friends with Astor and not even know it. We've been here such a short time we've not really had a chance to explore that possibility."

"Maybe check the land management records."

He smiled. She was able to think like a detective, and he liked that about her. "Yes, I should." Spencer reached over to push back an errant blond curl. Carrie didn't seem to notice. He liked that she was so comfortable with him that his action seemed natural.

"Use the distant family excuse. People respect folks trying to connect to family," Carrie suggested. "Papa was always talking about folks stopping by to ask him what he might know. I remember that quite well because my mother was worried about someone coming after us."

"For what reason?" Spencer stretched his legs out toward the fireplace.

"I mentioned it once when we were acting in that play we did about a group of orphans getting homes for Christmas. Don't you remember? There were these people who wanted to take me away from her after our father died." Carrie frowned and shook her head. "It wasn't a good situation. When our father died, the local pastor thought it unacceptable that my sister should take over raising me. She was young and unmarried. She had no means of supporting me. There was a wealthy and powerful family in the church who couldn't have children, and the pastor tried to arrange for them to adopt me. Mama was terrified of losing me. She and Papa married and came west to save me from being taken away. Besides, you told me you investigated me."

"I do remember it, now that you bring it up. Wasn't it the pastor who involved a local judge to take you from your sister?"

"Exactly so. Mama was beside herself because it always seemed rich people could buy whatever they wanted. After coming here, she was always quite adamant that I never speak to strangers unless she or Papa was with me."

"Seems a smart thing to teach children."

Carrie seemed lost in her thoughts. "I do recall, however, that once the railroad was completed a great many people began flooding our little town, and a lot of them came in search of family and friends. Your story won't be considered unusual at all."

"I suppose not. The problem is explaining the name change."

This drew her full attention. "Nonsense. The West is full of people who were looking for a fresh start and changed their names. Many of the immigrants did that too. I had a friend whose last name was Karpovsky, but it was too difficult for others to pronounce, so they changed it to Karp. If you just explain that to the people you talk to, they'll understand why you don't know what name he went by."

"Makes sense. Maybe I'll ask around tomorrow after Bible study with the men. Your father and Mr. Decker really seem talented in leading the men. The study has deepened my knowledge of the Bible."

"Mr. Decker has a vast education and has even filled in for the pastor on occasion. He runs a wonderful school for boys, and nearly everyone who attends his school ends up going to college. His son Michael, the one who's marrying my sister Greta, graduated college early and teaches at the school as well."

"The Deckers have ten children, if I remember correctly."

"Yes, they do. Mrs. Decker and Mama have been close friends since we first came to Cheyenne. They both wanted big families, but Mama couldn't have any more children after Daniel. Mrs. Decker said that was all right, she would have plenty and share them with Mama. We grew up like one big happy family. I got a lot of experience caring for babies that way."

"I think I would have enjoyed being part of a big family. Having had no siblings, I was often very lonely, and after losing my father, there was no one with whom I could share that pain. My mother was devastated and hardly able to console herself, much less her child. I tried to be strong for her, but I assure you, the loss was deeply felt."

"I'm sure it was." Carrie reached over and took hold of Spencer's hand. "I'm sorry you had to face it alone."

"My faith grew during that time." He drew her hand to his lips and placed a kiss on her knuckles. Spencer didn't know what had prompted him to this action, but Carrie seemed unconcerned. "I learned to talk to God more. I prayed all the time and found great comfort in that."

"Prayer has gotten me through many rough patches. I

suppose given all that has happened to you, my feelings of void and loss seem silly."

"Why should they? You lost a mother and father just as I did."

"Yes, but my sister and her husband stepped into the role so neatly that I didn't really suffer much. After all, I was just a babe."

"And you think that babies don't suffer loss?"

Carrie's brow furrowed. "You know, that poses an interesting line of thought, especially given my studies on the brain. I do believe infants can suffer from the loss of their parents. I don't think much has been done on this line of study, however."

"Maybe it will be another area where you'll excel and bring great results. The losses you've known have obviously had a profound effect on your life, despite having been nurtured and cared for by loving substitutes. If you were to find a way to help others with the void that is created in that loss, it might very well change the world as we know it."

"I suppose it might at that. If people could learn to manage the emptiness left by the loss of another person, especially at a young age, it would alter their behavior and, in doing so, alter life choices. This is quite interesting to me." She seemed momentarily lost in thought and for several minutes fell silent.

Spencer gazed into the fire and thought of how fascinating Carrie's studies were. They certainly had the potential for helping people to overcome problems in their lives. Hers was a task that truly mattered.

Whereas mine is a self-focused drive to avenge my father's death.

Spencer frowned. His entire life was wrapped up in that one goal. What would he do once he'd accomplished that task? He glanced over at his wife. She was everything he wanted in a mate. How could he ever walk away from her?

Eugene was glad to be home. His body was breaking down. He could feel life slipping away from him bit by bit. He had decided to see one more doctor in Kansas City and discuss options. The physician had described his terrifying estimation of what Eugene's death would be like. The weakness, the loss of sight, possible loss of hearing as well. The seizures that were sure to come and the eventual coma he'd slip into. The doctor added to this that even in the coma, his pain would be tripled. How he knew this, the doctor didn't say. He was, however, convinced that even in a comatose state, Eugene would still feel the intense pain.

"You won't be able to do anything about it or ask for medication, of course," the doctor had explained. "You'll be unconscious, and most people will believe that you will be unable to feel anything. But that won't be the situation."

Eugene had asked how the doctor could be certain of this ending, and he had replied that years of experience had convinced him of the matter. The doctor's last words of advice to Eugene still echoed in his thoughts.

"If I was faced with this knowledge, I would resolve the matter by taking charge and assigning my own end. I would never face such a death as I've described. I would take my life and avoid the misery."

That idea haunted Eugene on the train ride home. Across the vast empty prairies of Kansas, he had contemplated the doctor's words. It seemed more than reasonable. Who would choose a laborious, painful death if an easy one of peaceful, gentle passing could be had?

The small house was freezing after he had so long been absent. Eugene continued his contemplation on what to do as he began to build a fire. He opened the damper, then laid logs on the grate. Next, he took up a few pieces of kindling and arranged those on the floor beneath the grate. Leaving this, he went to a stack of newspapers that had collected in his absence. He took one from the pile and pulled apart the sheets.

Just then his gaze fell upon the headline. *LOCAL GIRL RETURNS TO CHEYENNE LAUDED PHYSICIAN.*

Eugene scanned the article reading about Carrie Vogel-Duval, daughter of the chief of police. She had been something of a scientific prodigy, concentrating her studies on injury and illness to the brain. She was noted for her ability to seek alternative methods of healing and help, going beyond what other doctors would consider acceptable practice.

A woman physician. A very young woman who was able to look beyond the problem to all the possible solutions. She wasn't stymied by the normal routines of the day. The smallest spark of hope ignited. Might it be possible that the help Eugene sought was right here in Cheyenne? If he was already condemned to death, what possible problem could it be to seek out the young woman and get her opinion on his condition?

He smiled and carefully folded the paper and set it aside. Picking up another copy, Eugene crumpled up a page and went back to the fireplace to start his fire. For the first time since leaving Kansas City, he had a renewal of hope. Maybe Dr. Carrie Vogel-Duval would be his salvation.

12

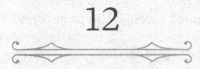

Carrie knew it wouldn't be easy getting patients in Cheyenne, though she secretly hoped that because she was known to so many and that folks highly regarded her parents, they might overlook the fact that she was a woman and take a chance on her doctoring skills. She knew it would be imperative for her to practice as a regular physician while doing her specialized research. She had to make a living, after all. If not, her savings would dwindle fast, and she'd soon be faced with having to move home.

At least, once Spencer caught his man and left Cheyenne. The thought of that saddened her more than Carrie liked to think. Spencer was a good friend, and while there were other friends in Cheyenne, none of them were as special to her as Spencer. When had that happened?

Each day she found herself longing for his company, eager for him to return from his duties. She cared deeply about his welfare, and when she'd heard him sneeze the day before, she'd hurried to his side to feel his forehead and ascertain whether he was coming down sick. She knew it was foolish to care so much. He was going to find Astor, and then he was going to leave. That was the agreement, and that would be the way things went. She desperately needed to remember this.

Sitting down to her desk, Carrie tried to focus on a new book. She'd ordered it just before leaving Chicago, and it had finally caught up with her. The book, *Handbook of Psychology: Senses and Intellect* by James Mark Baldwin, was touted as offering exceptional insight into the world of psychology.

Carrie thumbed through the preface, skipping it as she often did and going straight to the table of contents. She noted the introduction section with three chapters devoted to the nature of psychology, the psychological method, and finally classification and division. She continued down the list of chapters. Part I was titled "General Characteristics of Mind." That held great promise. She turned to the page and began to read. She wasn't much past the first couple of sentences, however, when a light knock sounded at the front door.

Getting to her feet, Carrie made her way to the door. On the other side she found a middle-aged woman dressed fashionably in a navy-blue wool coat trimmed in mink. A mink muff warmed her hands and a matching hat completed the outfit. She was obviously one of Cheyenne's wealthier citizens.

"May I help you?"

"I do hope so. You are Dr. Vogel-Duval?" the woman asked.

"I am. Won't you come in?" Carrie stepped back to allow the woman entrance. She closed the front door and led the woman down the hall to her examination office. "What can I do for you?"

"My name is Gloriana Bryant. I'm suffering from terrible headaches," the woman began. "I've been ignored by most of the doctors I've visited. They tell me it's my nerves and suggest I take laudanum. One doctor told me I was just a highly agitated woman."

"Goodness, that must be quite vexing."

The woman seemed momentarily surprised, then leaned toward Carrie, nodding. "It is. It is. There is something wrong with me. I don't know what it might be, but I hoped that you could help. My husband is quite wealthy. I will pay you any amount of money you ask, if only you can help me."

Carrie smiled. "While I appreciate being paid for my work, I'm not in this business for that reason. Why don't you have a seat, and I'll ask some questions and make notes before examining you."

When they had both taken a seat, Carrie began. "Now, tell me the general nature of these headaches."

Mrs. Bryant drew a deep breath. "They come at all hours of the day or night. Often I have warning."

"Warning?" Carrie asked.

"Yes. There's a sort of spell where my eye, usually my left, blurs like after having sunlight hit you unexpectedly. It's not the flash of light itself, but that blur of vision that comes afterward."

Carrie began to write notes. "I understand. Please go on."

"Then within a short time, I experience my vision darkening around the edges. When that happens, I know that in twenty minutes to half an hour, my head will begin to hurt and all I can do is go to bed. The pain increases to unbearable levels and lasts for several hours. Sometimes days, although that isn't as usual. Most of these attacks are maybe four to six hours."

"And what does the pain feel like? Is an intense sharp pain, a dull ache, a tightening—"

"Yes! A tightening. Like a band being fitted around my head and squeezed smaller and smaller."

"And how are your eyes during this time? Sensitive to light? Do they throb?"

"No, the darkening and blurring leave me. I'm usually in

my bed, and my maid brings me warm compresses, so I don't allow for much light. The shades and drapes are pulled."

"What about nausea?"

"Yes, my stomach roils. I also become very sensitive to smells and, of course, noise. It seems the tiniest of sounds causes the pain to increase."

"It sounds to me that you are suffering a special kind of headache called a migraine, Mrs. Bryant."

By the time Mrs. Bryant left, Carrie had a fairly good idea of her overall condition, as well as the headaches. She was forty-three years old, had been married for twenty years, and had given birth to three children. Her general health was good. She never had feelings of weakness or nausea that weren't a result of the headaches. She did not experience heart palpitations or pain in other areas of her body on a regular basis. She had suffered debilitating headaches several times a week for over three years and had tried a wide variety of cures, none proving very reliable.

Mrs. Bryant was beside herself dealing with the pain and had visited numerous doctors. She had avoided laudanum due to the results her sister had suffered after constant use. Having recently read an article on the continued experiments with theophylline, Carrie thought this might help. She suggested Mrs. Byrant have her cook make a batch of extremely strong tea, letting the tea bags steep for several hours. Theophylline was naturally found in tea leaves, and this had been known to eliminate head pain. Carrie also suggested a series of hot and cold compresses.

There was much experimentation being done, including incline therapy, in which the patient would lie on a sturdy board and allow themselves to be tilted down for increasingly longer periods of time. Carrie hadn't read much on the outcomes, however, and hesitated to recommend it. She was of the school of thought that believed the migraines were due to various issues with the blood flow in the head.

She suggested Mrs. Bryant return in a week's time so that they might go over her condition once again. The grateful woman agreed, paid her bill, and hailed her driver. For Carrie the entire visit had been most gratifying. She enjoyed giving patients hope of relief and had promised Mrs. Bryant she would work with her faithfully to find a solution. Where other doctors had cast her aside, Carrie was personally challenged to figure out how to help.

Nevertheless, for all of her skills, Carrie still found prayer absolutely necessary. She sat at her desk and bowed her head.

"Lord, please give me wisdom for helping Mrs. Bryant with her headaches. You alone know what she might need. Please let me know as well, yet no matter what . . . Your will be done. Amen."

The latter part of her prayer was always the hardest. Letting go of her own desires and praying for God's will in healing matters required utmost trust and faith. Many a time, patients had died despite Carrie's efforts. It was hard to look into the eyes of a person who had just come to realize there was nothing more that could be done. The understanding of their own demise was often more than they could bear. In that moment all their plans, hopes, and dreams were rendered useless. The reality of death was not easily accepted for many.

Carrie, however, didn't fear death. She remembered when old Granny Taylor had passed away. The woman was a pillar of strength when it came to her Christian faith. Death held no cause for concern. No regret. She had lived a life of grace and mercy in the Lord.

"*I shall but breathe out this old world and breathe in the presence of my King,*" she had said upon her deathbed.

It was the first time Carrie had witnessed someone die.

She could still remember the peaceful expression on the older woman's face. It had given her a perspective of death that remained with her even now. Death wasn't the end.

"Thank you for inviting me to this town meeting," Spencer told his father-in-law as they joined an audience of mostly men.

Edward Vogel gave him a nod. "Good to have you here. I think it's important to get a feel for the business end of the place you live."

They took their seats, and Spencer looked around the room to see whom he might recognize. It seemed unlikely that Astor would join in on such an affair. Of course, Spencer reminded himself that he didn't know this man the way he wished he did. Astor had done a good job of staying out of public view. He'd been quite skilled at disappearing and deceiving the agency. Had it not been for the letters they found at his mother's place, they wouldn't have even known he was in Cheyenne all these years. It was always possible that this was a lie, but it seemed to both Al and Spencer that Astor drew the line in trying to deceive his mother.

The meeting was quickly called to order, and Spencer put aside his concerns regarding Astor. He didn't want Vogel to think him disinterested in the town's procedures and news.

"As most of you know," a man began, "there have been many changes going on in Cheyenne of late. I'm going to introduce you to a man who is representing our largest and most active employer, the Union Pacific Railroad. The president of the UP has sent us one of his right-hand men, Mr. Claude Danby, to report on the various Cheyenne projects that are now in progress. Mr. Danby."

The audience clapped for the man as he approached the

podium. Spencer noted his gray suit, black tie, and white shirt. The balding man was of average height and weight and with no distinguishing marks. He was the kind of man who would easily blend into a crowd unnoticed.

"Ladies and gentlemen of Cheyenne, it is my pleasure to report that President Adams sends his regards. We at the Union Pacific are delighted to announce that Cheyenne continues to be one of the largest and most efficient stops along the line. The new depot has proven itself a masterpiece of creativity. It has already serviced over a thousand trains. At this time, we are at work to build a roundhouse with ten stalls as well as a shop to create railcars, a woodworking and paint shop, a warehouse, and a variety of other structures. The Union Pacific is here to stay in Cheyenne."

The audience broke into thunderous applause. Spencer knew that besides the Union Pacific, the only other major employer was Fort Russell. With those two employers expanding and adding new employees and soldiers, Cheyenne was bound to see prosperity.

"We will be adding several hundred new employees, which means that your town will see considerable growth in this year alone. Our company has always been big on hiring family men as they make for a much stabler workforce. This will in turn bring families to your community, and the railroad is ready to help with that as well. We are making new railroad land available for housing as well as community needs. We have expanded the UP hospital to provide adequate services, both routine and emergency. Furthermore, we were pleased to see a new school being built on the south side of the UP tracks and hold great pride in this fair community.

"The Union Pacific is proud to be a part of Cheyenne and will endeavor to do whatever we can to promote statehood for the fair territory of Wyoming."

There was more applause, and after Danby finished his

short speech, George W. Baxter, another of the city officials, came to take the podium and began speaking of the topic on everyone's mind: statehood.

"As most of you know, I was an active member of the constitutional convention we held last year to draft a state constitution." Cheers again erupted. Baxter held up his hands to quiet the room.

"We are pushing hard for acceptance into the Union for this year. Delegate J. M. Carey is even now lobbying with great enthusiasm in Washington to see that the House of Representatives passes a bill to admit us as the forty-fourth state in these United States of America."

As the audience again began to applaud, some of the men jumped to their feet to give shouts of approval. Spencer felt the excitement of those in the room. It was contagious. Even Chief Vogel clapped most enthusiastically. When they were once again calmed, Baxter continued.

"We feel confident that the vote will go our way, and then we will seek the approval of the Senate. These are exciting times in the life of our territory and soon-to-be state. We are on the cusp of a bright future."

He continued to speak about celebrations and new opportunities to serve in the government while Spencer gazed around the room, seeking anyone who seemed out of place or disinterested. At the moment, everyone in the room seemed caught up in the momentum of Baxter's speech.

Politics had never been Spencer's point of interest. He had no desire to run for public office or butter up those who did. He was content being out of the public eye. It served his position as a Pinkerton quite well. However, it was easy to see how a mob might be easily incited to do almost anything. These people were the kind who would get this matter resolved in quick order.

There were at least five other speakers, and by the time

they finished, Spencer was more than anxious to be on his way. But his father-in-law wanted to introduce him to a number of men. Cheyenne's city fathers. The people who made things happen in Cheyenne. Spencer took a bit more interest in this, knowing it was very possible one or all might be familiar with Eugene Astor. Still, it wasn't like he could just up and ask if they knew the man. Nothing would be more questionable than that, and Spencer hadn't gotten where he was with the Pinkertons by being amateurish in his duties.

He endured the introductions and made small talk with each. Finally, Chief Vogel signaled it was time to go, and Spencer happily followed. To his surprise, it had started to snow again. Would this winter never end? They crossed the muddy street, and Spencer let his father-in-law take the lead.

"How about some lunch?" Vogel asked.

Spencer didn't want to appear anxious to get away, so he nodded. "Sounds good."

They slipped into a local café and ordered coffee and the special. Spencer settled back in his seat and wrapped his hands around the warm cup. He took a long, slow sip and smiled. It was strong and hot and took the edge off his nerves.

"You seem wound up tighter than new springs. What's going on with you?"

He hadn't anticipated this question from the older man. He decided the truth was best.

"I guess I'm still a bit unsure of our relationship." Spencer shrugged. "I know Carrie and I married fast, and you question my love for your daughter. I think you're entitled to feel that way and don't blame you for wondering about me. I guess if Carrie were my daughter, I'd wonder too. Still, I can't help but feel I'm being constantly scrutinized." He held up his hand. "Not that you're wrong to do so."

"I'm glad to know you're an understanding sort." Vogel

leaned back in the chair and studied Spencer for a long moment.

"I'll answer any of your questions. I figure the only way you'll feel better about me is to get to know me."

Vogel nodded. "But I have a feeling there would still be things you'd keep hidden."

His comment took Spencer by surprise. He cleared his throat. "I suppose we all have things we keep to ourselves."

Vogel leaned forward rather quickly, and Spencer had to force himself not to jump. He knew Vogel would sense his tension and did his best to maintain eye contact.

"I know you're important to my daughter. I can see by the way she looks at you that she cares deeply. She never looked at Nelson that way. But I can also see that she has her secrets. She always has. I guess I'd feel a mite better if the two of you realized you could trust me."

The serving girl brought their food, but Spencer found his appetite was gone. Vogel knew there was deception going on. He was a good lawman and had studied the behavior of multiple individuals over the years. He knew Spencer was lying to him. Carrie had known her father wouldn't be easily persuaded by a pretense of marriage. And now, even though they had a marriage certificate and had gone through an official ceremony, Edward Vogel still seemed to know they were lying about something. Maybe everything.

"Look, I'm not trying to impose on either of you. I want you to know that I consider you a son now, same as I do my own boys. I want us to be close and to know we can trust each other to be honest. We hopefully have a great many years to get this relationship to a place of comfort and ease, but it's going to take honesty."

"I want that too." Spencer realized he meant it. He wanted to know this man better. He wanted Edward Vogel to trust him and count him as a son. He was ready then and there to confess what he was up to. Maybe telling his father-in-law would be beneficial in the long run.

"I guess one thing I'd like to tell you—"

"Chief Vogel," a man said, coming up to the table. "I wonder if we might have a word? In private. It's urgent."

Vogel gave Spencer a look that suggested his regret. "What is it?"

Spencer didn't know whether to be relieved or aggravated as Vogel got to his feet. His stomach churned. Lies never sat well with him. Especially when it involved someone he truly liked and wanted to show respect.

13

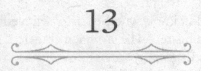

Over two weeks had passed since the article in the *Leader* was published, and plenty of people had offered their insight and thoughts on Carrie's choice of career. Some were quite open and supportive, telling her they were happy to have female doctors in town. Others were less impressed and tended to condemn such positions for women.

Carrie was used to the negativity, especially when it came to older women feeling it was inappropriate for a single young lady to treat the bodies of men. Such intimacy was far too great and would ruin her reputation and innocence. There was always someone who inevitably brought up the Bible and how women were to be workers at home. Carrie took it all in stride, however. She knew most of the folks who commented didn't mean to cause her trouble, and those who did or who wanted to belittle her weren't of great enough importance to even address. As her mother once had told her, *"I imagine if they had a desperate need, and you were the only doctor available, they would yield to your care fast enough."*

The newspaper had given her good exposure, and for that she was more than grateful. Several women had sought her out. Most were suffering a variety of headaches and female troubles. She dealt with them in her usual manner—questioning, observing, and doing her best to hear what they weren't saying. Most of the situations were fairly routine and of no great consequence.

During that time, Carrie also challenged herself to read a variety of books dealing with brain disorders and injuries, as well as the Baldwin book on psychology. She held herself at a high standard, testing herself on terms and conditions until she was almost able to repeat the writings verbatim.

That's why, when a visitor came unannounced, Carrie was more than ready to put aside her studies and receive the smiling woman who stood on the other side of the door.

"I don't know if you've heard of me, but I'm Dr. Buchanan," the woman introduced herself.

"I'm so glad you decided to stop by, Dr. Buchanan." Carrie ushered the woman into her front parlor and offered her a seat by the fire. "I have indeed heard of you. We both attended the Women's Medical College in Chicago."

"Call me Jennie." The petite-framed woman took a seat and arranged her wool skirt.

"Of course, and you must call me Carrie. My mother, Marybeth Vogel, mentioned you being here." Carrie remained standing.

"Yes, I opened an office here in Cheyenne with my husband. He's a dentist. We're located downtown at 307 Seventeenth, room 14."

"And do you have an ample number of patients who are willing to put their trust in a woman doctor?"

"I do." The woman gave a disarming smile. "Wyoming isn't like other places. We women have long held our own in the territory. We're the first to have the right to vote, after all. I have managed to gather a fair number of men and women in my practice."

"I've had a few women come to see me, but not many.

Of course, the newspaper article did stress that my area of specialty is the brain."

"Yes, I read that as well. I know Dr. Bruce Compton also has great interest in that field."

"We've already met. His interests do run in the same direction as mine."

"It's an important area that needs to be explored," Jennie said, nodding. "I greatly admire your interest. Humankind is bound to be indebted to all those who continue to ask questions and seek answers, especially where the brain is concerned. It is quite daunting."

"Would you care for tea?"

"No, I won't stay long. I came, of course, to meet you, but I wanted to invite you to join an organization I helped create. It's the Territorial Medical Association. We're led by Dr. Crook, and we even have another lady in our midst, Dr. Antonette Williams. There are nine of us doctors here in Cheyenne, five doctors from Laramie, two from Rock Springs, two from Evanston, and one from Rawlins. Of the nineteen members, only two are women. It would be nice to have another. Would you consider joining us?"

"I would love to associate with other doctors. It's always fascinating to hear about what others are learning." Carrie finally took a seat.

"We have a great group of people. Doctors who truly care about learning and teaching. Out here there aren't a lot of physicians available, and we've begun to discuss plans for enticing others to come west."

"I am hoping there might be enough interest on Dr. Compton's part that we might join together in our pursuits regarding the brain. I think Cheyenne could easily become known worldwide for brain research."

Jennie smiled and gave a nod. "It could indeed." The

grandfather clock chimed the hour. "I'm so sorry, I must go. I have a patient coming at one thirty."

"Of course." Carrie rose. "I'm so glad we could meet."

"I will get you the information on our next meeting," Jennie promised and crossed the room without even bothering to glance back.

Carrie followed her guest to the door. "Thank you for coming. While I have gained a few patients, I admit to feeling a bit unwelcome by people here. Despite there being two other women in town practicing as doctors, I have my doubts on how readily we are accepted."

"To be sure, there are still plenty of people who doubt the ability of a female doctor, but folks are coming around. I'll recommend patients to you as they come to me with brain issues. It is far from my area of expertise."

"Thank you."

"I'll send you the information on our organization and when the next meeting will be held. Good day."

"Good day."

Carrie watched Jennie head off down the walkway. She paused to let herself out of the picket fence gate and then headed toward town.

"Well, that was a pleasant surprise." She genuinely liked Jennie Buchanan and hoped they might become good friends.

She had no sooner closed the front door and taken a seat at her desk, when another knock sounded. This was a most unusual day to be sure.

Carrie opened the door to find an older gentleman. He took off his hat and smiled from behind a well-trimmed mustache and beard, both as gray as the hair on his head.

"How may I help you?"

"Are you Dr. Carrie Vogel-Duval?"

She smiled. "I am. And you are?"

"Rowland Knowles. I read the article about you and am seeking a doctor's opinion."

Carrie shivered from the chilly winds. "Won't you come in?" The old man did as Carrie asked, and she quickly closed the door. "It's rather cold out there today."

"It snowed a bit earlier but didn't last. That's typical of this time of year," he replied. "I've been here a great many years and have found the weather to be completely unpredictable."

"I've lived here most of my life, and I agree." Carrie led him to her examination room. "Mr. Knowles, please have a seat and tell me why you've come today."

He handed Carrie a leather satchel. "Inside are the reports from other physicians. I cannot begin to explain all that is going on in my head. However, to be simple and to the point, the doctors believe I have a tumor." He held his hand to the back left portion of his head. "Somewhere around here, but the pain has spread, and my vision blurs with exceeding regularity these days. They believe it may be something called a spider-cell glioma."

Carrie nodded but was careful to show no reaction. "So you have seen another doctor regarding this condition?"

"I've seen five. The first doctor I spoke to was in San Francisco. It's when I first felt the effects of the disease. After numerous tests, the doctor suggested a brain tumor. I've seen two additional doctors in Denver and two in Kansas City. All have reached the same conclusions. You'll find it all in those papers I've brought."

Carrie opened the satchel and took out the stack of documents. "I will of course need time to study these papers, but what was their conclusion?"

"That it's a fast-growing tumor that they suspect has spread out like a spider's web and is completely inoperable. They've given me a short time to live, with the progression of the disease gradually rendering me unable to function."

It was the exact answer Carrie had anticipated. Since the first discovery of spider-cell gliomas in the 1870s, there had been no good news associated with the diagnosis. As the name suggested, the cancer spread out across the brain in a webbing fashion. Little was known or understood about the condition. Most of the research had come purely through autopsies.

"I know there's probably very little you can do for me, but I thought perhaps, given what I read about you, that you might have some thoughts on the matter." He smiled. "If nothing else, perhaps my condition and demise will allow you to further study the disease."

Carrie nodded. "I am quite willing to study the matter and discuss it further."

The older man got to his feet. He closed his eyes for a moment, then blinked them open and held her gaze. "I appreciate your consideration, Dr. Vogel-Duval."

"Of course. Why don't you plan to see me again on Friday? Let's say, two o'clock?"

"I'll be here." He walked slowly to the hall.

Carrie put the papers on her chair and followed after him. "I am sorry for your diagnosis. I don't anticipate that there is much I can do for you, but I will help you in every way possible."

He paused at the door and extended his hand. "Thank you."

His eyes seemed almost pleading as he stared her in the face. Carrie felt immense sorrow for the man. Generally speaking, she didn't allow her emotions to be a part of her relationship with patients. However, there was something about this man that captivated her.

Eugene Astor had barely opened the door before finding himself colliding with another man. He looked up and smiled. "Excuse me."

Any further response stuck in his throat as the younger man momentarily glanced his way. Astor felt as if he'd been transported back in time to that moment in the alleyway in Philadelphia. The Pinkerton agent held him at gunpoint, and Astor was trapped.

"I'm so sorry," the man said, reaching out to steady Astor. "I wasn't looking where I was going."

"Quite all right." Eugene forced the words and lowered his gaze.

There was no doubt in his mind that this was the son of the man he'd killed. He was the spitting image of his father. There could be no doubt about it. Then realization hit. The woman called herself Vogel-Duval. The man he'd killed had been Harrison Duval. He hadn't thought about a possible connection. This was Cheyenne after all, and that incident had been twenty years ago in Philadelphia. Duval wasn't that uncommon a name.

Eugene didn't so much as look back as he walked to the gate. Would Duval's son recognize him? The younger man hadn't seemed to. There had been no narrowing of his eyes or questioning expression. His tone had remained cordial and even.

Astor took a deep breath and started down the road. Even if Duval recognized him, there'd be nothing he could really do. Eugene Astor would never face a court or execution for his sins. There wasn't time enough to even begin to set up a trial against him. He was already sentenced to death. What more could they do to him?

Marybeth Vogel checked the oven for the second time. She was making a batch of scones and was struggling to keep the oven at an even heat. The weather wasn't helping. The wind had been blowing all day, and now it looked as if it might start snowing.

She straightened and closed the oven as someone entered the house through the back door.

"Smells good in here," her husband called as he came in from the mud porch.

She smiled and went to embrace him. "And to what do I owe a visit by the chief of police?"

"Just thought I'd come home and have lunch with my favorite gal." He kissed her, then let her go. "Besides, you seemed out of sorts this morning. I was hoping you'd tell me why since everyone is out of the house."

She shook her head. "How did you know everyone was out of the house? Were you having me watched?"

He chuckled. "No, I listened well at breakfast. I heard Greta say she was going to be busy helping Melody clean out her storage room, and Rosie offered to go and help. I figured that would give us a little time alone."

"You are a good listener." She leaned back against the counter. "I guess I'm just worried about Carrie. She's up to something."

"I know."

"I just can't figure out what. It's clear she's uneasy about being around us. More so than usual. Usually she's just quiet and observant, but now she's guarded as well."

"Spencer is too. The two of them have a secret, but they aren't ready to tell us. I thought he might talk to me the other day. Seemed like he wanted to share something, but I got called away. I keep hoping he'll just stop into my office or come by one of these evenings."

"Maybe we should stop by and see them. Go check out the

place they're living in. I have some new crocheted doilies I could offer as a gift and an excuse for coming."

"We could do that. Maybe slip by after supper some evening."

"Yes, that might be good. That way we wouldn't have to worry about one of the other children or any of your officers showing up to interrupt."

She stopped and checked the scones again. They finally looked golden brown. She pulled them from the oven and placed the pan on the counter to cool. "I just want them to trust us. No matter what's going on."

"There's no guarantee they will. Carrie's been gone a long time. She's a completely different person now."

"Not completely," Marybeth said, looking at her husband. "She has changed some, but there is still the foundation of who she's always been. She's not comfortable living a lie or keeping a secret. She never could do it for long."

Edward laughed. "That's for sure. Do you remember that time you were planning a surprise party for my birthday? Carrie did her best to keep the secret. She even attempted to lie right to my face and tell me something else was going on."

Marybeth started moving the scones to a plate. "I do remember that and how at supper she finally blurted it out, telling us that she couldn't keep a secret anymore. I tried to distract her by calling her to come with me to the kitchen, but the damage was already done."

"I knew about the party before that happened. There's rarely much that stays secret around here." He stepped to where she was placing the scones. "Are those for eating or giving away?"

Marybeth looked at him and smiled. "For eating and for giving away. You want some coffee to go with it?"

"If it wouldn't be too much trouble."

He gazed into her eyes for a long moment and leaned forward to kiss her again. Marybeth forgot all about the scones and wrapped her arms around her husband's neck.

She sighed as they pulled apart. "It's never too much trouble to do things for you, Edward Vogel. You're the love of my life, and pleasing you pleases me."

"Strange. I feel the same way about you. Guess it's a good thing we're together."

"A very good thing."

14

Spencer did his best to keep quiet, even though he knew there was no one else around. The land management office was a part of his patrol, and fortunately for him, the back door wasn't locked. It gave him the perfect excuse to enter. If someone came upon him, he could explain that he had reason to believe someone was inside.

It was a lie, of course, and he didn't feel particularly proud that it had come easily to mind. Still, he was able to search through some of the old records to see if Eugene Astor had ever purchased land in Cheyenne or the surrounding area.

There was nothing listed under that name, however. He hadn't really expected there to be, but he'd hoped just on a chance that the man might have filed under his real name and then gone by another. Looking through the alphabetical files for 1870, Spencer found nothing that even suggested one of the owners might have been Astor. Most were men with families.

He gave cursory glances at the years that followed and still found nothing. Astor had probably lived in a boardinghouse or rented. Coming to Cheyenne that early in its existence, Astor might have even lived in a tent.

Spencer left the files and went out the back door. He hadn't taken two steps, however, when he heard someone tell him to stop. He held up his hands.

"It's me, Officer Duval," Spencer called.

"Well, that's a relief." The man stepped into the light. "What were you doing in the land management office?"

Spencer recognized his brother-in-law. "Robert. I thought you worked a later shift."

"I usually do. Was someone in there?"

"No, but the back door was unlocked." It wasn't exactly a lie.

"Yeah, they're bad about that. I saw the tiniest bit of light from the front window."

"I didn't want to turn on the electric lights, so I used a couple of matches. No one was in there, however." Spencer nodded toward the far end of the alley. "I'm making my way in that direction. Where are you headed?"

"Over to the jail. Like I said, I saw movement and light and figured there might be a thief." He grinned. "Glad it's just you doing your duty. I'll see you later." He started to leave, then turned back around. "Say, why don't you and Carrie come for supper tonight? Rosie's been nagging me to have you two over."

"If Carrie isn't too busy, I think that'd be great. But shouldn't we give your poor wife some warning?"

"I'll let Rosie know. She'll be happy as a lark. As for Carrie, I'll talk to her too. I've got seniority in the office, so I can come and go pretty much at will. I try not to take advantage of the fact, so I shouldn't have any trouble doing it today." He chuckled and tipped his hat. "See you tonight."

Spencer nodded and moved off in the opposite direction. His heart was still pounding at having been discovered. The entire situation couldn't have been much worse. Had it been another officer, he wouldn't have given it a second thought.

Now, however, he'd probably be questioned about it by the chief.

He'd very nearly shared with his father-in-law his real reason for being in Cheyenne. The man had a way about him that just made a fella feel at ease. Like you could tell him almost anything and he'd understand. But something always seemed to stop Spencer.

Last week, his in-laws had even shown up at the house unexpectedly, and it seemed the perfect chance. They had stayed for nearly an hour just talking and drinking coffee. His mother-in-law had brought a batch of scones and cookies. He'd had to sample them, of course. They were delicious. There was talk of how Carrie was a fairly good baker, but by her own admission, she just didn't have the time or interest in such things. The Vogels had left with Marybeth's promise to bring them baked goods from time to time.

Spencer kept looking for an opportunity to explain his Pinkerton mission, but for the life of him he couldn't manage to move the conversation in such a way that he could do so without making it a big ordeal. And Spencer knew it was going to be a big enough matter when they learned the truth without any help from him with bad timing.

The night before, Spencer had planned to say something to Carrie about it. He wanted her opinion. Despite feeling that she didn't belong in her family, she knew her parents. She'd be better able to gauge the situation for him. So when she had come to join him for reading by the fire, Spencer was determined to talk about the entire matter. Instead, she had spread a blanket over them both and snuggled beside him as though they were a happily married couple. Her action had taken him by surprise. It wasn't that she hadn't done it before, but tonight something seemed different. The intimacy of her actions had left him more than a little puzzled about the future.

It was confusing living with Carrie Vogel. She was devoted to her work, but at the same time she seemed eager for his company. She had agreed to a platonic marriage and yet seemed to almost be asking for something more. What did she want from him?

Many nights they had discussed the details of their day over supper, each adding comments and insights to problems that the other found of value. He was surprised how much Carrie shared with him about her research. But she always had, he realized. They had talked about her work in Chicago. She had eased him into the various terms and areas of work that fascinated her most. In turn, he'd shared a variety of cases that he'd worked on over the years. Carrie would ask questions about the background of his perpetrators. She believed that the science behind a person's actions was steeped in their neurological conditions and traumas. He could see where that made sense.

Later that evening, as they sat down to dinner with Robert and Rosie Vogel, he could see that Carrie was quite lost in thought. She'd had a few patients come to see her, and her practice, though still quite small, was giving her new purpose. Even Robert noticed.

"You seem quite pleased with yourself, sis. What's going on? Does this have to do with your research?"

"Actually, a patient. I've been able to help a woman who is suffering from severe headaches. It makes me happy to see her relieved of the pain she's been enduring." Carrie sliced into the pork steak she'd been given. "Other doctors hadn't been able to help, and she thought she'd be reduced to the drugged stupor that laudanum brings in order to find relief, but instead, we found another help for her."

"I suppose doctors all have their own way of doing things," Robert replied.

"Yes, that's exactly true. However, a physician must keep

up to date on new medicines and procedures. A lot of the older doctors rely only on their experience and believe the old ways are always the best. However, there is so much new evidence to consider because of research. I try to never discredit the findings of others. I give each new idea thorough consideration."

"That's because you're smart." This came from Rosie.

Carrie smiled. "So are you, Rosie. And an amazing cook."

Spencer had heard Carrie detail the problems Rosie had known from a difficult birth. She'd been deprived of oxygen due to the umbilical cord being wrapped tightly around her neck. The doctors had been certain that she would be unable to read or write or possibly even speak. They had encouraged the family to institutionalize her, but instead, they had hidden her away at home.

Rosie's brother's wife, Emma, had seen something more in the young woman and had worked with her. Rosie had learned her alphabet and numbers and then graduated to reading and writing. She was eager to learn after having been deprived of it. Carrie said she was still constantly seeking to understand new things. It fascinated Carrie, given her focus on neuroscience and the brain. Thankfully, Rosie wasn't offended by Carrie's interest, and the two spent considerable time together one afternoon a week. Rosie told Spencer she hoped that by Carrie studying her, it might help other babies who suffered as she had.

"So did you have other patients today?" Rosie asked Carrie.

"No. In fact, there's one man in particular who I thought would have come to see me by now. He was supposed to come last Friday, and when he didn't, I thought perhaps he misunderstood the day and would show up this afternoon. But he didn't."

"Maybe he decided he doesn't need a doctor." Robert shrugged.

"In a sense, he doesn't. He's beyond the help of a doctor. However, I'd like to see if he might sign a paper allowing me to perform an . . ." Her voice trailed off. "I am sorry, I don't want to turn this into a macabre conversation."

Rosie reached over and patted her hand. "I don't know what that word means, but there's nothing you can't talk about with us."

"My sister was probably going to say that she'd like the man to allow her to study him after he dies."

Rosie thought about this for a moment and then nodded. "I imagine that could really be useful to a doctor. I would sign a paper to let you study me if I died."

Spencer was amazed at the way Rosie just spoke her mind. Apparently no one had ever suggested to her it was unacceptable to talk so casually about autopsies.

"Thank you, Rosie. It does help doctors tremendously to be able to study the dead in order to help the living. But let us talk about something more uplifting." Carrie smiled at Spencer, and he gave her a wink.

"I've heard from the area ranchers that it looks like it'll be a good calving season. If the weather stays mild, that is. We've all seen March and April turn ugly, but hopefully, it won't come about this year." Robert held up the basket of dinner rolls. "Mama's been teaching Rosie to make bread and rolls. These are delicious. Be sure to get one or two . . . or more."

Spencer took the basket. "You don't have to ask me twice."

Back at home, Carry quickly changed out of her clothes and put on her nightgown and robe before returning to the parlor. She'd become so casual and comfortable around Spencer that it never dawned on her to do otherwise. She knew she was in trouble, though. She enjoyed his company far too much. Their evenings together were the highlight of her day. That was something she never thought she would say.

Until now, medicine had been everything to her. Even when accompanying Oswald to various functions, her mind had remained on her work. She had longed to be back in the laboratory researching or at least at home reading. Spencer had changed all of that for her. He was easy to talk to, and his stories and way of looking at life gave her completely different perspectives.

As she brushed her wavy blond hair, Carrie caught sight of her face in the mirror. She looked different in so many ways. When she thought of Spencer, her expression softened. She couldn't help but observe the effect, like the physician she was. Pleasant thoughts altered expressions. Just as anger changed a person, so did pleasure. Carrie hadn't allowed herself a lot of pleasure in her adulthood.

She frowned, and that, too, caught her attention. She tried to think exactly of what had caused the frown. It was involuntary. She hadn't meant to frown. She hadn't considered a specific unhappy thing except that pleasure hadn't been a priority in her life.

Perhaps this frown was one of regret. She had focused on her studies since she was twelve. She'd buckled down and devoured learning like a starving man would food. She hadn't allowed herself time for a beau or any of the local parties. Carrie had made a plan that allowed for neither.

She graduated early and went off to college, where she did the same again. She finished at the top of her class, accomplishing the requirements in less time than most. Her professors called her most talented, even suggested she was a medical prodigy. She loved medical studies. Oswald Nelson did too, or so she had thought. As she'd come to realize his lacking and deception, Carrie knew he didn't care about it nearly as much as she did.

Knowing Spencer was waiting for her in the parlor, Carrie finished with the brush and didn't even bother to braid her hair for bed. There would be plenty of time for that. Spencer always had to go to bed by nine in order to get up for his early shift. Seeing that it was already eight fifteen, Carrie hurried to join him.

"You are clearly the most beautiful woman in the world," Spencer said as she entered the parlor.

Carrie gave a nervous laugh. "You haven't seen all the women in the world."

"Then you're the most beautiful woman I've ever seen. You can't argue that one."

He patted the sofa beside him, and Carrie grabbed up a folded blanket by the hearth and took a seat.

"I wasn't trying to argue," she said, spreading the blanket over her lap.

Spencer took hold of the blanket and drew it across his lap as well. "Did you enjoy yourself this evening?"

"I did. I enjoy Robert and Rosie's company. Robert, as an adult, has become far more interesting to me. As a child he was just annoying, though I'm told most little brothers usually are."

"I always wanted a little brother or sister. I would have loved that."

"Until they got into your things." Carrie reached over and took up the *Handbook of Psychology*.

Spencer restrained her from opening the book. "Why don't we just talk tonight? We've been so busy lately that it seems like we haven't had any fun. What if we were to go to the opera tomorrow night or see a play?"

"Maybe we should find a theater group to join."

"That's come to mind more than once. We had a lot of fun playacting."

"Our entire life is playacting right now." She hadn't meant to sound harsh, but even to her own ears there was a note of dissatisfaction.

"Are you unhappy?"

"No, not really." She leaned back and gazed up at the ceiling. "I suppose it's more a sense of concern for the deception we're practicing."

"I know. I have nearly told your father the truth a dozen times. I'm afraid to do so, however, for fear he'll want you to move home immediately."

"I know. I don't want that to happen either. Were you able to learn anything this morning at the land management office?"

"No. I suppose I didn't really expect to, but it would have been nice had I found Eugene Astor's name listed among the landowners."

"I am sorry that it didn't help you. I wonder if you just went to the Union Pacific offices and told them what you were doing and asked to see their employment records. Seems like you'll have to trust someone sooner or later."

"Al has been working at his end. He even made a trip to Omaha to see UP officials and explained that he needed information for a government case. They were cooperative, but it didn't really help. He's sending me a list of men who started with the UP in Cheyenne in 1870 and 1871. It's better than nothing and will allow me a chance to see names without giving away my hand."

"When you get the list, you might talk to Papa about everything. I don't think he'd give you away, even if he happened to be best friends with Eugene Astor. Papa is a good man and serves the law faithfully. He can be very merciful when mercy is deserved, but he wouldn't allow a killer to go without punishment, even if it were his best friend."

Spencer seemed to consider this a moment and then nodded. "I'll talk to him, then. But I plan to do what I can to keep the issue from interfering with us. I've gotten used to you, Dr. Vogel-Duval."

Carrie laughed and waved her arm over them. "We do act like an old married couple at times. I find you very comfortable to be with."

Spencer surprised her by pulling her into his arms. "I find you so much more."

He turned her toward him and kissed her. It wasn't just a peck on the lips, either, and Carrie found herself breathless from the encounter. When he pulled back, he looked at her as if to ascertain her opinion. Then without a word, he kissed her again.

Carrie wrapped her arms around his neck and shifted her body toward him. She lost reasonable thought and acted solely on her feelings. She very much liked what was happening between them. Better still, she didn't want it to stop. However, it was inevitable that it would.

Spencer broke the hold and got to his feet. "I have to tell you . . . my feelings for you have changed. I think I'm falling in love with you, Carrie." He shook his head. "No, I'm certain that I've already fallen."

Carrie couldn't even force her thoughts into order. She was still living in the moment of warmth and seduction that had come from those few minutes in Spencer's arms. She looked at him, and all she could do was nod. Her feelings told her that she was just as much in love as Spencer. So why couldn't she rationalize it all in her logical manner of thinking?

"I think I'd better go," Spencer said, looking at her with such longing. "Or I won't leave at all, and this marriage will completely change." He strode from the room and down the hall. Carrie heard his bedroom door close and realized she was still holding her breath.

She let out a sigh. There was something of regret in her feelings, as well as relief. But neither offered her any satisfaction whatsoever.

15

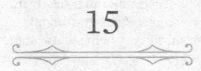

It was well past the day of their agreed upon appointment when Rowland Knowles finally returned to Carrie's office to discuss his condition.

"I must say, Mr. Knowles, I was beginning to give up hope of seeing you again."

"I am sorry," the older man replied, taking off his hat. "I've been feeling progressively worse and had much to accomplish. I meant to send word, but . . . well, here I am."

Carrie nodded and directed him to a chair in her examination room. "I can well imagine you are having an increasingly more difficult time. After going over all of your files, I can honestly say that I'm surprised you are still alive."

He chuckled and sat down. "Frankly, I'm just as surprised. The doctor in Denver thought I'd certainly be dead by now. The one in Kansas City gave me a little more time. Do you suppose I should write to the Denver physician and tell him he was wrong?"

The man was teasing, and Carrie smiled. "Doctors seldom like to know they were wrong. It's a pride thing, I suppose."

"And what was your conclusion? Do you have a new date to offer me?"

At least the man was able to deal with his condition without rage or tears. Carrie found herself liking Knowles.

"I agree that given the information we have, your situation is grave. I would also agree that given your symptoms, it is most likely that you have a fast-growing tumor in your brain. I wouldn't go so far as to say it's a spider-cell glioma. That can really only be ascertained after death during an autopsy.

"And while I also agree that the tumor is most likely inoperable due to brain surgery being in its infancy, I would like to consider options to at least give you relief for the time you have, because even if the tumor is benign, at the rate it's growing, I can't say that the odds of recovery are any better than were it malignant. If my colleagues' assessments are correct."

He smiled. "You are most kind, Dr. Vogel-Duval. What kind of options do you have in mind?"

"Well, there is the possibility we could drill into the cranium and relieve the pressure on the brain. This won't stop the tumor's growth, but part of the reason for your pain is the increased pressure caused by the enlargement of the tumor. Drilling several holes in the bone could allow relief."

"Could, but not necessarily would," Knowles said, shaking his head ever so slightly. "That type of thing was discussed in Kansas City." He gave a shrug. "I have already pretty much come to terms with the fact that little can be done."

"I am sorry. The brain is quite complex. We are just starting to learn about it. When you consider all human organs, the brain is not only the most difficult to understand, but also the hardest to gain access to thanks to being encased in bone."

"I do appreciate that you would take time to consider my case."

"I will endeavor to help you through to the end." Carrie

wanted to make it clear that he needn't face this alone. "If you like, I can come and check on you every day and make sure you have enough medicine to help with the pain."

"That's very kind of you. It would be something of a comfort to know that someone would be aware of my condition and know when my final hours come. I would like that very much, Dr. Vogel-Duval."

"Just call me Dr. Duval." She wasn't sure why she'd said that. Taking Spencer's name had only been planned for a short time. Now, however, things were changing, and she had to admit confusion over where it would lead.

"You're newly married, the newspaper article said."

Carrie was momentarily taken aback. "Yes, uh, we married shortly before moving to Cheyenne."

"And your husband? Where is he from?"

"Philadelphia originally. Though the last few years he lived in Chicago. That's where we met. I attended college there."

"So he's a doctor as well?"

"No." She thought of Spencer's attention to detail and knew he'd make a good doctor if he wanted to go in that direction. "He's a . . . city police officer. He's been in law enforcement for years."

"Ah, a good job to have, keeping law and order. And did he make the suggestion to move to Cheyenne?"

Carrie wasn't sure how to respond. She didn't want to give insight into Spencer's real task. "No. I am from Cheyenne and wanted to move home. My family is here. But surely you read that in the newspaper as well."

"I hadn't recalled that until just now." He smiled and got to his feet. "Dr. Duval, I do appreciate all that you've done. What do I owe you?"

Carrie hoped that he wouldn't be offended with what she wanted to offer next. "I . . . well, I don't want to make you uncomfortable, but I am a research doctor. I'm working hard to gain information on the brain and to be able to find solutions for a variety of problems that stem from injury and disease. I would like to propose something that might seem odd."

"You have me intrigued, go on." The man looked more than a little curious.

"I would treat you free of charge. I would come daily to your home and assess your situation and aid in seeing that you have the best medicine available to ease your pain and suffering. In return, I would only ask for permission to perform an autopsy on you after your death."

"That's all?" He chuckled. "I'll be dead and will hardly care what you do at that point. Of course you may perform your autopsy. Perhaps it would even help someone else in years to come."

"That's exactly what I hope to do with the research gained."

Knowles got to his feet. "I've already arranged for my burial with the local undertaker. Do I need to sign something for you? Perhaps let him know?"

Carrie nodded and produced the legal form. "It would be best if it were witnessed by a friend or notary. That would prevent any problems in the future. I would like to be able to keep your brain for study. Often times, organs are studied quickly and replaced in the body cavity for burial, but we would take your brain out and keep it for long-term study." She looked at him, hoping he wouldn't change his mind. "It would benefit us both if you were to notify the funeral director. Or I can."

"I'll get someone reliable to witness my signing and deliver this paper to you by this afternoon. I'll let the undertaker know as well." He took the paper and glanced at it. "I haven't lived the best life. It would be nice to know that I might do something, even in death, that would benefit mankind."

"This definitely would." Carrie hoped her assurance

wasn't overly eager. It was hard for nonmedical persons to understand just how much could be learned about the body with the use of autopsies.

She showed Mr. Knowles out just as Dr. Bruce Compton was coming up her walk. The wind seemed determined to blow in gusts, nearly taking the hats of both men as they tipped in acknowledgment of each other in passing.

"Dr. Compton, won't you come in?"

"Thank you." He entered the house with a firm grip on his hat. "Good day to you, Dr. Vogel-Duval."

She started to correct him but held her tongue. "What can I do for you today?"

"I wanted to discuss your interest in the brain."

"You just missed meeting a patient of mine. Quite a complex individual with a probable brain tumor that is growing at an alarming rate."

"Do tell."

She ushered the doctor into her examination room. "Have a seat. Would you care for tea or coffee?"

"No, but thank you. I just wanted to stop by. I've meant to do so since our first encounter. I realized Dr. Lyons was hardly receptive, but I was most intrigued. Especially after learning that you were engaged to marry Dr. Oswald Nelson."

"But I also told you that he stole my research."

"Yes, and so I reread the last few articles that he wrote." Dr. Compton fixed her with a questioning look. "Do you swear to me those things he wrote were based on your own findings?"

"I do. God knows the truth of it, Dr. Compton."

"Then I want to make a proposition. I've discussed it at length with my wife, and she agrees with me."

"About what?" Carrie was more than a little confused.

"It is my desire that we work together. I have a large laboratory and examination area. I have been working to create a hospital of sorts that would work solely with patients who were suffering from brain injury and disease. My wife's father recently passed, and she is about to inherit a large enough sum of money that I can build a place just east of town. I think together you and I can accomplish great things."

"I don't know what to say. I hardly know you and certainly have no idea of your work, nor you of mine." Carrie was more than intrigued and excited at the prospect of creating such a place as Dr. Compton described, but she didn't want to put herself in another position like that which she had with Oswald.

"I realize that," Dr. Compton began. "I have some things I've been working on, as well as my journals. I'd be happy to let you read them to know the direction in which I've been working. I don't expect you to make a decision this moment. Pray about it. I know from talking to your father that you're a woman of God."

"I'm rather surprised at your willingness to set up business with a woman." Carrie couldn't help but voice her concerns. "Most male doctors have little tolerance for women in the medical field."

Dr. Compton's laugh wasn't what Carrie had expected. "My own mother was a physician. It was her love of medicine that sent me in this direction. She was of the utmost intelligence and ability when it came to surgery. There was none like her, and she saved many a life and limb during the war."

The pride he held for his mother was evident. "Maybe I've heard of her. What was her name?"

"Dr. Sarah Compton."

The name was unfamiliar to Carrie, but that hardly mattered. "I don't know of her, but I must say I'm intrigued by your idea. It's been the same I've longed for."

"I hope you'll give it consideration. Your intelligence and experience in this field is just what is needed. I hope to get several others to join us in time. For now, however, we will have to build our reputation and knowledge."

"I will discuss the matter with my husband and, as you suggested, pray about it."

Dr. Compton got to his feet. "You have a great personal reputation in this town, Dr. Vogel-Duval."

"Dr. Duval is just fine."

He nodded and smiled. "No matter what you call yourself, people think highly of you. They may not yet know you as a physician, but that will come in time. I know your passion and your heart to help others. Given the findings you've made, even if credited to another, I believe we can make great progress in our research."

She smiled at his encouragement. "I will thoroughly consider your proposition. But I must tell you that Dr. Nelson was less than pleased when I broke off our engagement. He . . . well, he was dependent upon me in our research and holds a grudge. He threatened to see that I would never be acknowledged in this area of study. He wants me to face complete disgrace and failure. I've no doubt he'll go out of his way to tell others what a waste of time I am."

Dr. Compton gave her a wry smile. "Sour grapes."

"What do you mean?"

"Aesop tells the story of the Fox and the Grapes. The fox wants the grapes but cannot reach them or obtain them in any way. Therefore, he declares them undesirable. Dr. Nelson can no longer reach you or obtain your work, and therefore he's declaring you undesirable—sour grapes." He surprised her by chuckling. "I'm unconcerned with his threats. I believe once we start making headway in research, others will know the truth for themselves."

Carrie shook her head. "I had prayed God would send the right people into my life regarding my work. Looks like once again I stand in the presence of answered prayer."

"Dr. Duval, I feel the same way exactly. For now, however, I will bid you good day." He picked up his hat. "Oh, I wonder if you and your husband might come to supper next Friday evening?"

Carrie knew of no reason they shouldn't and gave a nod. "I believe we are free to accept. Thank you."

"Wonderful. You shall meet my wife and daughters. My oldest would like to be a doctor one day. Perhaps you can offer her encouragement."

"I would be honored."

Spencer had known he'd have to come up with an excuse to go knocking on the doors of each man on Al's list of UP workers who'd been in Cheyenne since 1870. He figured if all else failed, he could go from man to man on the pretense of hunting for a friend or family member. An idea had come to him to say that he was looking for an acquaintance of his father. A man who'd come west after the war, but whose name he didn't know. He'd wrestled with the idea of what excuse he could give for looking for this man and hit upon his father owing the man money. He could say that he'd promised his father to repay his debt and now he was looking for the man he owed but couldn't remember the man's name. All he knew for certain was that he'd once lived in Philadelphia, still had a mother there, and he worked for the Union Pacific. There was no need to mention that the mother was dead or that the man he truly sought was a criminal.

He felt almost certain he would recognize Eugene Astor even with all the years between them. The man couldn't have changed that much. Furthermore, Spencer knew he looked like his father. It might be shock enough for Astor just seeing him. Surely he could remember the face of the man he'd killed.

But maybe not. Maybe Astor didn't even remember much about the murder. Perhaps he'd murdered a great many people, and Harrison Duval was just one of those who'd inconvenienced Eugene Astor. The very thought of him not even remembering what he'd done bothered Spencer in a way he couldn't talk about. He'd once confessed to Al that a day didn't go by without him remembering that day in the alleyway. Al told him it would be better to let it go.

"Give it over to God, Spence. He'll take care of all business in His time."

But Spencer had wanted to take care of it himself. He wanted to be the one who got justice for his father and made Eugene Astor pay for what he'd done.

He went over the details of what he knew once more. Astor had been alive as of a week before Christmas. He'd last mentioned Cheyenne to his mother in a letter written in November. He'd told her about the clock finally being fitted into the Union Pacific clock tower and how it had been a wonderful addition to have. He spoke of the cost and of the UP's belief that the clock would draw more people to the station if for no other reason than to get the accurate time.

If Astor had moved, it had been since December. It seemed unlikely to Spencer that he would just up and leave for no good reason. He supposed, however, that Astor could have been tipped off that his mother had died. That might cause him to leave the area. There were all sorts of possibilities, but Spencer's Pinkerton job had equipped him with a great many searching skills. He felt confident that he would get his man. Even if it had taken more time to pin Astor down than Spencer had figured.

And then what?

That question had haunted him. After he caught Astor, what would happen next? He had fallen in love with Carrie, and she was in love with him as well. Even if she hadn't exactly said it, he could tell her feelings for him had deepened. He had never planned to marry anyone. He'd always figured he'd work as a Pinkerton all his life and avoid commitments to anyone. It wasn't that he didn't desire a home and the love of a good woman, but he knew the potential for pain and suffering that came with it. His mother had been devastated after losing her husband. He had been heartbroken by his father's death. How could he put another woman and child through the possibility of losing him as he continued to work for the agency?

But after capturing Astor, maybe he didn't have to continue working for the Pinkertons. After all, he could just as easily serve the local law enforcement. He was college educated and could even make himself useful to those in business or the government. Wyoming was standing on the threshold of becoming a state. There would be plenty of government positions available, and a man with his education could be a tremendous asset.

He let out a heavy breath. Could he be happy with a desk job?

Spencer looked again at the list of names on the telegram Al had sent. The first name was John Bushton. He wondered if there was a city directory that might list the man's name and address. The easiest way to find the addresses for each of these men was probably to go to the Union Pacific. But he'd already talked to several people there. It would only raise suspicions if he went back with a list of names and demanded addresses.

He supposed he could break into the offices and search through their records. He'd done things like that before. The ends justified the means as far as he was concerned. But he doubted his father-in-law would see it that way.

Again, Carrie came to mind. It was such a dichotomy. How had he lost focus of what he was doing so much so that he had fallen in love?

Who am I fooling? I've always loved her. Since we first met, I was taken by her appearance and attitude. I fell hard for her and ignored it because she belonged to someone else.

But now she belongs to me.

He'd really made a mess of things. At least he'd confessed his feelings to her. Of course, he hadn't stuck around to discuss them, and the next morning he'd been particularly careful not to wake her as he was leaving for work. He had no desire to discuss the matter just yet. He wasn't even sure what he hoped to gain from it.

Spencer shoved the list back in his pocket and went to grab his coat from the station's coat-tree.

"You finally done with your paperwork, Duval?" a young uniformed officer asked.

"Yeah, everything is logged. I'm heading home."

It was well past his usual time to leave. Thankfully, no one was there to question him for his lengthy stay. The last thing he wanted was to have to explain to Carrie's family why he wasn't exactly eager to head home.

He pulled the coat on and stepped outside to a light rain. He hadn't even noticed the sky had clouded up. The days were getting longer, but even so the sun had set probably half an hour ago, and twilight had been hastened by the rain.

What was Carrie doing? Had she fixed them supper? Had she wondered why he was late? Spencer was eager to see her, but at the same time dreaded it. He had to somehow ignore his feelings for her. It was interfering in his duties. He was failing to move quickly toward Astor's capture.

He started to head down Sixteenth, then changed his mind. He couldn't go home yet. He had to try to figure out where each of the men on his list lived. Without giving it any other thought, he turned toward Capitol Avenue and headed toward the train station. Maybe he'd have an idea of what to do once he reached the depot.

16

"Greta! I wasn't expecting to see you today." Carrie ushered her younger sister into the sitting room. "It's been such a busy week, and tonight Spencer and I are supposed to have dinner at Dr. Compton's house."

"I'm sorry if this is a bad time. Mama says you've been very busy with your work, but I wanted to see how you were doing."

Greta was already untying her bonnet. With her blond hair and blue eyes, she looked a great deal like their mother. Carrie had never really noticed it before.

"I've missed you so much, Carrie. It's been hard not having you around these last years."

Carrie was surprised by her sister's words. Greta had always been such a self-sufficient soul. She had numerous friends and was the center of attention at home. Carrie had always seen Greta as her parents' favorite child. Well, of course Robert was their first son and special in a way that only he could be, and Daniel was the baby, so he, too, was favored. Carrie supposed she saw all of her siblings as holding special regard in the household.

"Would you like something hot to drink? I can make coffee or tea."

"No, I'd much rather just have a chance to talk." Greta looked so completely delighted to be with Carrie. She patted the sofa. "Please just sit with me."

Carrie nodded and took the place beside her sister. "I suppose you're busy planning your wedding."

"It's all been pretty much figured out. My gown has been made for months now. It's quite lovely. You should stop by to see it. It has large puffed sleeves and a high neckline with lots of lace."

Carrie could well imagine how lovely her sister would look. "And where will the wedding be held?"

"We'll marry at the church, and there will be a reception afterward in the large hall at the opera house. There will be food and drink and dance."

"And have you picked out a house where you'll live afterward?"

"Oh yes. Michael purchased one a few months ago. We've been working on repapering some of the walls and painting. It was the old Cooper boardinghouse. You remember it, don't you?"

"I do. That's a very large house to have starting out."

"Michael wants a big family like he grew up with." Greta giggled. "I'm not sure about having ten children, but I told him I loved the idea of a lot of children."

Carrie nodded. "I'm sure you'll be a good mother."

"So long as they all feel special and loved. I always knew I was loved, but I never felt I held any special place in the family. Not like you."

Her words so surprised Carrie that she couldn't even speak. Finally, after a lengthy bit of silence, Carrie asked her sister, "What do you mean by that?"

Greta shrugged and laughed it off. "You know. You were

always the favorite of the family. The fair-haired girl who could do no wrong. Always the smartest and the most driven. Always the perfectionist. I wanted so much to be like you, but I'm afraid that just was never meant to be."

"Greta, you are mistaken. You were the favorite. Mama and Papa, especially Papa, doted on you. I'm the one who didn't fit into the family. I was the one who had no real understanding of my place. Was I a sister or a daughter? Were we sisters, or was I just an aunt?"

"Carrie, I never saw you as anything but my sister. You were the one I esteemed. I wanted to grow up to be just like you. How can you say that I was the favorite? I never felt that I was anyone's favorite. At times, I even wondered if I was adopted. Or maybe that the entire family would have been better off had I never been born."

Carrie shook her head. "I don't know how you could feel that way. I was the adopted one. I was the one who didn't belong. You and Robert and Daniel all had the same mother and father by blood. I was from entirely different parents."

It was Greta's turn to shake her head. "No, you were the reason for everything. For all of us being a family. You were the linchpin, our keystone. You were the very person upon which the entire family had been built. I always admired your position, even before I understood about the past and how Mama was also your sister."

"Admired my position? I disdained it. I always felt I could never fit." Her sister's words were causing her to look at the entire situation with new eyes.

"Oh, Carrie, I don't know how you could ever feel that way. Robert adored you and followed you everywhere, and when I was born, I followed right behind."

"I figured he was bored and thought I would help him to find something exciting to do. As for you, I always thought you were following Robert. He was, after all, your brother by blood."

"That never mattered to me. You were my sister. You were Carrie, the smart one, the one everybody loved. Oh, how I wanted to be you."

Carrie didn't know what to say. All of her life she had been certain that she didn't belong. At first it was just a niggling doubt in the back of her mind, but as she grew older and could reason the situation for herself, that doubt grew. Now her sister was telling her that she'd been the keystone. That certainly couldn't be true.

"But then you went away. I was devastated when you left. I cried for days, even weeks. Mama did her best to encourage me, but she was just as lost."

Carrie frowned. "She said that?"

"She didn't have to. The whole house went into mourning when you left. We none of us were the same. Even Daniel moped and cried. Oh, Carrie, you have no idea how much you were missed. I remember Mama closed the door to your room. She might as well have hung black crepe."

"I really had no idea of that being the case."

"You were the one who told us interesting stories at the table, inevitably coming up with fascinating tidbits about a wide variety of subjects. I remember when you read in the newspaper about a cowboy who rode ahead of a flash flood and saved a whole valley of settlers. You told us he was like a modern-day Paul Revere, but we didn't know who that was so you explained that as well. Oh, how I loved your stories."

Carrie barely remembered telling tales to her siblings, much less the story of the cowboy and a flash flood.

"And anytime one of us got hurt, you were always so good to help us. I suppose that need to be a doctor was in your heart even when you were little."

"I suppose so." Carrie had always loved helping when her siblings were sick or hurt.

"When Robert broke his arm after jumping off the roof at the Decker School for Boys, Daniel came and got you because he couldn't find Mama. You went and secured his arm and brought him home. You weren't even the least bit afraid, while I bawled like a baby and so did Daniel. We were so afraid, but you told us that Rob would be just fine. You told us to pray for him."

"I do remember that. I was almost fifteen years old. I knew that I wanted to become a doctor, and tending to Rob made me feel like I was on my way. The doctor even told me later that I'd done everything right. Of course, he didn't think girls should be doctors, but he thought I might make a good midwife and mother."

"I can't believe you didn't feel like you fit in our family. I thought I was the only one who felt that way. I couldn't do the things you did, and I wasn't at all talented in sewing. Mama tried so hard to teach me. I can mend a torn seam and repair a hem, but making clothes always turns out badly. I feared no man would ever love me."

"I suppose we can all be in error as to what we think and feel."

"Mama has always maintained that the devil is looking to separate us out, like wolves getting a calf to leave the herd and especially its mother. If he can get us alone, convince us that no one cares about us, that we don't belong, then he can cause us no end of trouble."

Carrie nodded. It was all true, so why had it been so hard for her to see? Why had she been so willing to buy in to the lie that she was somehow not as good as the rest of her siblings? That she somehow didn't belong because she'd been adopted by her sister? Greta had given her a great deal to think about, but especially to pray on.

"And this is my husband, Spencer Duval," Carrie said, introducing Spencer to Dr. Bruce Compton and his lovely wife, Rachel, later that night.

"We're so pleased to meet you, Mr. Duval," Dr. Compton replied.

"I'd just as soon get rid of titles, if that's all right with you. Call me Spencer."

Dr. Compton nodded. "And you both should call us by our given names."

"Please come in. Dinner is nearly ready," Rachel instructed. She led them to a beautiful music room. "These are our daughters, Mineola and Francesca."

"What beautiful names." Carrie bent to greet each child. "I'm very pleased to meet you."

"They call me Mini," the youngest explained. She had brown hair and braided pigtails and offered up the sweetest smile. "I'm six years old, and I go to school."

"And I'm Frannie," the taller child declared. In every other way she was the spitting image of her sister. They were even dressed alike. "I'm eight, and I want to be a doctor like my papa. He says you're a doctor."

"I am. I think it's wonderful that you want to take after your father and be a doctor. It's a wonderful job to have."

"I don't want to be a doctor," Mini felt the need to throw in.

"And what is it that you would like to do, Mini?" Carrie couldn't help but wonder what kind of answer she might get. It didn't take long.

"I want to have about a hundred horses and ride them all."

The child's honest answer made Carrie smile. "I think that would be a great deal of fun. I hope you both get your way."

She straightened and smiled as Spencer put his arm

around her waist. She met his gaze and saw the love he held for her reflected there. They still hadn't really talked about the other night. It was almost as if they were both afraid to broach the subject.

"I'll go check on our supper." Rachel left, and Bruce directed them to sit and relax.

Carrie and Spencer sat close on the high-backed sofa, while Frannie went to her father and pulled on his coat. Bruce bent over to allow Frannie to whisper in his ear.

He smiled and straightened. "Frannie would like to play you something on the pianoforte. Would that be acceptable?"

"Oh, please do," Carrie said, looking to Spencer.

"Absolutely. I love good music."

Frannie skipped over to the piano and pulled out the seat. She climbed up and adjusted her skirt and then carefully aligned her fingers on the keys. She began to play and, much to Carrie's surprise, was quite talented. An old hymn was immediately recognizable. By the time she finished, her sister was ready and waiting to pick up where Frannie left off. Her abilities weren't as polished as her sister's, but the effort given was admirable.

"What a rare treat," Spencer said, clapping after the girls had finished. "I haven't heard anyone play the piano in a very long time."

Rachel appeared in the archway to announce dinner. "Everything is ready for us. Please come this way."

Spencer helped Carrie to her feet and held on to her hand longer than he needed to. A delightful shiver went up Carrie's spine. She was no longer trying to hide her feelings. She hoped that Spencer sensed her pleasure at his touch. She tried to push down any thoughts of him and of what would happen after he caught Astor. For now, she would simply enjoy being Mrs. Spencer Duval.

Supper was a pleasant time. Bruce and Rachel were more than happy to share stories about their life, while Carrie talked about Cheyenne in the early days. Spencer joined in from time to time with tales about his own youth. Mini was particularly delighted when he shared about the time he'd had to climb a very tall tree to rescue a kitten only to get stuck himself.

"My father had to climb up and get us both. The other children thought it quite funny."

"Do you have children?" Frannie asked without warning.

Carrie glanced at Spencer, who was grinning. "Not yet," he told Frannie. "We've only been married a very short time."

"Do you want a lot of children?"

"Frannie, you are imposing on Mr. and Dr. Duval."

She sobered and looked at her mother. "I'm not imposing. I just wanted to know if they were going to have a lot of children. Papa said that Dr. Duval might work with him. If they have a lot of babies, then I could help take care of them."

Spencer chuckled. "I would very much enjoy having a lot of children, Miss Frannie. Furthermore, I believe you would make an excellent helper in taking care of them."

The little girl straightened and beamed a smile. His answer had obviously delighted her. Spencer wondered what Carrie thought of his comment, but he said nothing and didn't even look at her.

Mini, who sat on Spencer's right, reached over to pat his arm. "May I help too?"

He gave her hand a squeeze. "Of course you may. And you can teach them to ride horses."

She looked most serious as she nodded. "I have to learn how first."

The adults appeared to fight off outright laughter. No one wanted to cause the little girl distress at her shortcomings.

The rest of the evening passed quickly, and on the walk home Spencer brought up the topic of children.

"We've never really talked about our thoughts on children. Do you want a family of your own?"

She didn't answer right away, and Spencer worried that perhaps Carrie was upset by the conversation.

"You don't have to answer. I didn't think about how Frannie's questions might have made you feel."

"I'm all right. Her questions were those of an innocent child."

"Whereas mine are more intimidating?"

"I suppose you could say that. But we've always been able to talk about anything, so, yes, I want children."

They walked another block or so, passing one house and then another. Neither one saying a word. Finally, when they were standing in front of their own house, Spencer stopped Carrie and pulled her close. "Do you think you'd like to have my children?"

Carrie's face was aglow beneath the light of the streetlamp. Her eyes searched his face as if trying to find answers to unspoken questions. She gave the slightest nod, and it was all the encouragement Spencer needed. He pressed his lips to hers. He'd only just started to kiss her when he heard someone approach.

"Unhand that woman!"

17

Spencer quickly tucked Carrie behind him and turned to face their assailant. Much to his relief, he heard laughter and found his brother-in-law approaching.

"Sorry, I couldn't resist. I hope I didn't scare you, sis."

Carrie came from around Spencer and shook her head. "I didn't have time to get too scared. Spencer had me safely behind him, ready for a fight."

Robert nodded and grinned. "It's nice to know he can protect you."

"You working tonight?" Spencer asked, eager to move the conversation along so that he and Carrie might be alone once again.

"Rosie sent me. She's up and decided we need a picnic tomorrow. The weather has been so fair that she's certain it will continue. I told her to have a plan just in case it rains or turns chilly. We've all seen that happen around here."

"What time does she want this picnic to be held?" Spencer asked.

"Noon," Robert replied. "She knows we have our men's Bible study in the morning and wanted us to have plenty of time for that."

"What can we bring?" Carrie asked.

"Not a thing. She's been cooking up a storm all day. She even talked Mama into fixing a few things. We'll have more than enough food."

"Sounds good." Spencer looked at Carrie, who gave him a nod. "Where are we meeting up for this picnic?"

"The park at Lake Minnehaha. Rosie loves it out there. We take horseback rides there most Sunday afternoons during the warm weather. You can just catch the trolley, though. It goes all the way out there now. We'll just meet everyone there at the trolley stop."

"It is a lovely area. Tell her we'll be there." Carrie looked at her husband. "If that's all right with you."

"Absolutely. I wouldn't miss it."

Robert gave a nod. "Then I'll head back. I still have to extend the invitation to the Deckers bunch."

"Have a good evening, Rob. Give Rosie my thanks and love," Carrie called after him.

Spencer linked his arm with hers and headed up to the house. He knew they needed to talk. He'd tried to refocus on capturing Eugene Astor, but his feelings for Carrie kept getting in the way. Perhaps if they discussed the matter and truly shared their hearts, he'd be able to get his thoughts in order again.

It was funny how catching Astor didn't seem nearly as important as it used to. Since Astor killed his father, Spencer had thought of very little but seeing the man brought to justice. How funny that one beautiful young doctor could so easily distract him.

"Would you lay a fire? I'm chilled tonight." Carrie discarded her hat and gloves on the table by the door. "I'm going to go change my clothes, and then I'll join you by the fire."

Spencer could see in her expression that she understood the need for them to talk. He didn't hesitate to do as she asked. He built a large fire in the grate and was just adding another log when she returned dressed in her nightclothes.

She had no idea how beautiful she was, and Spencer couldn't help noticing she'd left her hair down. She knew he liked it that way when they were alone. But tonight, it was her alluring eyes that caught his attention. Those blue eyes seemed to take in every detail at once and never miss a thing. It was one of the things he really loved about her. Even now she seemed to search his face for answers.

He sat down and waited for her to join him on the couch. His stomach tightened as if to remind him that they were on the verge of a most important conversation. Perhaps the most important of their life.

Carrie grabbed the blanket and came to sit with him, tucking her legs up under her and spreading the blanket across her lap.

"Everything has changed," she whispered, "and I really don't know what to say, but it's been on my mind since you said what you said."

"I know. I was thinking about that very thing." He turned slightly to better see her. "I never expected to feel this way."

"Nor I." She met his gaze. "It's practically all I've been able to concentrate on."

"Me too." Spencer gave a sigh. "I love you, Carrie. I think I have since we first met. I ignored my feelings for you because of your relationship with Dr. Nelson, but I can't ignore them any longer. You are, after all, my wife. I see you day and night and just sitting here like this is driving me mad."

She nodded. "I know. I feel the same way. Not that I fell in love with you when we first met. I did, however, have special feelings for you as a friend. I always looked forward to my time at the theater because I knew you'd be there and we'd have time to talk. You always treated me like an equal, whereas Oswald was happy to remind me that he was so much more experienced and knowledgeable. I never felt good enough with him, but you were another story. You always made me feel . . . Well, I'm not sure that I can explain it."

It was hard to be this close to her and not touch her . . . hold her. Spencer planted his hands on his thighs. "I've lost sight of why I even came here. I try to think about my duties, about my desire to get justice for my father and catch the man the government has had a bounty out on for over twenty-five years, but I keep coming back to you."

Carrie laughed. "I've got it just as bad. I thought for a few moments yesterday that I was coming down with something. I felt flushed and anxious. My heart seemed to beat faster, and I was so restless. As I assessed the situation, my feelings for you seemed to be the answer. I've fallen in love with you."

Spencer smiled. "Good thing we're married."

"But we never intended to remain married after you accomplished what you were here to do. We never really thought about a future together . . . forever."

"I guess I've been thinking a lot about that the last few days. Maybe longer than that." He couldn't help himself. Spencer put his arm around her and pulled her closer. "Carrie, I want to be married to you. I want to be a real husband to you."

She placed her head on his shoulder and sighed. "And I want to be a wife to you. I've honestly not thought of what that future might look like, however. You know my passion for medicine, and I don't know where that might lead me."

"I know what it means to you, and frankly, I don't care where it leads us. I can be a Pinkerton or a lawman wherever we go. I have a college education and feel certain I could go in any number of directions where work is concerned. If we need to move because of your research, then that's what we'll do. I want you to know I fully support your position as a research doctor."

"As you already know, I'm not good to keep up with housework, cooking, or laundry." She pulled back and looked him in the eye. "If not for restaurants and my mother, we'd starve."

He laughed. "And don't forget the Chinese laundry. We wouldn't have any clean clothes at all if they weren't situated just a few blocks away."

"It's true. I've been trying to figure out how many months I could pay a housekeeper-cook with my savings since I'm not yet making much in the way of a regular salary."

"We've got my pay. Remember I'm working for the Pinkertons as well as the city of Cheyenne. Everything I have is yours, and I don't mind at all if you want to hire someone to take care of us since we're both rather pathetic at it."

"So we're going to make this real, no more pretending?" she asked.

"No more pretending." He looked at her, hoping she could see all the love he felt for her. "I love you more than life itself, Carrie. When Robert startled us, I was ready to die for you. I will always do my utmost to protect you. I know you've told me how you never felt you belonged, but that's all behind you now. You belong to me in every way, and I belong to you."

He pulled her back into his arms, turning her in order to kiss her. He pressed his mouth to hers and felt her arms go around his neck. In that moment, Spencer knew he could never again be without her in his life. She completed him.

Carrie had never known such an overwhelming flow of emotions. Spencer's declaration of love and willingness to follow her wherever she needed to go was more than she had expected. She'd never been much given to tears, but they came now, even as Spencer's kiss deepened. He understood her. He comprehended her need to belong. But even as she lost herself in his touch, Carrie felt herself pulled back to the moment.

She put her hand up to his face and withdrew from his kiss. "I want to get married."

Spencer looked at her oddly. "We are married."

"I mean in a church." She wiped the tears from her eyes, causing Spencer to notice them.

"You're crying. What's wrong?"

"Nothing." She smiled. "I'm very happy. It's just that if we're really going to stay married, I want us to take our vows again. This time with God at the center of it all. The only reason I felt right in agreeing to marry you was because a civil ceremony didn't mean that much to me. It was just another legal matter, nothing more than a business dealing. But if we're to have a real marriage, then it needs to be sacred. It needs to have God at the center of it."

"All right. I understand that. So what do we do about this?"

"I suppose we start by being honest with my family."

He nodded and dropped his hold on her. Carrie got to her feet, knowing she couldn't remain in his arms without things getting passionate again.

"We can do it at the picnic tomorrow. We'll tell them everything."

"I should probably tell your father and Robert about my Pinkerton arrangement in private. There's still such a risk of Astor finding out I'm here."

"All right. Why don't you tell him and Rob tomorrow after your Bible study. Even tell them the truth about the marriage, and we can speak more about getting married in the church at the picnic."

Spencer looked up at her, longing to have Carrie back in his arms. He knew without her saying it that she would want to wait to consummate their marriage. He knew it would be important to both of them, but it was hard to know she was right there and he couldn't be with her.

"I'm going to my room." She pulled the blanket around her as if suddenly shy of this very intimate situation.

Spencer nodded. "I understand." He watched her go and let out a long, heavy breath. Maybe they could get married on Sunday. Or even tomorrow. One thing was certain. He wasn't going to get much sleep tonight.

Eugene waited until the dizzy spell abated before trying once more to make coffee. He hadn't been able to sleep much. Either the pain woke him up or his own fears of what was yet to come refused to let him rest.

He'd never been a religious man, but he had attended church in Cheyenne as was expected of decent folks. He'd picked the Catholic church, where Father Nugent offered three different services. Eugene's mother had been Catholic and had raised her three sons that way, while their father had cared very little for religion. It was an attitude Eugene actually shared, but Cheyenne was not so large a town that he could ignore religion altogether.

Decent folks expected that you would go to church on Sunday. Even his colleagues at the Union Pacific had been given over to discussing Sunday church attendance. Quickly after his arrival, Eugene had seen the need to comply, and after all, it didn't require that much on his part. An hour or two of inconvenience on Sunday. Occasional visitation to the confessional and faithful giving of his tithes. All to maintain the appearance of being a godly man of integrity.

He put the coffee on and made his way back to the table.

Eugene always went to the most popular service in order to blend into the crowd. In fact, blending in to the church and his community had been a practiced routine. In twenty years, he'd made few friends, and none of them were at all close. He had acted the part with the neighbor on his right, mainly because the man worked in the UP offices just down the hall. They sometimes took the trolley to work together. Other times they discussed the weather and town affairs while standing at their property line.

But Eugene had made himself scarce in all other settings. He didn't speak regularly to anyone or keep company with any special lady. In his younger days, he hadn't been opposed to slipping off to the less favorable side of town to enjoy the various evils offered there. The Cheyenne city fathers were even now anxious to find a way to eliminate most all of the questionable activities that the notorious west side had to offer. The problem was that Fort Russell soldiers were some of the town's biggest spenders, and the city fathers also wanted to keep them happy. Allowing for a variety of vices was good business. Eugene knew that as long as there were men with money to spend, there would be allowances for all sorts of evil.

Still, as he sat staring at his kitchen stove, Eugene wondered about the days to come. What would happen to him when he was bedfast? There was no one to see to him, except Dr. Duval. She had come to check on him daily, as promised. In fact, she was due to see him that morning. But sooner or later he would need constant care, and she couldn't offer him that. Worse still, when he died, no one would even care about his passing, except for Carrie Duval—the wife of his enemy.

Eugene shook his head. Spencer Duval wasn't an enemy. He no doubt wanted justice for his father's murder. Perhaps that was even why he'd become a lawman. How could Eugene fault him for that? A thought came to mind. Cheyenne had a decent jail. What if he turned himself in? Someone would definitely have to see to his needs day and night. He didn't have that much time left, so he doubted seriously that he'd get as far as being hanged for his crimes.

"And even if I did," mused Eugene, "wouldn't a quick death be better than the one I'm dying?"

The thought intrigued him. In jail, he could have care and a doctor to look in on him. It could even be the lovely Dr. Duval. Her father was chief of police and would no doubt allow for her to continue as his physician.

Going to jail could be the answer to all of his problems. Of course, there was always the possibility that Spencer Duval would rather shoot it out with Eugene. That would be an even quicker death.

"I could leave him with the sense of avenging his father."

But even at this thought, Eugene knew that wasn't the answer. He had been made to live with his killing, and the memories haunted him even now, twenty-five years after the fact.

A knock sounded on the front door, and Eugene got to his feet. He fought back the momentary blurring of his vision and made his way to admit Dr. Duval.

But to his surprise, he opened the door to find his neighbor's wife, Mrs. Cranston.

"Hello, deary. I meant to bring this over to you last night," she said, extending an envelope. "I picked up our mail yesterday, and it was slipped in by mistake."

Eugene took the letter. "Thank you. That was kind."

"Brought you this as well." She reached into her apron pocket and pulled out a wrapped bundle. "It's some of my apple cinnamon cake. My old man loves it with his coffee in the mornin'. I thought you might as well."

"That is a welcome sight. Thank you, Mrs. Cranston."

Eugene took the offering and gave her a nod as she turned to go. There was no lost conversation about the weather or the state of affairs in the world. She was a woman who kept things together most of the time, and Eugene appreciated it greatly, as well as her occasional treats.

He took the letter and cake back to the kitchen table and sat down. The cake was still warm, and he quickly unwrapped it and began eating, even though the coffee wasn't ready.

The letter intrigued him. It was from his old friend Simon Dade in Nashville. The Dades had been longtime family friends from Philadelphia who moved to Nashville shortly after the war. When it became clear Eugene would have to go on the run, Simon had been one of the men he'd entrusted to send letters to his mother. He opened the envelope and unfolded the brief missive.

The news brought instantaneous regret. His mother had passed away. She had died the previous December. Simon offered his condolences but little more.

Eugene dropped the letter to the table. He had known his mother was bound to die sometime soon. She was, after all, in her eighties. He supposed her still being alive had been a burden on his heart. He had arranged to leave her his money, but he had hated knowing she would be alone in the world. Now he was the one completely alone.

A knock sounded again at the door. This time Eugene greeted Dr. Duval. "How are you today, my dear doctor?"

She smiled and followed him into the house. "I'm doing very well. The skies are cloudy and the winds a bit cold, but the morning is nevertheless invigorating. I hummed a tune on my trolley ride here."

Despite his sorrow, Eugene grinned. "You sound like a woman in love."

To his surprise she sobered. "You know what?" She paused at asking this and nodded. "I am. I'm very much in love."

Eugene laughed despite the pain it brought. "Well, I would hope so, otherwise your husband would be very dismayed."

A wave of dizziness washed over him, followed by immediate nausea. He grabbed the back of the chair.

Dr. Duval was immediately at his side. "You need to sit."

That was all he heard as he sank to the floor, his consciousness fading fast.

18

Coming out with the truth about their marriage weighed heavy on Spencer's heart. He met up with his father-in-law and Robert Vogel at the men's weekly Bible study that morning and was still uncertain as to how he was going to tell them the truth. It distracted him so much, in fact, that he could hardly focus on the Scriptures they were going over. By the time they ended in prayer, Spencer decided the best way to handle things was to just ask the men to meet with him privately afterward. There was nothing else he could do.

Charlie Decker finished praying, and one by one the men left the schoolhouse. Spencer waited until everyone had gone but Decker and the two Vogel men.

As Edward Vogel moved toward the door, Spencer approached. "I, uh, I need to talk to you and Robert."

Robert had just joined them by the door, and Charlie Decker followed after. Spencer thought this was as good a place as any to talk to his in-laws.

"Mr. Decker, I wonder if you might allow me a few minutes here to speak to my father-in-law and Robert? I need the privacy and don't really know where else we might go."

Charlie looked surprised, but then nodded. "You're welcome

to stay here as long as you like. I have some things to take care of in the house. I'll lock up later." He glanced at his good friend Edward Vogel. "See you at the picnic."

"It'll need to warm up a bit more, but otherwise we can all gather at my house," Vogel replied. "With all the food those gals put together, I know we'll be happy wherever we decide to eat."

Decker laughed. "I've yet to go hungry when our women were in charge of the menu."

Once he left the room, Spencer looked at his father-in-law. "There's something important I need to tell you."

"Finally."

Spencer looked at him and could see Vogel's raised brow. "Yes, finally. I apologize for keeping it from you both for so long."

His father-in-law motioned to the table where they'd just had their Bible study. "Let's sit."

They reclaimed their seats, and Spencer drew a deep breath. "I haven't been completely honest with you about why I'm here in Cheyenne. The truth is, I'm a Pinkerton agent."

Edward gave him a nod. "I know."

Spencer couldn't hide his surprise. "You know?"

"You aren't the only one who has friends in the agency," Edward replied.

"I didn't know," Robert threw out. "Why wouldn't you want us to know something like that? There's certainly no shame in being a Pinkerton."

"It's a long story, but I'm chasing down a man I've been after for the last fifteen years. Really the ten before that, as well, but I was too young to go after him. The man killed my father. I was there when he shot him."

"Why didn't you think you could share that with us?" Robert asked.

Spencer didn't have a chance to reply. Edward Vogel spoke up. "Because he couldn't be sure that the man wasn't a friend of ours since he was living in Cheyenne all this time. At least that's my guess."

"You're exactly right. My sources tell me he's been here for the last twenty or so years. I'm sure he's chosen a different name to go by, but his real name is Eugene Astor. He was a bounty jumper during the war. He and his brothers would sign up to fight and take the bonus, then desert. His brothers were killed rather than be captured.

"The Pinkertons figured out their mother still lived in Philadelphia, and so they had her watched, as well as her mail. Astor sent her letters, or we presumed them to be from Astor. We sent men to the towns where he was supposedly living. Usually, it was just me who went. She passed on last December, and the agency was able to get hold of Astor's letters in her personal things. In them he told just enough to make it clear he'd moved to Cheyenne and was working for the Union Pacific, most likely in accounting, since he'd worked at that prior to the war."

Robert considered this a moment. "So you figured to come here and catch him."

"Yes. But Astor has always been quite good at giving us the slip. My father chased him all over the northeast. He finally caught up with him in Philadelphia the day after the war ended. That's where Astor shot and killed him. I made it my life's ambition to get justice for my pa, but Astor always seemed to know what we were planning to do and stayed two steps ahead of us."

"Then you found out he was here." This came from his father-in-law.

"Yes. My supervisor, who also happened to be my father's best friend, gave me the news. He helped me so much after Pa died. He knew what it meant to me to catch Astor and arranged things with the Pinkertons. Of course, I had other jobs to do for them, but since Astor managed to swindle the government out of a lot of money, they wanted the agency to catch him no matter how long it took."

"Still, he did kill an agent," Edward Vogel said, leaning back in his chair.

"Yes, which was in part how we justified my continued search."

"And how does Carrie fit into all of this?"

Spencer couldn't quite meet the older man's gaze and looked at the table. "Well, I didn't lie about loving her. I fell for her from the first moment I met her. Still, we didn't really have a chance to court after she ended things with Nelson. I heard about Astor being in Cheyenne and asked her to be a part of the plan to come here.

"See, I . . . well, I figured if I just showed up in Cheyenne alone, it would take me twice as long to make friends or earn trust than if I came as Carrie's . . . husband. And we needed to move fast. As it is, I've not gotten very far at all."

"You might have gotten further if you'd just come as an agent and told me the truth," Vogel replied.

"But Astor could have been a good friend of yours."

"And you think I wouldn't have turned him over to you?"

Spencer forced himself to glance up and meet his father-in-law's stern gaze. "I didn't really know you, sir. I'd listened to Carrie's stories about her family, but I couldn't take a chance."

"So that's why you two married?"

"No!" Spencer hadn't meant to sound quite so firm. "I love Carrie. I've never lied about that, and she loves me now as well. We just had a long talk about this, which is why we felt it was important for me to come clean. We want to have a real marriage."

"You aren't married?" Robert asked, his eyes narrowing.

"We are." Spencer held up his hands, hoping to calm them both. His father-in-law had said nothing, but Spencer could see he'd stiffened up considerably. "We married in a civil ceremony arranged by the Pinkertons. We're legally bound, but to tell the truth—"

"Which you'd most assuredly better do." The irritation in Robert's voice was quite evident.

"Calm down, son. Let's give him a chance," Edward said, watching Spencer with tense reserve.

Spencer drew a deep breath. "We've lived apart. I've not taken advantage of her in any way. We had married with the thought of annulling the marriage after I caught Astor. But now . . ." Spencer couldn't help but smile. "We're in love and quite happy to remain married. We want to be there for each other and grow old together."

Edward Vogel leaned forward at the table. "So all this time, even under my roof, you two didn't take advantage of the fact that you were married?"

"No, sir. I completely respected her position, knowing that we would go our separate ways when the job was done. I didn't want to compromise her in any way. Again, I love her too much to do something like that."

"I still don't understand why you thought you had to be married," Robert said, shaking his head.

"I don't suppose it would have had to be that way, but it saved a lot of time. Being your kinsman, I was immediately welcomed into your circle of friends and was able to ascertain if any of them were Astor."

"So you know him by sight?" the elder Vogel asked.

"I think I would. I can't say for sure. It's been a lot of years, and I was just a boy. It's possible I wouldn't know him."

Spencer folded his hands atop the table. "Look, I'm sorry for the deception, but Carrie and I plan to get married again, this time in the church. We'll do it soon and right here so that you can all be a part of it. And for now, we'll remain here in Cheyenne. It's all up to Carrie. I don't have to be a Pinkerton to be happy, but I do need her to be so. She needs to continue her work. Wherever she wants to go to do that . . . well, I will see to it that she gets where she needs to be."

"You love her so much that you'd give up on what you want in life?" Edward asked.

"Carrie's the only thing I really want. She even had me forgetting about my need to catch Astor. That's part of why I still haven't gotten very far."

"Are you willing to let us help you now?"

Spencer looked at his father-in-law and nodded. "I'd like whatever help you can offer."

"Are you two going to be honest with the rest of the family?"

"Yes, sir. Although I'd rather not give too many details on the man I'm hunting down. The fewer who know, the less chance of someone saying something by accident."

"I agree." Edward Vogel got to his feet. "There's also the matter of what happens now between the two of you."

"I don't understand." Spencer stood, as did Robert.

"Well, until you're married in the eyes of God, I'm wondering where you'll live."

"I don't think we should have them living separate," Mama said after Carrie and Spencer shared the details of their quick marriage and relocation to Cheyenne.

The weather had been much too cold for a lakeside picnic, so the families had gathered at the Vogel house. Spencer had told Carrie in a hurried whisper that he'd shared everything with her father and brother. She'd worried about how the news would go over with Mama, so it was hard to wait until the Deckers went home to share the truth with her mother and sister. Michael Decker had stayed with Greta since they had plans for the afternoon, but Carrie figured they could trust him.

"If they live separately now," Mama continued, "folks will question whether they were ever really married. It will ruin their reputations. Since they are already married, I can just make it clear to my friends that I wanted very much to see Carrie get married. I think everyone will understand my desire for a church wedding."

"Yes, I think that makes sense," Carrie said, nodding.

"I have a wonderful idea!" Greta all but squealed. She looked to Michael. "What if Carrie and Spencer stand up with us and marry in a double ceremony? Robert and Rosie married with Rosie's brother and Emma Johnson. We could carry on the tradition."

Michael nodded. "That's fine by me."

Greta looked at her mother and then to Carrie and Spencer. "What say you? Just think how special it will be. Sisters having a double wedding."

Carrie looked to Spencer. "Would you mind?"

"No. Whatever makes you happy."

Carrie smiled. "Greta, I would love that. This way we can stand up with each other just as we always planned to do." She glanced over at Rosie. "And you can be our matron of honor, Rosie. We'll share you."

"That's perfect because Robert is going to be my best man," Michael added.

"Would you be mine as well?" Spencer asked.

Robert gave a shrug. "Might as well be."

They laughed, and the tension of Carrie sharing the truth faded. She was relieved to see everyone so amiable about the matter.

"I'm so glad to have this matter settled," Mama said, shaking her head. "And the double wedding is the perfect excuse. No one will be the wiser."

"It's not like we're hiding anything . . . not really," Papa said. "Maybe we're not filling everyone in on all the details of how things got first arranged, but it's no one else's business."

"I'm just so excited," Greta said, reaching over to give Carrie's hand a squeeze. "This is absolutely wonderful. But we're going to have to go immediately Monday morning and have you fitted for a wedding dress."

"That's right. We'll need to get right to it. The wedding is in just about a month. The dressmaker will need time to get your gown made."

"I don't have to have a fancy gown, Mama. You didn't have one, and the marriage has lasted just fine."

"Oh, but it's going to be such a beautiful wedding. We're having flowers brought in and everything," Greta said, sounding so hopeful that Carrie couldn't ignore her desires.

"Very well. I'll go with you Monday to see the dressmaker." She looked at Spencer, who seemed rather preoccupied. "Can we afford a wedding dress, Spencer?"

He looked at her with an odd expression. "We can afford whatever you need."

"We'll pay for the dress," Carrie's father announced. "Just as we did Greta's. That matter isn't up for discussion." He gave her a wink.

Carrie could see the love in his eyes. She really did belong and always had. Why had it been so hard to see when she was younger? God had given her a solid foundation of loving parents and siblings. It was her own misguided doubts that had left her feeling somehow less than worthy of love.

"Why don't we go cut the cake," Rosie said more than asked. "Everyone should have room for it now."

Papa rubbed his stomach and laughed. "If not, I'll make room for it by moving everything around."

Everyone laughed, but Greta and Michael got to their feet. "We have plans and will eat cake later. We'll be back around five."

"All right, you two, I'm sure you have plenty to discuss and plan. Behave yourselves," Mama said, waving them off. "Let's head back to the dining room, I'm sure we'll be more comfortable there."

As everyone moved from the front room and down the hall, Carrie noticed Spencer was still quiet. She took hold of his arm and held him back a moment.

"Are you all right? Are you regretting us telling them everything?"

"No," he said, reaching out to touch her cheek. "I'm glad we did. Your father and brother have agreed to help me in any way they can. I'm going to need their help to get this wrapped up."

"Then what? I feel like something isn't quite right."

He laughed and leaned closer to her ear. "The wedding is May third. That's over a month away."

Carrie nodded. "Yes."

Spencer sighed. "Seems an awfully long time."

She laughed, finally understanding his line of thought. "Good things are worth waiting for."

19

If Eugene Astor had any doubts about his days being numbered, that was in the past. The dizzy spells and blurred vision came more often. Twice he'd actually blacked out only to wake up on the floor, just as he had that Saturday when Dr. Duval had been present.

Now he was having trouble controlling his left hand and arm, and the head pain was constant. He made his way to Dr. Duval's knowing there was little she could do. She had talked about drilling a hole into the cranium in order to relieve the pressure, but she wasn't at all certain it would help. And if it did help, it probably wouldn't help for long.

He knocked on the door, feeling the world begin to spin once more. He closed his eyes and drew a deep breath. How much longer did he have? He had already outlived all of the doctors' predictions.

Then there were the questions of how the end would come. Would he be conscious and know what was happening? Would it be painful or a soothing release? He had so many unanswered questions about his condition, not to mention some of his other issues. Who was he to leave his money and house to now that his mother was dead? Who would see to his arrangements? He had an appointment later in the day with Colton Benton, the lawyer who had set up his will. He would ask him what he suggested be done.

Dr. Duval opened the door and gave him a quick glance from top to bottom. "I wasn't expecting to see you, Mr. Knowles. Please come in."

"I'm afraid . . . I'm worse. I've passed out twice, and my hand and arm are causing me trouble now. My vision is worse at times, and the dizziness and pain are nearly constant."

She nodded and took hold of his right arm. "Come into my examination room."

She wasted no time helping him up on the examination table. "Now, tell me what preceded your fainting spells. Did you feel them coming on?"

"I remember feeling warm all of a sudden, and then it was as if my vision began to tunnel on me. Like the blackness was coming in from all sides. Then I knew nothing."

"And was this different from your regular blurred vision?" She widened his eye with her thumb and index finger and bent closer.

"Yes, it was different. The pain in my head was worse in the morning but constant now."

She finished looking into his eyes and took hold of his hands. "Hold your hands out in front." She let go and then reached to place her hands atop his. "Don't let me push your arm down."

Eugene was able to keep his right hand fairly firm, but he had no strength in the left. After that there were a series of tests on his hands.

"Close your eyes and tell me when you feel me touching you." She started with the right hand, and Eugene had no difficulty detecting touch. When she moved to his left, he was completely lost. Without looking, he was convinced she wasn't touching him at all. When he opened his eyes, he could see that she was running the end of a pencil over his fingertips.

"I had no sense of that whatsoever. Is that normal for my disease?"

"It's normal for a tumor in the brain. You are clearly worsening, but I don't believe you've had a stroke. I have been speaking to a colleague of mine, Dr. Compton. He shares my interests in the brain. We would like to continue to care for you and share the responsibilities. He has a better setup than I do. He suggested that when the time is right, you should close up your house and stay at his facility. I will come and take turns with your medical needs. You will have round-the-clock care."

"That's quite generous of you both." He rubbed at his temples. "And how do we gauge when the time is right?"

"I believe that time has come, Mr. Astor. You are going downhill fast, as you already know. There's very little time left. Frankly, I'm surprised that you're still with us."

He looked into her eyes. Such a beautiful shade of blue. It reminded him of an icy mountain lake he'd once seen back in Pennsylvania. "Then this is the end?"

"I believe so, Mr. Knowles. I'm sorry." There was such sincerity in her voice.

Eugene gave her a smile. "Don't be sorry. We knew this was coming." He slipped off the examination table. "I will go put my things in order and allow you to escort me to Dr. Compton's." He started for the door, then turned back. "What do you suppose all of this care will cost? I'd like to bring you money when I return. You deserve to be paid, and you can hardly get coins from a dead man."

"You've already agreed to let us autopsy you. I won't be charging you further."

"Your help has been important to me, Dr. Duval. I want to pay you as I have the other doctors."

"No pay is due, Mr. Knowles."

She smiled at him, and it was such a kind look that Eugene almost turned away. He wasn't deserving of such innocence and tenderness of spirit. She was married to the man who surely wanted him dead. If he knew who it was his wife was treating, he'd probably throw Eugene out onto the street. Perhaps she would as well, but something in her countenance suggested to him that she wouldn't.

"Have you a faith in the Almighty, Dr. Duval?"

"Absolutely," she answered, her expression growing quite serious.

"My mother had a deep abiding faith, and I recall to mind her quoting a verse about the laborer being worthy of his reward."

"Yes, I believe that verse is found in the fifth chapter of First Timothy. But you are paying me in the only way that I truly wish. Your autopsy will allow Dr. Compton and myself to learn more about the disease that is taking your life. In turn, it may well save the life of another. You are more than paying your way as far as I'm concerned."

A thought came to Eugene and brought a smile to his face. "Perhaps the Good Lord has another reward in mind for you."

When he left, he headed directly to Colton Benton's office. He now knew to whom he intended to leave his fortune.

Spencer had narrowed the list of suspects down to just three. With the help of Carrie's father and brother, they had managed to cross every other name off the list that Al had provided. They split the list between them, and Spencer was now off to see what he could learn about Rowland Knowles. The name was familiar to him for some reason, but he wasn't sure why. Neither Edward nor Robert knew of the man, yet Spencer was certain he'd heard the man's name mentioned.

He headed home to check his journals, where he made meticulous notes on his cases. Surprisingly enough, the house was quiet. Carrie had told him that she would be spending more time at the Compton house during certain days. The two were trying to figure out a way to go into business together. Spencer had done his best to encourage his wife to pursue her dream in whatever manner seemed appropriate. He only wanted her to be successful and garner the credit she deserved.

He went directly to his bedroom and opened a trunk at the end of the bed. He pulled out the book in which he'd been keeping all his notes on Eugene Astor. He glanced through the list of names that Astor had been known to use. There was nothing to connect him to Rowland Knowles. Spencer continued to scan through his notes but found nothing that seemed to offer any help. He replaced the book and closed the lid of the trunk.

Why was that name familiar?

He heard the front door open and made his way to see who it was. Carrie hurried in pulling her hat from her head.

"I wondered where you were."

She startled at his voice and took a stance with hatpin in hand as though she might attack. "You scared the life right out of me." She shook her head and glanced at the pin. "I thought I might have to do battle."

"With a hatpin?" He grinned. "I don't know that you'd get very far."

"You'd be surprised just how effective an eight-inch-long pin can be, especially when poked into certain parts of the body." She tucked the pin into the straw brim of her bonnet and placed it on the foyer table. "What are you doing home at this hour?"

"I've been looking for some information." Spencer waited as Carrie finished pulling off her gloves. "Does the name Rowland Knowles mean anything to you?"

She looked at him oddly and narrowed her eyes. "I should say it does. He's a patient of mine."

"A patient? Have you mentioned his name before?"

"I'm sure I have. He's the one I visit every morning. In fact, that's who I was arranging for just now. We're going to settle him in at Dr. Compton's house. Bruce and I are going to take turns caring for him."

"Caring for him? What's wrong with him?"

Carrie frowned. "He's dying. He has some sort of brain tumor. At least that's what a half dozen doctors have determined. He has only a short time. Days or a week at the most."

Spencer felt his heart rate pick up. "Knowles is dying?"

"Yes. I don't understand your sudden interest in him."

"He may be Eugene Astor. I've narrowed the list to three men, and your father and brother are checking out the other two. Knowles was left to me."

"Well, if he's Eugene Astor, there's little you can do about it. He won't live much longer, and I intend to see him made comfortable. He's given me permission to autopsy his brain, and it will be very helpful to us in our research."

"I still need to speak to him."

She gave him a look that suggested frustration. "Spencer, if he's your man, you won't be able to arrest him. He's not going anywhere. Certainly not back to Philadelphia or Chicago or wherever it was you had in mind to take him for his comeuppance."

Spencer had never considered the possibility of Astor being too ill to face responsibility for what he'd done.

"I've chased down this man my entire adult life. He needs to face up to what he did, and I mean to make him pay."

Carrie moved past him toward her examination room and office. "Rowland Knowles is a dead man, and as his doctor, I must insist you allow him to die in peace."

Spencer wasn't at all sure what to think or say. His purpose in life had been to get his father justice, and now his killer was going to avoid any kind of punishment? It wasn't fair. It wasn't right. Astor had killed a good man. Was it true he was dying? If Carrie said he was too ill to live much longer, Spencer believed her. She was an astute doctor. She wouldn't say such a thing just to throw him off the trail.

He followed her to where she was gathering some of her things and putting them into her black bag.

"Look, where is he now? I need to talk to him."

Carrie looked up. "To what purpose, Spencer?"

"The truth. I need to know if he's Astor. I need to . . . I need to find out if he's the man who killed my father. At this point, he shouldn't feel the need to hide the truth."

"It won't change anything," Carrie all but whispered.

"I need to know. It's important to me. Can't you understand that?" Spencer realized he sounded much harsher than he'd intended. He tried to calm himself. "You know I've been looking for this man for a long time. It's the reason I came here." He looked away. "Part of the reason."

He paced off a few steps and tried to put his thoughts in order. "Look, I just need to talk to him. Obviously if he's dying I can't very well take him in, but I can make him admit what he's done."

"And if he's not Astor?"

"He has to be."

"You said my father and brother are checking the two other men. You don't know that Mr. Knowles is your man. You don't know."

"I will know if I talk to him. There's no reason he should lie to me if he's dying. I'll make him tell me."

Carrie put her hands on her hips. "Listen to yourself. You're going to make him tell you. Will you knock him around if he refuses to speak? Perhaps draw a gun and scare him with the threat of a bullet in his head? He's already got a bullet in his head, for all intents and purposes."

"I thought you understood. I thought you cared." Spencer frowned and immediately regretted his words. He knew she cared, but he also knew she was devoted to her patients. Her considerate nature and determination to heal was what drove her passion for medicine.

Carrie's expression hardened. "I do care. And although you may not like to hear it, God has brought Rowland Knowles, or Eugene Astor, into my life. He needs my help—not to live, but rather to die."

"He killed my father."

"You don't know that." She squared her shoulders, and Spencer knew he was in for a fight. "I know you've searched for this man for a great many years, and I wanted very much to help you find him. But if Knowles is Astor, then as his physician I must insist that you listen to me. He is going to die, and I am going to do what I can to make that passing easy no matter who he's killed. Do you understand me?"

"He deserves torment and pain," Spencer heard himself all but growl. What had gotten into him? How could he act so callously? He could see by the look on her face that she was thinking much the same.

"I'm sorry, Carrie. I just . . . I need to know if it's him. If need be, I'll get your father's help on this."

"You're obsessed with making someone pay for your father's death."

"I want him to pay. Eugene Astor needs to pay for my father's death!" Spencer got to his feet and stormed out of the house.

She didn't understand, but then how could he expect her

to when even he didn't understand this sudden hardening of his heart? Astor deserved to face the truth, but if Knowles and Astor were one and the same, then he was going to die no matter what the truth of the past might be.

But I need to know if it's him.

20

Carrie was shocked by Spencer's anger, but at the same time she understood it. She had considered how she might feel had someone murdered her father. It was bad enough that her birth father had died when she was so young. She believed God was all powerful and therefore able to prevent her father's wagon from going off the icy bridge. God could have kept the situation from becoming a tragedy in the lives of the two sisters left behind. But He didn't. Just as God hadn't kept Spencer's father from being murdered.

She went to the window and put up the shade. She hated that Spencer had left in such a rage. She'd never seen that side of him, but she had seen her father angry at injustices. She'd heard him rant at her mother when something had gone wrong and the bad guy was kept from paying his dues.

Spencer was in pain. There was no doubt about that, but Carrie wasn't sure that Spencer would find relief even if Knowles was his man.

Movement caused Carrie to look out the window once more. Perhaps Spencer was coming back. To her surprise it turned out to be her mother. What in the world had caused her to come calling at this hour?

Carrie opened the door before her mother even knocked. She forced a smile. "Good afternoon, Mama. What a surprise."

"I know it is, but I felt compelled to come see you. Call it intuition or God's nudging, but I just felt like perhaps you needed me. Or at least needed to talk."

"Come in." It seemed strange that God would have sent her to Carrie. She hadn't considered needing a mother's ear, but maybe that was exactly what was called for. Carrie hadn't taken her troubles to Mama in a long time.

"Oh, and I brought this letter for you. It was posted to our address."

Carrie took the letter and opened it. "It's from Jason Frommel. He was one of the research assistants at the clinic Oswald headed up."

"I don't remember you ever mentioning him."

"There was no reason to mention him. He was an acquaintance, someone I worked with. Nothing more. We had very little interaction." Carrie scanned the letter and threw it aside. "Oh, that man!"

"Jason?"

"No, Oswald Nelson. He infuriates me in more ways than I can even tell. Jason says he received acclaim in New York last month for his latest research. Or should I say, my research. Remember I told you about him stealing my work and having published an article?" Mama nodded while Carrie picked up the letter from the floor. "That's the same work for which he's being heralded as a genius."

Carrie made her way into the front room with Mama following behind. She knew she wasn't being much of a hostess, but she was too distraught. "Why would God allow that? It's not like it's a questionable matter. I did that work. I found the discoveries. Oswald had nothing to do with it. God could have kept my work safe . . . could have kept me safe."

"I believe He has kept you safe, my love." Mama reached out to touch Carrie's cheek.

Carrie crumpled the letter in her hand. "But Oswald is getting the credit for something he didn't do. That finding could have given me the extra attention needed to get the medical world to take me seriously. It might have attracted sponsors, donors. Research doctors need those kinds of people since we don't make much money in any other way."

"But you once told me, if you'd presented the information as a female doctor, they might have ignored you altogether and the article would never have been published. The findings would have remained unheard of. At least this way the evidence is out there."

"Not that Oswald will ever figure out what to do with it." She met her mother's gaze. "My findings are the very early stages of what is yet to come. However, Oswald won't have any idea of where to go from there."

"And so perhaps the world will see him for the fraud he is." Mama put her arm around Carrie's shoulders and led her to the sofa. "Sit and calm down. Everything will seem better in a few minutes."

"I wish that's all it took." Carrie took a seat, and her mother did likewise. "Spencer and I argued."

"As do all married couples."

"This was about the man who killed his father."

"And why would you fight about that?" Mama asked.

"Because he thinks the man may be my patient."

"Well, I know your father and brother have been trying hard to help Spencer find his man. Although I admit, I don't know much other than that. Why should this new knowledge cause a fight?"

"Because I saw something in Spencer that I didn't like. He was angry and so focused on Astor paying for what he'd done to his father that he held very little compassion or sympathy for the man. A man who has only days, maybe hours to live."

"I'm not sure I understand." Mama shook her head and pulled off her gloves. "Why don't you start at the beginning and tell me everything."

Carrie began with Spencer learning that Rowland Knowles was her patient. She told her mother all the details of Knowles's condition.

"He's in hideous pain and is losing the ability to use his hand and will probably lose his vision. I told Spencer it would be impossible to bring him to justice. He's going to die right here in Cheyenne. Spencer insists on confronting the man and learning the truth."

"Maybe it would do both men good."

Mama's comment surprised Carrie. "Why would you say that?"

"Maybe Mr. Knowles needs to confess. The man is going to die soon. Perhaps he regrets what he did. Maybe speaking to Spencer would help him die in peace."

Carrie hadn't considered this aspect of the matter. Her mother was absolutely right. Dying had a way of making people speak on things they might otherwise have left unsaid.

"Perhaps. I admit that I hadn't really thought of it being beneficial to Mr. Knowles, but you may be right. I mean, what does he have to lose in admitting the truth? If it were me and I had something like that in my past, I would want to clear the slate, so to speak."

Mama nodded. "As would I. Of course, there are truly evil people who wouldn't concern themselves with such things."

"Mr. Knowles doesn't seem that type. Then again, I've known him such a short time that I could hardly tell you what the man would want. I feel bad for both men. Spencer has waited nearly his whole life to bring that Astor to justice. If Astor is Knowles, that isn't going to happen."

"Spencer will need you to help him through this. I'm sure there's a part of him that supposes he owes this to his father. He might believe that if he can't bring his father's killer to justice, then he's failed him."

"I could see him feeling that way. After all, he's devoted his life and career to catching this man. Every important decision of his life has been made with that task in mind."

"Including marrying you."

Carrie considered that. "Do you suppose he'll regret it now if he can't take Astor to face charges? Especially since he's my patient." She shook her head. "Will he blame me?"

"Spencer loves you. I'm convinced of that. I've seen it in his eyes. Heard it in his voice. Your father is confident of it, as well, and you know how good he is at discerning the truth."

"I've let myself fall in love with him. I don't honestly know what I'd do if I lost him now."

Mama patted her hand. "You aren't going to lose him. Just be understanding of his situation. Nothing you do will keep Mr. Knowles from dying, is that true?"

"Yes. He will die no matter what I do."

"Let Spencer have time with him. If he is the man who killed his father, then Spencer can put an end to his search and lay this to rest. It might not be the ending he'd hoped for, but it will be an ending nevertheless."

"Thank you, Mama. I appreciate your wisdom." Carrie looked at her mother for a moment. She was starting to get lines around her mouth and eyes. She wasn't all that old, but the years were starting to show.

"There's something else I need to say." Carrie drew a deep breath. "I spent a great deal of my growing-up years feeling like an outcast, which I vocalized quite loudly at times."

"I prayed constantly that you would realize how important you were to our family. How you weren't at all an outcast.

"When I first thought I might lose you, I was ready to fight to the death to keep you with me. You were my child in every way but birth. I was the first one to cradle you. The first to feed and bathe you. You never knew any mother but me. And in truth, Edward was really your only father. Our blood father was a good man, a brave man, but I believe babies were the one thing that scared him to death."

Carrie smiled. "I saw many a man react that way when I was helping you with some of the births around here."

"The only man I've ever seen take to babies with the natural instincts of a mother is Charlie Decker. He positively loves children, and babies don't cause him even a moment of hesitation. Even your father was scared and uncomfortable. Until your brothers and sister got to be around two years old, he would just as soon have very little to do with you. Not because he held no love, but because he was afraid of being too rough or not attentive enough."

"I can understand that. I guess what I really want to say is that I know you loved me. I know I belong to this family. Greta said some things that made me see myself differently. I guess we all just have those questions about ourselves. We all wonder if we truly have a place . . . if we really belong."

"We all struggle to fit in. And just look at you. You've gone and picked a profession where you'll continue to struggle." Mama put her arm back around Carrie's shoulders and pulled her close. "You're a fighter with a compassionate heart and inquisitive mind. You are exactly as God created you to be, and I know you will be a blessing to a great many people. Stop worrying about Oswald Nelson and let go of the past. Your future is far more important. I know without a doubt that you are going to do great things."

Spencer didn't know where he was going. He just had to walk off his anger and frustration. He wasn't really mad at Carrie. He was just struggling to deal with life. The truth of the situation was difficult to accept. He'd always seen in his mind how things would play out with Astor. He would find the man, and one of two things would happen. Spencer would either have to take the man's life when he refused to give up and go peaceably to face justice, or Astor would go willingly and realize his death by hanging. Spencer could accept either outcome. It was this third and unplanned ending that he hadn't counted on.

Of course, it could still be that Knowles wasn't his man. But everything in Spencer told him that wasn't the case. It was almost as if God was telling him that Knowles was indeed Astor and that this was how things would be. It seemed almost cruel. There was no satisfaction in badgering a dying man. All the things Spencer had practiced saying in his thoughts and dreams now held little importance. Knowles wouldn't care. He would soon be beyond all caring.

Spencer found himself amidst the downtown traffic and noise. People were rushing from one place to another, seemingly unconcerned with all the wagons and mounted riders or other fellow Cheyenneites. Realizing he'd walked all the way to the police station, Spencer made his way inside. He hadn't planned to go see his father-in-law, but somehow that seemed the right thing to do.

"Is the chief in?" he asked the sergeant.

"He's in. And he's alone. One of those rare occasions."

"God must have known what I needed." Spencer moved past the receiving desk and made his way down the hall to Edward Vogel's office.

The door was open, and Spencer could see Vogel at his desk, looking over papers. He gave a light rap on the jamb.

Edward looked up and waved him in. Spencer closed the

door behind him and made his way to where his father-in-law sat looking rather quizzically at him.

"I wasn't expecting to see you today."

"I wasn't expecting to be here, but I had a fight with your daughter and needed to . . . well, needed someone to . . ."

"Commiserate with?" Vogel asked, smiling. "She can be formidable. It's that brain of hers. She's too smart for her own good."

Spencer felt the tension ease and smiled. "Exactly."

"Sit down."

Taking the chair opposite his father-in-law, Spencer eased back and waited for the older man to say something more. When he didn't, Spencer glanced up and gave a halfhearted smile.

"I shouldn't be bothering you."

"I'm here for all my children and their spouses. What's going on?"

Spencer spilled out the details of all that had happened. "I know I sounded heartless, because . . . I felt heartless. If Knowles is Astor, I don't think I care that he's dying or that he's in pain. I've spent so much time hating that man for what he took from me. I hate that I feel this way, Chief."

"Call me *Dad* or *Pa* or something other than *Chief*. This isn't in the line of work."

"I'll call you *Dad*. I called my father *Pa*, and I don't think I could ever call anyone else by that name."

"Good enough. Go on."

"I don't know what else to say. I know Carrie is just doing her job as a doctor to look out for her patient. I guess I just have so much anger and rage built up against him. I want him to suffer as he's made me suffer."

"And will that make things better?"

Spencer shrugged. "Somehow, I always thought it would."

Edward smiled. "I can tell you from experience that it

doesn't. But I suppose you have to deal with that for yourself. Some things in life can't be taught through words."

"I'm disappointed in myself. I thought I'd handle this so much differently. But then, I thought the end would be different."

"What were you expecting?"

"I always figured I'd find Astor and arrest him. I'd transport him back to stand trial for my father's death and the bounty jumping, and the judge would pass sentence to hang him. Then I'd go to the hanging and somehow that would allow me to finally have peace of mind."

"For losing your father? Astor's death would actually give you that kind of relief?"

Spencer considered his question a moment. "I don't know."

"It won't bring your pa back from the dead. It won't change what you saw and felt that day. And it sure won't wipe away the years you had to live without him or the strain it put on your ma. All of those things are still going to be a part of your past."

"But if he faces punishment for what he did, then I would have accomplished my job. I would have gotten justice."

"Justice or revenge?"

"Both maybe?"

Edward nodded. "At least you're honest. I like that about you, son. But let me give you a piece of advice. You need to forgive Eugene Astor."

The words hit like a slap in the face. Spencer straightened and shook his head. "How can I forgive him? He killed my pa. I was there. He had no remorse. All he said to me was, 'The score has been settled, son. This is a day to end all wars.' But for me the war had just started. My war with him. It's consumed me."

"Your youth became a casualty of it in many ways. Are you going to throw the rest of your life away on it?"

"You think my desire to bring Astor to justice was a waste of my life?"

Vogel shrugged. "You're the only one who can say for certain one way or the other. However, to keep carrying this after Astor is dead and gone would be a waste. As a father, I would never want that kind of thing for my son. And I don't want it for you either."

"So what do I do?"

"Find out if Knowles is your man and ask him the question that's on your mind."

"The question?" Spencer could see great compassion in Edward Vogel's eyes.

"Yeah. Why? Why did you kill my pa? That is the question on your heart, isn't it?"

Spencer swallowed the growing lump in his throat. "Yeah."

21

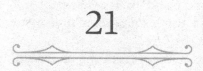

Spencer made his way home and wasn't surprised to find Carrie waiting for him. What did take him aback was that she was ready to take him to Knowles without further ado. All the way back from the jail, Spencer had tried to figure out how he could convince her to let him talk to Knowles, but here she was urging him to come with her to Dr. Compton's house.

"I think you should talk to him, but please promise me you won't argue with him or try to hurt him. He's quite sick."

"You must have a pretty low opinion of me to think I would strike a man who couldn't fight back."

Carrie shook her head. "I don't have a low opinion of you, but I know that people tend to forget themselves and the situation when they let their anger take over. You have a lifetime of rage built up against Eugene Astor. If Knowles is your man, well, isn't it possible you'll forget yourself?"

"I suppose it could be. It depends on what he says. If he doesn't care about what he's done . . . if he's not sorry . . ."

She placed her hand on his arm. "Even if he's sorry, Spencer, it's not going to take away your pain."

"Your father said I needed to forgive him. I don't know if I can."

"Ask God to help you. He forgave us, and we killed His Son. Or rather our sin did. Nevertheless, we played our part. Forgiveness isn't saying that you approve or even accept his reasons for doing it. My mama always said that forgiveness was letting go of a burden we were never meant to carry."

"Your ma and pa are pretty wise people."

She gave his arm a squeeze. "I'm just starting to realize how very wise they are."

They made their way from the house and headed north. These days they walked everywhere, and while Spencer didn't mind it, he did worry about Carrie. Traffic was terrible, and not only that, but as a doctor she might need to get somewhere quickly.

"I should get you a carriage."

She shook her head. "I don't mind walking. I used to walk all over Chicago. Cheyenne is certainly less of a risk."

"That's true, but I worry about you all the same."

"I'm sorry I got so angry earlier," Carrie said after a moment of silence. "I haven't worked a lot with living patients. This man's condition has played with my emotions. I'm frustrated that there's so little I can do. It really makes me angry."

"I was wrong to lose my temper, and I apologize. I had a talk with your father, and he helped me to better see things."

"He has a way of doing that."

Spencer reached out to take hold of her gloved hand. "I don't want to fight with you."

She nodded and stepped a little closer. "I don't want to fight with you either. I may seem controlled and logical most of the time, but I can get quite passionate about things. You might as well know that about me."

"I do. It's part of what I love about you." He gave her a smile.

Carrie seemed not to notice. "If Rowland Knowles is Astor ... then so be it, but I've only known him as a man in desperate need. Unlike you, knowing him as a killer and threat to your own well-being. It's funny how that makes such a big difference."

"What do you mean?"

"Well, it's just that when I was younger, I noticed how people often took up offense for their friends or family when someone was doing them wrong. While I might not have liked having my family or friends hurt or treated wrong, I wasn't someone who did that. I mean, I reasoned through things and thought very simply about it all. That didn't lead me to being offended on their behalf. But with my patients, I feel quite guarded about them and their needs."

"Being protective of them makes sense to me. You understand what's wrong with them to begin with, and you don't want anyone to cause them further harm. I can understand your reasoning."

"Even as I read through the notes other doctors had made on Knowles's condition, I wanted desperately to find a solution, some small thing I could do that those other doctors had somehow missed. I wanted to save his life."

"You're a good doctor, Carrie. Of course you would want to do that. I admire that in you."

"I'm glad you do. But I also understand you've searched your entire adulthood to find this man and see him pay for what he did. I want you to be able to talk to Knowles. At the same time, I want to spare Mr. Knowles any additional trauma or pain."

"I promise to go easy on him. Honestly, Carrie. I just want the truth from him. I want him to tell me why he killed my father."

She met his gaze, and her blue eyes searched him as if looking for some hidden detail. He stopped and pulled her closer. "I promise. You may not know me as well as I'd like, but you can count on my promise. I won't hurt him."

"I believe you."

They began walking again, and when they reached Bruce Compton's large house, Carrie took hold of Spencer at the door.

"Let me examine him first and make sure he's up to having a conversation with you."

"All right." As anxious as Spencer was to see the man, he knew it was important to do things Carrie's way.

"Oh, Carrie, I didn't know you'd returned," Mrs. Compton said, coming into the small front office. "I heard the front bell."

"Spencer wants to talk to Mr. Knowles, and I thought I'd better check him out beforehand. Where's Dr. Compton?"

"He's gone at the moment. A message came that someone needed to see him at the Inter Ocean Hotel."

Carrie put her gloves and hat aside and took up her black bag. "I'll go to see Mr. Knowles, Spencer, and then come back to get you in a moment. You might as well take a seat."

He nodded and smiled at Mrs. Compton before she turned to leave. He sat feeling awash in emotions. If this man was Astor, it would be the first time he'd seen him since that day. The longings of that ten-year-old boy edged to the forefront of his feelings. He had wanted so much to save his father's life. To somehow bring him back from the dead. For the shooting to have never happened.

Then Spencer remembered a moment from a few weeks ago. He had stumbled into a man as he was leaving the house, and Spencer was returning home. That had to be Knowles, yet Spencer hadn't recognized him. Perhaps he wasn't Astor.

"Spencer, you can come ahead," Carrie said from the doorway.

He was surprised at how quickly she'd returned. He gave her a questioning gaze, and she shrugged.

"He wants to see you."

"He wants to see me?" Spencer felt his heart pick up its pace. "He knows who I am?"

"I don't know. I only told him that my husband wanted to talk to him."

Spencer followed her through the door and down a very short hall. There were two doors on either side, and Carrie opened the one to the right.

She touched Spencer's arm. "Try to keep things calm."

"I will as best I can." Spencer stepped into the room and fixed his gaze on the older bearded man lying in bed. He was propped up slightly with extra pillows and gave the slightest smile.

"I figured it was time we had a talk."

Spencer felt a shiver go down his spine. The voice was familiar. The wrinkled, bearded face not so much.

"Eugene Astor."

The older man nodded. "I am, although folks around Cheyenne know me as Rowland Knowles. Come sit with me."

It was hard to accept the frail-looking man in the bed was the same one Spencer had spent a lifetime searching for. Nevertheless, he came and drew a nearby chair up to the man's side and took a seat.

"I wondered when you'd come."

"You knew I was here?" Spencer couldn't imagine Astor sticking around if that were the case.

"The day I came from having seen your wife and ran into you, I knew you. I could never forget that face. You look just like your father."

"The man you killed."

"Yes, for which I've never stopped paying." He frowned and slowly shook his head. "I never intended for him to die.

I wasn't shooting to kill. I'd never killed anyone before . . . or since."

"What do you mean? You knew he was after you. If you didn't mean to kill him, why did you shoot?"

"I was only going to wound him. I figured to graze him in the hip or leg. I'm an excellent marksman. Just before I fired, however, your father dropped to his knee. It startled me, and I fired. The bullet I intended for his hip hit his head and killed him. I was stunned, but at the same time I knew I'd sealed my fate as well as his and yours."

Spencer felt as if Astor had struck him in the gut. "My father knelt to fire when it was . . . was important." His breath seemed to catch in his throat, and the words wouldn't come. He kept seeing his father lying there in his arms. Blood poured from the head wound as his life slipped away.

"I'd never seen death up close and personal like that. I'd avoided the war, as you probably know. I'd never been one for fights or spilling blood. When my brothers were killed, I wasn't anywhere around. I wasn't able to attend their funerals without being found, so even then I didn't witness them in death.

"I know it's probably difficult for you to believe me on this, but I didn't have any intention of killing your father or anyone that day. I don't even carry a gun anymore. I've spent my entire life haunted by your face and scream. You were just a little boy . . . what were you, ten? Twelve?"

"I was ten. It was the first time I'd witnessed death."

Astor drew a ragged breath. "I hated myself for what I'd done, but I didn't want to die, and I knew your father would kill me if I tried to run. After I shot him . . . killed him . . . I knew your father's fellow Pinkertons would hunt me down and that would be the end. They'd pass judgment on me and hang me from the nearest gallows. I didn't want to die any more than your pa wanted to."

"But he didn't get a choice."

"No. And for that I am sorry. I don't expect you to forgive me, but I do wish you would. I know from bitter experience that holding on to the wrongs done to you only serves to make you bitter and hard-hearted. You don't want to be that way. Although, I suppose a certain amount of that has driven you to continue hunting me."

"I became a Pinkerton with nothing else in mind." Spencer felt his anger fade. He didn't know if he could forgive this old man, but for the first time since his father's death, Spencer was willing to contemplate the matter.

"I'm sure you've been a good one. How did you find me here?"

"Letters. Your mother kept your letters, despite you telling her at the end of each one to burn them. Your scheme of having them sent through friends living elsewhere was brilliant. We searched those various towns thoroughly hoping to find you."

"I was quite the trickster in my youth. I figured someone would be watching my mother's house and mail. There was never really any way for her to write to me in return without risking the truth. I could send letters to my friends and include letters for her, but the minute she had an address to write to . . . well, that would have been the end of things. The Pinkertons and local law would have harangued my friends until they gave up the truth of things. In many ways, I lost my mother the day your father died."

"We could never read the letters, of course, but when your mother died, whoever cleaned out her things threw them away. Our people took them and read them for every detail. That's how we realized you were in Cheyenne and probably always had been since 1870."

"That's true. I moved around the first few years. That's when I established good friends who would help me in forwarding the letters to my mother. You see, the only reason me and my brothers ever bounty jumped was to provide for our mother. The war presented an easy way to get a good deal of money without much effort. We each did our part, and it helped us to buy her a house and see her fed and clothed. We didn't want it for ourselves. It was always about her."

Spencer hadn't known what had prompted the illegal activities of the Astor brothers. Though knowing it wasn't for personal gain but for taking care of their mother didn't change the fact that it was against the law and had caused a lot of problems for others.

"My father was determined to see you pay for your law breaking." Spencer shook his head. "I don't think he ever knew it was for anything other than greed. Not that it would have stopped him."

"No, I don't suppose so." Astor's face betrayed signs of pain as his brow wrinkled, and he closed his eyes. He put his hand up to rub at the center of his forehead for several silent minutes.

"Never doubt," he finally said, "that I'm getting my payback. When the symptoms first started, I went to the doctors. They were completely baffled at first and then came up with the idea that I had an inoperable brain tumor. I don't think they ever understood how appropriate that seemed to me. I thought it almost like God reaching down to deliver the final blow. I'd killed your father with a shot to the head, and now this tumor was in my head, killing me. The irony was not lost on me."

Spencer realized that he had nothing more to say. Astor had explained away all of his questions. There was really no need to tell him how much he'd hurt Spencer and his mother. Astor already knew. It should comfort Spencer to know that Astor had suffered over the years ... had been haunted by the moments when he murdered another man.

But it didn't, and it couldn't bring Pa back. Neither would seeing the man hang.

To his surprise, Astor pushed back the covers and swung his legs over the side of the bed as he sat up.

"I have something I need to give to you."

"Stay in bed. I can fetch it."

Astor shook his head. He got to his feet and padded in old-man fashion across the floor to the small chest of drawers in the corner of the room. He pulled out the top drawer.

"I've kept meticulous records. You need to know about my further illegal activities." Astor swayed slightly as he took a thick book from the chest. "I had figured to ask your wife to have you come see me so I could get this off my chest and be done with it."

Spencer got to his feet and moved toward the man, fearing he might fall at any moment. Astor straightened, however, and steadied himself with one hand while extending the book to Spencer.

"This is a record of every penny I stole from the Union Pacific. I had arranged to send it to my mother when I died, but when I learned she was dead, I had no need. They'll want it back. In fact, there are rewards given by the UP for those who expose wrongdoings. You should be able to get something for this. There are twenty years' worth of my dealings and embezzlements recorded there."

"And where's the money?" Spencer took the book.

"In the bank. The name and account is listed at the beginning. Actually, there are two accounts. One is my personal account, and the other contains the money I stole. I've done very well for myself. I was once considered something of a money genius. Had I done more to stay on the legal side of things, who knows what kind of financial baron I might have become."

"I wish you had."

Astor met his gaze. "I wish I had too. At least as far as it concerns you and your pa." He shook his head. "Nothing I do will ever right that wrong, but maybe getting the Union Pacific reward will help you to have a better life. My lawyer will be talking to you about the rest of my things. His name is Colton Benton."

Spencer recognized the name of Rosie Vogel's brother. "Your lawyer will talk to me?"

"Yes. He's handling my affairs, and it includes that sweet wife of yours. She's been such a kind soul. Her concerns about my disease and pain were truly beyond what I had anticipated. She's a brilliant woman, and I have no doubt she'll go far with her research."

"I don't either. It's been hard for her. Most men are opposed to her being in their field of work."

Astor moved toward the bed. "She'll be better for it. Her strength is what will get her through."

"Her faith in God is more likely to help."

The older man stopped and nodded. "She is a virtuous woman, more valuable than rubies, as the Proverbs state. She spoke to me of her faith on one occasion. Reminded . . . it reminded . . . me of my . . . mother." He swayed and then fell to the ground.

Spencer dropped the ledger and came to where Astor had fallen. Carrie was there almost immediately.

"What happened? What did you do?"

"I didn't do anything." Spencer lifted the man and carried him to the bed. "He got up to get me that ledger." He nodded toward the book on the floor. "He was on his way back to the bed when he passed out."

Carrie began checking him over. Spencer could see there was a knot growing on his forehead where he'd struck the edge of the nightstand.

She glanced across the bed to Spencer. "I'm sorry. I didn't

mean to sound accusing." Her attention went immediately back to her patient. "Mr. Knowles?" She patted his face. "Mr. Knowles."

"His name is Eugene Astor," Spencer said with great resignation. His search had come to an end.

22

Carrie and Spencer sat with Eugene in his final hours. He didn't regain consciousness, but Carrie had known the time would come when he wouldn't. His pulse was very weak, his breathing shallow. From time to time, he would stop breathing altogether and she would think the end had come, but then he'd gasp a breath, and their vigil continued.

At 5:15 p.m., Eugene Astor drew his last breath. Carrie listened to his chest to see if there was any heartbeat. She straightened and looked at Spencer.

"He's gone. I hope he found peace." She pulled the sheet and blanket over his face. "His mother had taught him all about God. He knew the truth and hopefully acted on it."

Carrie stood and looked at Spencer for a long moment. "Did you get your answers? Did he tell you why he felt compelled to kill your father?"

Spencer stared at the covered body. "Yes. It was an accident. He said he never meant for it to happen. He hoped to wound him so that Pa couldn't follow him. Astor was just going to graze his leg or hip, but Pa dropped to his knee, as he always did, to steady himself. Astor was startled by his movement and fired anyway."

"Does it help that it wasn't his intention to end your father's life?"

Spencer met her gaze. "I don't know. I suppose it helps me to see him as something other than a ruthless killer. He said my having been there has haunted him all these years. He knew me instantly because I looked so much like my pa. When he saw me at the house after seeing you, he knew it was me. I didn't recognize him."

Carrie came around to where he stood. "I'm glad you at least got to talk it out with him."

"He wanted me to forgive him."

"And will you?"

"I want to."

She put her arms around him and hugged him close. "In time, hopefully you can."

"And will you forgive Oswald Nelson?" He returned her embrace.

"I already have. Oswald is pathetic and miserable. He knows he isn't able to see things in the way I do. He knows he's limited in what he can achieve. That is punishment of a most painful kind. Still, he'll find his way around it. He'll find someone willing to let him take control of their work. Oswald has a way about him."

"Sorry to interrupt," Bruce Compton said, coming into the room. "My wife tells me our patient died."

Carrie released her hold on Spencer and stepped away. "Yes. Shall we do the autopsy tonight or wait until morning?"

"Let's wait. I'm quite exhausted. Treated one of the area ranchers for a serious dog bite. Sewed up a lot of damage."

"Rabies?" Carrie asked.

"I don't think so. The man said his two dogs were fighting over food, and he foolishly tried to stop them. Once he managed to separate them, they calmed down and were again the boon companions he'd always known them to be. However, I will have them checked and watch the man carefully."

"Then I shall return in the morning." Carrie looked at Spencer. "Are you ready to go home?"

"Yes, just let me get this book Astor gave me."

Carrie waited by the door for Spencer. She hoped his time with Astor had helped, though she knew it was probably much briefer than Spencer had planned for. She remembered the first time she'd met the old man. He still had hope that someone might be able to help him. When that hope had left him, she had known her own momentary despair. She had become a doctor in order to heal and cure. Instead, her patient had died, but in doing so, he would give her better insight into the next patient to suffer his condition.

"Are you ready?"

She looked to Spencer. "I am."

As they made the walk home, neither spoke for several blocks. Carrie was already thinking about the autopsy she would help to perform the next day. In her mind, she had already determined what she thought they would find. She had mapped it out on paper both with words and drawings. It would be interesting to see how close she had come to the truth.

"Are you all right? I know you cared about him."

Carrie smiled at the compassion in her husband's voice. "Yes, I'm fine. I'm already thinking ahead to the autopsy."

"I hope it helps you to learn more about the brain."

"It will. I've no doubt." She noted the book. "What book is that?"

"Astor kept a ledger of the money he embezzled from the Union Pacific. Apparently, it's all in the bank. He had planned to use it for helping his mother, but since she died, Astor figured the UP would want it back, and he wanted me to know the details so that I could claim the reward."

"Reward?"

"Yes, apparently the UP offers rewards for help with such crimes, but as a Pinkerton, I can't accept it."

"Mr. Astor was a strange man. There was a gentleness to him. I know he's been the bane of your existence, but perhaps his sins and the years that passed changed him."

"I wondered that myself," Spencer admitted. "Astor was nothing like what I expected. I always figured him to be a heartless killer."

"And now?"

"It's kind of soon to sort it all out."

Carrie could understand that. "People do have the ability to change."

"If he was truly repentant, he could have given himself up."

"But that would have most likely meant he'd pay for his mistakes with his life. The human mind is all about preserving life. We like to go on living, even when things seem difficult. We fight hard for our place in this world. I'm sure when Astor considered that he would probably be hanged for what he did, confession seemed less necessary. But he could still be very sorry for what he'd done."

"He said he was. I guess I have no right to doubt a dying man's last words."

"Well, this is fortunate for me," Robert Vogel said, coming alongside them from one of the side streets. "Mama tried calling you at home. She wants you two at the house right away. Didn't say why, but I'm guessing for supper since it's that time."

"Where are you coming from?" Spencer asked.

"Work. I checked out that name you gave me. It's not your man. This fella is from Texas, came to the territory with a family—five children in fact. We talked at length, and I'm convinced he's not Eugene Astor."

"No, he wasn't. Rowland Knowles was my man."

"Was?" Robert's eyes narrowed. "You didn't . . ."

"He didn't kill him, if that's what you're asking," Carrie interjected. "Knowles was a patient of mine, and he was dying from a brain disorder. Probably a tumor. He just passed, but Spencer was able to take his confession."

"Truly?" Robert looked at Spencer in surprise. "That's great."

"He even gave me this ledger that shows a record of the money he embezzled from the Union Pacific. And he told me his lawyer would be in touch. Colton Benton was his lawyer."

"Rosie's brother." Robert shook his head. "Why should he be in touch with you?"

"Astor was grateful for Carrie's kindness and treatment. I think he left her something."

"Me?" Carrie was surprised by this announcement. "Why would he do that? I told him his permission to autopsy his brain was more valuable than anything else he could pay me."

Robert looked at her a moment and shook his head. "You are a strange gal."

Spencer chuckled and put his arm around Carrie's shoulder. "Yeah, but she's my gal."

They turned to head toward the Vogel house, and once there, Carrie was surprised to see one of the livery's rented carriages parked outside with driver in attendance. They gave the man a nod and headed in through the back door at Robert's suggestion.

"No telling who has come. Besides, Rosie will be in the kitchen with the cook. Maybe she'll let us sample what's for supper." He elbowed Spencer and laughed.

Carrie stepped into the back mudroom. The delightful aroma of fried chicken and other treats wafted through the warm air.

"Oh, it smells wonderful in here," she said as Rosie came to give her a hug.

Rosie frowned. "Someone has come to see you."

Carrie pulled back. "Who?"

Robert went to Rosie. "Yeah, who came, Rosie? Ma said nothing when she called me at the jail."

"It's that man who wanted to marry Carrie. That bad man who stole her work."

"Oswald?" Carrie looked to Spencer. "What in the world does he want?"

Spencer put his arm around her shoulder. "Don't worry, he can't hurt you now."

Carrie lost no time. She marched out of the kitchen and through the dining room, where Greta was setting the table.

"We have company," Greta said in little more than a whisper.

"I heard."

Carrie made her way into the front room, where Oswald was sitting in conversation with her folks. He was dressed impeccably in his gray tweed suit, looking every bit the proper gentleman. Good thing Carrie knew the truth.

"What in the world are you doing here?" She barely held her temper.

Oswald looked up and gave her a broad smile. "There you are at last. How I have missed you."

"What do you want?" Carrie crossed her arms. She sensed that Spencer was standing right behind her and drew strength from it.

"I'm here to apologize and win you back." He frowned as he seemed to recognize Spencer for the first time. "What's he doing here?"

Carrie shook her head. "Spencer is none of your concern. In fact, neither of us are. I would appreciate it if you would leave."

"My love, please give me a chance. I miss you terribly. I was just telling your folks that life in Chicago means very little without you."

"I heard that you've received awards for your research—or rather mine." Carrie fought to keep her expression indifferent, but her tone spoke volumes. "You should be quite pleased with yourself. You are the great man of the hour, and no doubt will continue to draw attention to yourself in one way or another."

"Carrie, my love, we worked so well together. I can't believe you're willing to just throw all of that away. You know full well that what I did, I did for us both. Your research would never have been considered on its own."

"Yes, well, you didn't even think to have it considered with me as a full partner. So once again, I must ask you to leave. I have no desire to see you, much less to discuss this further."

"I know I should have handled things better. That's why I want you to return with me to Chicago. We'll be married and see a lawyer and arrange for things regarding our research. You'll be fully credited, and together we will make history."

"You'll make history, all right," Spencer finally spoke up. "But not for brain research. See it's a little thing called bigamy. Carrie's already married. To me."

Carrie saw the strange look that crossed Oswald's face and thought it rather satisfying. He was so used to having charge over everything and everyone.

"We married back in February before coming here to Cheyenne," Carrie said, moving a little close to Spencer and lowering her arms. "So, you see, there truly is nothing here for you."

"You can't be serious. You married this . . . this actor?"

"He's a Pinkerton and now one of Cheyenne's law officials. He works with my brother and father." Carrie smiled at Spencer as he put his arm around her shoulders. "We're all one big happy family."

"I don't know what to say. I'm hurt, of course. You wasted no time at all in marrying him. I suppose you two were carrying on all the time, just as I suspected."

"We were good friends. That much is true. Spencer, however, never lied to me about his goals, motives, and aspirations. He never pretended to love me so that he could use me for his career."

Oswald scowled and looked to Carrie's mother and father. "You knew this all along and yet let me go on and on about how much I loved her? How I'd come to talk her into coming home with me? I suppose this whole family delights in humiliating good people."

Carrie's father got to his feet. "I've had about enough of you, Nelson. I never cared for you. Knew you were up to no good from the first moment I met you. You might recall the conversation we had about my suspicions. I told you then, and I'm telling you again, I'm mighty protective of my family and have no intention of standing by to let you hurt any one of them. Now it's time for you to go. I understand there will be an eastbound train out of Cheyenne tomorrow, and you'd do well to be on it."

"I'll come help you," Robert volunteered. "I'll carry your bags to the station."

Oswald looked as if he might say something, but instead, he gave a curt nod and headed for the front door.

Carrie turned to her family. "I'll see him out."

She didn't wait for anyone to give their approval and followed after Oswald. She grabbed his hat from the side table in the foyer and extended it as he opened the front door.

He turned and snatched the hat out of her hands. "You've made a big mistake. I will ruin you."

She smiled. "You will try, but when it comes to light that you can't even figure out the next step in my research, which is probably what is already happening and has you feeling a bit frantic, then people are going to see rather quickly that you aren't the doctor you claim to be. Little by little, they'll start to realize that you came up with nothing much on your own. They'll see it was only after teaming up with me—a female physician of all things—that you started having brilliant discoveries."

Carrie shook her head. "I feel sorry for you Oswald. But even more so, I feel sorry for your next victim. I'm going to pray no one else will be fooled by your false promises."

She all but pushed him out the door and closed it behind him. Carrie leaned back against the door and glanced up to find Spencer and her father watching her. They had both been close enough at hand to rescue her but stayed out of Oswald's sight in order for her to have her say.

Papa and Spencer both broke into grins. She could see that they were proud of her and pleased with the way she'd handled the situation.

She heaved a sigh and pushed off the door. "That felt good, and now let's eat. I'm starved."

Spencer put Astor's ledger aside. The man had been clever, skimming bits of money from one place and then another, never taking so much as to be noticed. He had started his career in bookkeeping, and numbers had been his area of expertise. Then the war came, and Astor had walked away from a solid job in accounting to venture into illegal bounty jumping. Why had he thought it so necessary to cross that line?

He supposed the Astor brothers felt they couldn't risk volunteering to serve and then dying on the battlefield. They loved their widowed mother so much that they couldn't leave her childless with no one to fend for her. Spencer had to admit they had taken very good care of her. She never suffered in the way many widows did. Certainly not the way his mother had. His mother had worried about paying the rent and keeping food on the table for her son. The minute Spencer was old enough to work part-time, he had given her money to help with the household expenses.

But in considering his own mother, Spencer realized that there wasn't much he wouldn't have done for her. If not for the help of Al, Spencer might have thought he had to go into something illegal to see her taken care of properly. Not that it would have been the right thing to do, but it did give him an understanding as to why a man might sink that low.

Spencer figured he'd send Al a telegram on Monday and let him know about Astor. He'd follow it with a detailed accounting of his search and the outcome, but the telegram would allow Al to close the file on Eugene Astor.

Spencer still wasn't sure what that would mean for him now. Would he resign from the Pinkertons? Stay on with the Cheyenne police force? Would he and Carrie move elsewhere? There were a lot of unanswered questions, and all because one old man had died.

It seemed strange to know that tomorrow Spencer would wake up and have nothing to see to . . . nothing to accomplish. He'd been after Astor in one way or another since that fateful day in 1865. What did he do with himself now?

He glanced into the dying embers of the fire. Carrie had long ago gone to bed, and Spencer missed her company. Were they living as husband and wife, he would have her to share his bed. Her company would at least allow him to not feel so alone.

"Lord, I need some direction. I don't know what I'm supposed to do now."

23

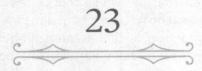

Carrie secured the lid on the two-gallon glass jar that now held Eugene Astor's brain in a mixture of alcohol and water. She and Dr. Compton would study the organ for some time, doing their best to glean all the secrets and details that would help them further an understanding of this particular brain disease. She even had plans to write and share the information with those doctors who had seen Astor and diagnosed his condition. As a physician, she knew they would appreciate further insight into the case.

She put the jar into the icebox that Compton had purchased for such purposes and closed the door. She was more than a little anxious to get started with their research, but she and Dr. Compton had agreed that they would work together, and he'd just been called away to see his dog-bite victim.

Returning to the operating room, as they had designated the second examination room, Carrie went to the covered body of Eugene Astor. The undertaker was to come for him later in the afternoon, and she wanted to check to make sure he was ready for transport. She pulled down the sheet and rechecked the head. Amazingly enough, he didn't look much different than he had before the surgery. She had taken great care to stuff newspaper in place of the brain and secure the scalp flap in place with the best of stitching.

Bruce had talked with the undertaker about keeping the fact that Astor's brain had been removed absolutely hush-hush since many people were highly offended at research that involved the dead. Various religious orders, including Christianity, had a variety of thoughts on the matter of autopsy and dissection. Carrie had seen mobs gather at the medical college to argue against dead bodies being studied for scientific purposes.

Often Christians felt it interfered with the proper passing of the soul. They argued that the body must be left intact for the resurrection of the dead. Others felt it was simply an abomination and obscene practice. But how else was a doctor to learn? There was so much they didn't know about human anatomy.

She felt sad for Astor. He must have lived life constantly looking over his shoulder, more than a little aware that he was a hunted man. Humans fought hard to stay alive, and Astor was no exception. He knew that if the Pinkertons caught him, he would most likely hang for his offenses. After all, he had committed treason in his fraudulent acts.

Still, Carrie couldn't help but wonder what might have been for all of them had Eugene Astor never taken that first step into illegal activities. Might Astor have done something great with his life? Might he have married and had a family? A hundred questions danced through her thoughts.

Carrie put the sheet back into place and then pushed the table to the far end of the room near the door that would allow the mortuary easy access to the body. After that, she finished cleaning up and then headed home.

Working with the dead man had made her quite reflective of her own life as well as his. She had worked on many dead bodies during her time in research, but she'd never known any of them personally. She didn't know Astor well, but well enough that his passing had affected her more than she'd thought it might. With his connection to Spencer, Carrie felt that she knew more about this man than she had any other patient.

It seemed strange. In all of her time after graduation, she had worked with very few living patients, and most of them were seen by the nurses first, and only after their particular conditions were assessed to fit the criteria needed had the doctors involved themselves. Truth was, so much of Carrie's work had been based on tissue samples and detailed patient intake information, with very little time spent with the people themselves. She had a feeling that was all going to change now. The patients she'd had in Cheyenne were mostly women struggling with headaches in varying degrees of severity. Still, she and Bruce had a very detailed plan for what they hoped to accomplish in the future. They wanted to become well known for brain studies, and that was going to require new and innovative equipment and living patients.

Working with Astor had rearranged her thinking about brain studies. She had seen this man gradually give way to his condition. She had heard the disappointment in his voice at being told she could do nothing for him. She had observed his deterioration, seen death claim his body firsthand. But there had been the very real, very human side of Astor as well as the clinical and scientific. She had known about his past ... about his regrets. She knew he had been haunted by his taking of another life. He had lived a criminal life, but not solely to better himself. Rather he was devoted to his mother, a woman he had to give up ever being with or risk his own demise. Both had been made to suffer the absence of the other when all they really longed for was a life lived together.

But in knowing him more intimately, Carrie saw aspects of his condition that pushed her to pursue avenues that she might not otherwise have tried. She had always been cautioned as a doctor not to allow herself to become emotionally involved with her patients, but there had to be a fine line. Knowing them more intimately opened doors to learning about behavior and past experiences. These were the very kinds of things that she felt certain would have great effects on brain disease and trauma.

She glanced once more at the covered body. Her brief time with Astor had given her a completely different view of ways that she might accomplish her desired purpose. She was more than a little thankful that she'd allowed Spencer to talk her into marriage in his pursuit of Astor. She had to shake her head at the way God had so intricately orchestrated her life to bring her full circle—back to Cheyenne.

Everything had changed. She had fallen in love, happy that she hadn't settled for what Oswald was offering her. She had grown in understanding of her past and the choices made by her parents. Carrie had even come to realize that others saw her much differently than she saw herself. She pulled on her coat and stepped outside into the warm spring air. Glancing heavenward, she smiled.

"Thank You, Father. Thank You for opening my eyes to the truth. I'm so very blessed and grateful for all You've done."

At home, Carrie settled down to her desk to read a medical journal article on Dr. Victor Horsley, an English surgeon who was the first to successfully resect a spinal tumor. The patient had been an army officer who was in terrible pain. The man was for all intents and purposes paralyzed and incontinent. Within a year of the surgery and removal of the tumor, he made an almost complete recovery.

Carrie reread one of the paragraphs several times, realizing that her focus wasn't at all on the information. She was still thinking about the brain of Eugene Astor and what they might learn from him. Carrie put the article aside and glanced at the clock. It was nearly four, and Spencer would be home in an hour or so. She should try to figure out something for their supper. It wasn't that she couldn't cook or do the other tasks required of a homemaker, but her heart definitely wasn't in it. She would just as soon grab a quick bite and be back to work. However, Spencer changed all of that for her. She found herself happy to come home, just at the prospect of seeing him again. Where thinking constantly of her work had once been her only drive, now her love for Spencer and his company often interfered with that focus. She wanted to care for him as he cared for her.

She looked at the clock again. Spencer had planned to speak to the Union Pacific officials today about the ledger Astor had given him. Was he there now? Was he worn out from all that had happened? Had things gone well?

He hadn't gone to bed very early the night before. She had heard him in the front room. From time to time, he stoked the fire, and sometimes he paced back and forth. She had almost gone to him several times but always felt something stop her. He needed to process all that had happened. He had spent most of his life chasing Eugene Astor. Now his job was done. He had to be wrestling with his feelings. After all, what was he to do now?

"This is all quite fascinating, Mr. Duval," the Union Pacific official said, closing the ledger. "We had known there were discrepancies in various areas but never suspected this had been going on for twenty years. Nor that so much money had been taken."

"Eugene Astor was a brilliant man. Had he used it for good instead of self-serving reasons, he might have been able to truly benefit his fellow man. However, that aside, he wanted me to bring you this and let you know that the money is in an account at the bank. How you proceed from here is up to you. I would suggest you start with his lawyer, Colton Benton. His office is on Eighteenth." Spencer got to his feet. "I'm just the messenger."

"Far more than that. There will be a reward coming your way for such an outstanding find."

"I was working in an official capacity for the Pinkerton Agency," Spencer explained. "Any reward is due to them alone. I'm sure they would happily accept a check from the Union Pacific." Spencer handed the man a card. "This is the man to contact and his address in our Chicago offices."

The man took the card and glanced at it with a nod. "It would seem I've got all of the needed information. We will see this matter resolved, to be sure. It's hard to believe Eugene Astor was orchestrating all of this deception. I honestly liked the man. He was quiet and kept to himself, but he was pleasant enough when pressed."

Spencer thought of the misery the man had caused him and of the years spent pursuing Astor. Mostly, however, there remained thoughts of Astor's desire for forgiveness. How was Spencer to go about that? The man had taken so much.

Spencer got to his feet. "I'll leave you to it, then. I'm sure you'll have plenty to oversee in this matter."

"Actually, someone else will be put in charge. My focus is working with the powers in Washington to see this territory becomes a state. We have most of them convinced, but to assure statehood comes this year we must press forward and do so in a very persuasive manner."

"Well, good luck to you."

The man laughed. "The Union Pacific doesn't rely on luck, to be sure. We have too much at stake. Especially given people like Astor, who seem determined to take what they can from us. Those folks in Washington will also take what they can, so we have our work cut out for us."

"Yes, sir." Spencer picked up his hat. "I suppose rather than luck, then, I should ask God's direction and mercy for everyone concerned."

With that Spencer left the Union Pacific office and headed back downtown to the jail. He wanted to let his father-in-law know what had taken place before going home. Edward Vogel was just pulling on his outer coat and hat when Spencer knocked on his door.

"Spencer, good to see you. How's it going?"

"Good. I just met with a Union Pacific official and went over the details of Eugene Astor and his thievery. They were shocked at the amount of money he managed to steal but grateful that at the end he wanted to give it back."

"Are you heading home?"

"Yeah, Carrie will want to know all about this."

"We can walk part of the way together."

Spencer nodded and followed Vogel out onto the street. Traffic was as bad as ever, with more bicycles these days than Spencer had ever seen, even back east. The horses didn't like them, but they were growing in popularity with the people. Carrie had even talked about getting a bicycle for herself.

"So what's next, Spencer?"

The question took him off guard. "I suppose I'm asking myself that."

"It would seem God's giving you a chance to start everything anew. The past is cleaned up and put to rest. Time to focus on something else."

"I've thought of that myself, but there's something I haven't yet come to terms with."

Vogel glanced over. "What would that be?"

"Forgiving Astor. He asked me to, I'm just not sure how."

"Are you opposed to forgiving him? I mean, he did a terrible thing that changed your life and that of your mother."

"I don't feel it's so much that I'm opposed to it, but I've hated him for so long. Blamed him for every bad thing that happened, including my mother's death. It was easier to blame him than accept what was happening around me. I've spent most of my life hating that man and wanting him to pay for what he did."

"And instead, he up and died."

Spencer thought about that for a moment. "Yes. He got away with it all."

"Did he?"

"What do you mean?"

They paused at the busy intersection of Eighteenth and Capitol while several freight wagons passed.

"Astor's life was hardly ideal. He might have found ways to rob the Union Pacific, but that didn't make him happy. He was close to his mother but could never be with her. He knew that seeing her, or even receiving a letter from her, would cause him to be captured. He bore the guilt of what he'd done, and I don't care how hardened a man you might be, unless you're just plain evil, that's going to eat at you."

"Astor wasn't evil. He told me he never meant to kill my father. It was an accident. He was only going to graze him to stop his pursuit. My father moved, and that changed everything. Astor said it haunted him for the rest of his life."

"So he did care."

"Yeah, I guess in his way."

"But he also cared about himself. Keeping alive is what we do best. We fight the elements, circumstances, and other people in order to keep alive. It's deep in our nature. We even battle God on occasion, begging and pleading, promising whatever we think might prove our worthiness, all in order to go on living."

"True enough."

"But, Spencer, I can tell you one thing. Harboring unforgiveness is one of those things that will rob you of your life. It will deplete your health and happiness. It will interfere in every corner of your world. Refusing to forgive another person does absolutely no good."

"I guess I can see that for myself. I want to be forgiven, and the Bible says I must forgive for that to happen. But it's hard to know how to go about it, especially with Astor."

"Why especially?"

"Because I've hated him for so long. He's been the focus of my days up until now."

"Then make something else that focus. Put your energy into knowing the Lord better, making a good marriage with my daughter, deciding what you want to do with your life."

"And forgive Eugene Astor?"

"I think it probably starts there, son. Just take it one step at a time. Pursue forgiveness like you pursued Astor. One step at a time, one moment."

Spencer looked at his father-in-law and smiled. God had given him a good mentor in Edward Vogel. Marriage to Carrie was going to have far more benefits than Spencer had ever imagined.

"I'll do my best, but I would sure appreciate your prayers."

"Son, you've had my prayers since I first learned you were married to Carrie." He smiled and gave Spencer a pat on the back. "I won't stop now."

24

"I'm pleased to meet you both," Colton Benton said as he welcomed Carrie and Spencer into his office. "My little sister speaks highly of you. I can hardly believe we've not met before now."

"Rosie's amazing," Carrie replied. "The way she manages my brother is proof enough. He was always a handful for our mother, but Rosie seems to keep him in line without any trouble."

Colton chuckled. "She was always able to keep me walking a straight line as well. I thought I was in charge of our family, but I'm beginning to think that was just a ruse."

Carrie laughed, and Spencer did likewise. He liked Colton Benton. He'd already done his research on the man via the Pinkerton Agency. Benton was quite wealthy and yet generous to charities and family. He had also recently become a deacon at the church.

"I suppose Mr. Astor told you to seek me out after his death." Colton got right down to business.

"So he told you his real name." This surprised Spencer. "I wasn't sure that he had. For years he depended on being Rowland Knowles to keep ahead of the law."

"He didn't tell me until our very last meeting. He made me get my secretary to adjust everything to show his real name and alias so that there would be no question as to the legalities. I wasn't anticipating problems until he told me in detail about his dealings with the Union Pacific."

"And how did that go?" Spencer asked.

"It complicated matters, but not overly so. Given Astor was the meticulous soul he was, the Union Pacific feels confident that the accounting of what he took is in good order. They aren't going to contest his will as it relates to you two."

"I'm so surprised by all of this." Carrie shook her head. "He was a patient of mine. Certainly not a family member. It seems odd that he should leave us anything."

"As I understand it, his relationship to Spencer was more complicated. He told me everything. I've never had a client such as Eugene Astor, but I mean to see his wishes met and can't imagine anyone more deserving."

Colton pulled up a folder and opened it. "Mr. Astor's house has been sold, and that money, along with what he had in his personal account, is now yours. Astor was quite the investor. I suppose when you aren't worried about whether you can access more money, you aren't afraid to invest in risky things, and that's what Astor did. There is a process to go through, of course, but in a short time the two of you will inherit some seven thousand dollars."

"Seven thousand dollars!" Carrie was aghast.

"Are you certain that it doesn't belong to the government or even the UP?"

"As I said, there is a process to go through, and we will make certain to cover every possibility. I wouldn't want you to receive the money only to have it stripped away. I have already been making inquiries but basically have left it in the hands of the Pinkertons. Their fees will come out of the balance, but I think you'll still be left with a substantial amount of money."

"You can set up your research center," Spencer said, looking to Carrie. "Wherever you want to have it."

"I heard something about that." Colton leaned back in his chair. "I'd like to know more. My wife, Emma, suggested we should have dinner together this evening. I believe Dr. Duval and my wife know one another."

"We do. We met at school when we were younger, although we weren't exactly close friends, since she's older than me."

"Well, Emma believes medical research can benefit us all, and so do I. If you aren't already busy tonight, please join us for supper. Say, six o'clock?"

Carrie and Spencer exchanged a glance and nodded. Spencer looked back to Colton. "We'd love to come."

Colton wrote down something on his business card and handed it to Spencer. "Here's our address. We're up near the Capitol. As I said, we're both fascinated by Carrie's interest and can't imagine any better organization to help support. As you know, my own sister suffers from damage done to her brain during birth. If there are ways to prevent such things or help in the aftermath through your research, then I would like to donate to that cause."

Carrie appeared overwhelmed, but Spencer was more than able to speak. "I'm glad you're interested because, frankly, I believe my wife and Dr. Compton are going to make incredible discoveries together."

"I'm looking forward to hearing more and working toward a plan for the future."

Carrie appeared uncomfortable enduring their praise and folded and unfolded her hands several times. Spencer took hold of her gloved fingers and gave a slight squeeze to encourage her.

She seemed to calm. "I'm honored that you would put your faith in me that way. You must know that short of naming something for you, there's nothing in the way of financial gain. Unless, of course, I managed to invent some sort of machinery or instrument to sell." Carrie folded her hands together. "However, the work we do will change the future of medicine and allow us to cure more brain diseases and trauma injuries. And hopefully, we can better understand the brain's role in a more intimate fashion."

"I'm completely intrigued by the prospects," Colton admitted. "And financial gain wasn't at all my concern. I would love to see you find answers to problems endured by so many. I am talking a donation, not an investment, although I feel as though it's an investment in the future. Who can say, I might one day need help for something brain related, and you will have the answer."

"I pray that you never need that kind of help, but if you should, I will happily be there for you."

Spencer grinned at Carrie. "She's going to make the world a much better place using the unique talent God has given her. I couldn't be prouder."

"Your home is so beautiful," Carrie told Emma Benton after they retired to a small parlor after a wonderful supper.

"Colton insisted on building me a palace," Emma said, shaking her head. "I would have lived happily in a tent so long as he was at my side."

"Well, this is a magnificent house. Mama told me they just finished building it last month."

"Well, actually, they are still working on parts of the third floor. It can be quite noisy here some days. I usually make plans to visit the ranch or at least make extended visitations to friends."

Carrie couldn't imagine trying to live with the noise. She

was about to ask Emma when they planned to be finished when the men joined them.

"So we want to hear about the plans you have for your research hospital," Colton declared, taking a seat beside his wife. "Spencer tells me that you and Bruce Compton have been talking about all the possibilities."

"We have. In fact, I went to see Bruce after you told us about the inheritance. He was quite excited when I mentioned that you were considering becoming a patron to our cause. We went from imagining a small single-floor laboratory and clinic to a two-story hospital and research center."

"Perhaps you should think even bigger," Colton said with a shrug. "You will want to entice the best minds to join you. I'm sure there will be a great need for space."

Carrie couldn't contain her excitement. "We talked about that as well. We both know doctors we'd like to encourage to come to Cheyenne. Of course, we'll need someone to help us with the budget and securing other donors and such. We both thought you might be the perfect man to join our board of directors. In fact, we think both of you would be worthy of a place on the board."

Emma looked quite surprised and laughed. "Me? Cheyenne only knows me as a troublemaker. When I was young, I was quite the hoyden, as you well know."

Colton laughed. "What better way to make it up to them. I, for one, would be honored to serve and help you get this thing up and running."

"Well, at least that way you can oversee things and make sure that you get your money's worth." Carrie sobered. "I must stress something else. My former fiancé, Dr. Oswald Nelson, has promised to ruin me in any way possible."

"Nelson stole much of Carrie's work and claimed it for his own," Spencer interjected. "The man is despicable. He knows Carrie will have a hard time as a female physician anyway, but he has threatened to make her life miserable."

"Well, that's where the help of a good lawyer should benefit you," Emma said, giving Colton glance. "Colton is quite good at what he does. He's been challenged by some of the most devious businessmen and robber barons. I think you'll find him more than capable of putting Dr. Nelson in his place."

"Absolutely," Colton said, frowning. "You can fill me in on all the details later. Perhaps come to my office, and we'll discuss it at length. I can then figure out how best to handle the matter."

"That would be wonderful, Colton," Spencer said, giving Carrie a wink. "With him out of the way, I've a feeling there will be no stopping Carrie."

"Good, then that's settled." Colton reached over and took hold of Emma's hand. "I've already got one additional donor for you, Carrie. When I mentioned to my sister what you were about to do, she wanted very much to help as well. Robert was in complete agreement."

"I honestly don't know what to say." Carrie was deeply humbled at the love and support she'd found. Things had seemed so bleak and impossible when she'd left Chicago. Now the possibilities seemed endless. Two wealthy donors wanting to fully support her desires. "And frankly, I'm not even sure where to start."

"Like I said, we'll meet this week and establish a plan. We'll lay out cost projections and establish salaries for you and Dr. Compton. You might want to speak to him and get a list together of people you'd like to encourage to join you. Then we can discuss what might be an enticing salary to encourage them to come to Cheyenne."

"We could speak with our builder and architect," Emma suggested. "You and Dr. Compton could tell them what you have in mind for your place. That will help us establish what kind of money will be needed."

Carrie could hardly think clearly. "This is happening so fast."

"Sometimes God moves that way," Emma said, her gaze moving to her husband. "I know He did for me."

"As long as God is at the center, I know it will be perfect no matter how fast or slow we go." Spencer took hold of Carrie's hand. "You just have to let Him take charge."

"Have you decided what you're going to do now that the search for Eugene Astor is over?" Carrie asked her husband that evening as they sat once again in front of the fireplace.

Spencer put his arm around her shoulders and pulled her snug against him. "I figure I'll focus on loving you."

She smiled and placed her head on his shoulder. "I hope that won't prove too arduous."

He chuckled. "I haven't found it to be so as of now. It's easy to love you, Carrie. You're smart and pretty and charming too. And your faith in God is understated but strong. I like that about you. You really are more precious than rubies."

"What?"

"Eugene Astor mentioned that reference from Proverbs thirty-one. 'Who can find a virtuous woman? for her price is far above rubies. The heart of her husband doth safely trust in her, so that he shall have no need of spoil.'"

"'She will do him good and not evil all the days of her life.'" Carrie remembered the verses from Sunday school when being taught what a godly Christian wife should be. "I'm afraid I will never be the woman that Proverbs portrays. Working at home with my maid servants and planting vineyards and bringing honor to my husband."

"You will be very much like her. As I recall, she's quite active outside of the house as well as in. She has many duties and handles them all with wisdom and dignity. Just as I know you will. I especially lean toward the verses that say, 'Strength and honour are her clothing; and she shall rejoice in time to come. She openeth her mouth with wisdom; and in her tongue is the law of kindness.' You are very much like that and always will be. God has given you a brilliant mind and an understanding of things that will merit and benefit many. Just like the woman in those verses. I am more than blessed to call you my wife."

"But I'm completely unconventional."

"Are you?" He shook his head. "I don't see it that way at all. The Proverbs thirty-one woman is mindful of her household, her servants, and her husband. You might not work with wool and flax or plant vineyards, but you work willingly with your hands at the tasks God has given you. For who has given you the desire to find help for injured or ill patients if not the Great Physician Himself?"

"I've never really considered it that way. I always figured my mother was the better example of the virtuous woman. Working at home, sewing and gardening, cooking and cleaning. She has made a great home for my father and for her children. We always had her love and protection. I just couldn't always see it or appreciate it. I do now, however."

"And that's what matters. It's a part of our growing in the Lord. His wisdom and direction will help us through. There are many examples of virtuous women, Carrie. They don't all look the same, not even in the Bible. And if God blesses us with children, they will rise up and call you blessed one day. Perhaps not when they are young and unable to see the truth of why you do what you do, but, Carrie, I know you will love them, and you will love me. Your work will be important to you, but I've no doubt we will be even more so. I also don't doubt that there will be a way for both if that's what the Lord desires and designs. Perhaps there won't even be children for us, but no matter the future, I know there will be love."

He gently touched her chin and raised it so that he could kiss her. "I love you, Carrie, and I always will. No matter where life takes us. So long as we are together and put God first, I know we will be blessed."

25

"I can hardly believe you came to Cheyenne," Spencer said, welcoming his former boss and dearest friend.

Aloysius Gable embraced Spencer with a powerful grip. For a man in his sixties, he was still as strong as a man half his age. "I figured I missed the first wedding. Didn't want to miss the second. It's so good to see you, Spence."

Spencer hugged the older man tightly, then released him. Stepping back, he couldn't believe it had only been a matter of months since he'd last seen his friend. It seemed years had passed. "It's been so long."

"It has been too long."

The busyness of the train platform created a cacophony of sounds that made normal conversation difficult. Spencer reached for Al's suitcase.

"Let's get out of here so we can talk." The older man nodded and allowed Spencer to take the case and lead the way.

Once they passed through the depot and out onto the street, a whole new scene just as noisy as the last greeted them. Freight wagons were busy lining up to receive shipments of goods while the trolley noisily clanged away. There appeared to be even more people rushing from place to place than had been inside.

"So the wedding is on Saturday," Al began. "Are you still determined to see this through? No more merely posing as a husband."

"I am more than happy to become a real husband to Carrie Vogel. Al, she's everything I've ever wanted in a wife and more."

"I've heard you talk enough about her this last year that I easily recognize your admiration of her. These last few months playacting as husband and wife must have been interesting for the both of you."

"It was . . . at times very hard. I have to admit." Spencer shrugged. "She completes me in ways I didn't even know I needed completing. We both have a strong faith in God, and even as it has been tested, we've drawn closer and closer."

"Have you had any fights?"

Spencer saw an opening on the busy street and motioned Al to cross. Once they were safely on the other side, Spencer gave his answer.

"We've had a couple of misunderstandings and arguments, but my wife is extraordinarily logical. When her emotions start to get the best of her, she retires to think things through, and in those moments of quiet contemplation, we both tend to rethink the matter and see things in a different light."

"Sounds most unusual, to be sure."

"Carrie is most unusual. She's older in some ways than her twenty-four years."

"I hope she'll be a tremendous blessing to you, Spence. I've only ever wanted good things for you. Your pa and ma wanted that for you as well. I know they'd be proud of you."

"Even though I've quit the Pinkertons?" Spencer smiled. "My pa was mighty proud of being a Pinkerton man and looked forward to me being one as well."

"And you were, and you did the jobs you were given. Now God is calling you to another season of life. Do you know yet if you'll stay here in Cheyenne?"

"I do. Carrie and Dr. Compton, the man she intends to partner with on brain research, have concluded that Cheyenne is a perfect place to set up business. It's on the main rail line, so getting supplies and patients won't be difficult. It's also home to both Dr. Compton and Carrie. They know so many of the people here. And as the territory is about to become a state, there are all sorts of opportunities for me with the government."

"Will you now go into politics?" Al asked, looking at Spencer with a concerned expression. "You never struck me as a politician."

Spencer chuckled. "I only meant that they will be expanding the government operations here. I believe I'll have ample opportunity for employment. I have a college education and can move in a variety of directions. I've even considered becoming a state attorney. I'm very familiar with the law and qualifying to practice wouldn't be impossible."

"Give it a lot of prayer, son. Government work can be vexing. You know from working with the agency that there's a lot of paperwork to sort through. New laws every day, it seems."

"Yes, that's true, but someone has to keep the place running in an orderly fashion."

They reached the Inter Ocean Hotel and stepped inside. The place was always busy as far as Spencer had seen. The large lobby was a popular meeting place for businessmen and proved no different today.

Spencer helped Al register and then went upstairs with him to his room so that they could drop off his suitcase.

"I really want to show you around town. I'm thinking, once you retire, you might enjoy moving here."

Al looked at him with a wry smile. "So you're going to sell me on Cheyenne, eh?"

Spencer unlocked the hotel door and stepped inside the room. "I plan to try."

The room was well-appointed with a full-sized bed, small night tables on either side, and a washstand across the room. The papered walls were evidence of quality, and the fine bed linens suggested great care had been given to making the visitor feel a sense of opulence.

"I don't know that you'll have to do much selling, to tell you the truth. After all, it has one thing that I truly appreciate and find valuable in my daily life."

"What's that?" Spencer asked, placing the older man's suitcase on the bed.

"You." Al folded his arms and fixed Spencer with a serious look. "You're the only family I have anymore. Never married or had children. My folks are long gone, as is my brother and his wife. You're all I have left to consider as family."

"And I am your family, Al. You've always been there for me, and I intend to be there for you. You could move here, and we could go into business together. I'm not sure what we'd do, but I'm willing to take a chance at most anything."

Al laughed and gave an enthusiastic nod. "Let's get some lunch and talk about the possibilities that await us."

Spencer had hoped this might be the man's response. "I know just the place. There's a restaurant down the street that serves the best steaks you've ever had. You thought Chicago was famed for fresh beef, but you'll be amazed at what you get here."

"The dress fits you perfectly," Mama told Carrie as she checked first one side and then another.

Carrie felt like a princess in the beautiful white satin gown. Greta had insisted on advising Carrie of the latest fashions but made certain the dress was completely to her sister's liking. Having never been one who worried about such things, Carrie had appreciated her sister's insight.

Catching her reflection in the mirror, Carrie had to admit the gown was beyond her expectations, especially the bodice with its intricate workings of lace, silk, and satin. The rounded neckline was finished to the middle of her neck in a delicate lace that was as soft as angel's wings, according to the woman who'd made it. Carrie had to smile remembering that she had wondered at the woman's reference. How did she know what angel's wings were like?

However, wearing the gown and experiencing the lace firsthand, Carrie thought the woman might very well be right. Such fine work seemed almost heavenly in origin.

She turned to see the skirt and train that were created in banded silk and satin. The shimmering piece fell gently over a small, bustled back and splayed out across the floor in an elegant half circle.

"I'm sure I've never worn anything so fine." Carrie turned to look at her sister and mother. "Thank you for insisting I have a special dress."

"You only have a day like this once," Greta said, smiling in a dreamy way. "I just want it to be perfect and lovely. I've never been happier in all my days. I get to marry with my sister and family around me."

"And half the town," Mama added. "Goodness, but this wedding will be even larger than the Kuydendall-Moore wedding at St. Mark's Episcopal."

"And bigger than Ida Bergman's ceremony," Greta added. "Not that size is all that important."

"I should say not. Mama and Papa got married in a very

simple way, and no one could have a better marriage than them," Carrie said.

"Well, just remember nothing matters as much as keeping God at the center of your marriage," Mama said, smiling at her girls. "The most important day of your life is when you seek Jesus as your Savior. The second most important might well be your wedding day. It's important to be matched with someone who believes as you do. The Bible makes it clear that being unequally yoked with unbelievers is not to be done. It only leads to heartache, whether in business or marriage. If you can't at least agree upon your positions of faith, there's little hope for much else."

"Well, on that account you needn't worry, Mama. Our men are solid in the Lord," Greta countered. "They are good, Bible-believing Christian men who love God."

"And love you both as well," Mama said, embracing both of her daughters. There were tears dampening her eyes, and it made Carrie realize just how special this moment was. How glad she was that she hadn't missed out on it.

I truly belong and always have. I just couldn't see it in full until now. Carrie swiped at the tears that came. She would never again feel that sense of loss.

"Do you, Greta, take Michael to be your lawfully wedded husband in the eyes of God and man?"

"I do," Greta replied, looking to Michael Decker with great solemnity.

Carrie watched as the minister continued to lead them in their vows. She waited patiently for her own turn, knowing it would still be hours before she and Spencer would have time alone. She looked at the man who would soon become her husband once again, but this time with a pledge of commitment to God as well.

Spencer gave her a reassuring smile and squeezed her fingers. In a matter of moments, the minister was leading Carrie and Spencer through the same recitation of vows that Greta and Michael had just made.

"Carrie, do you take Spencer to be your lawfully wedded husband in the eyes of God and man?"

"I do."

Someday she'd tell their children that their parents were double married. First in Chicago and three months later to the day in Cheyenne. No doubt they would ask questions about why it had happened that way, and Carrie and Spencer would fill them in on all the exciting details of their work for the Pinkertons.

The minister combined the ring ceremony for both couples, having them place their rings and pledge their lives together at the same time. When all was said and done, the organ began to play, and the grooms gathered their brides up for a kiss to seal the deal.

And then they were surrounded by friends and family with congratulations and tears flowing all around. *It really was a perfect celebration,* Carrie thought as they made their way to the catered reception downtown at one of the second-floor opera house halls. There would be feasting and dancing throughout the evening, but for the moment, she was seated beside her husband in a carriage, with well-wishers she didn't even know waving to them from the side of the street. Cheyenneites never needed much of a reason to celebrate.

"Are you sure we have to go to the reception and dance?" Spencer asked, leaning his head toward hers.

"It was all planned for Greta and Michael long before we decided to join in, but I do believe we're obligated to share in the festivities."

Spencer laughed and followed her in waving to the people who had stopped to cheer them along the way.

"We're Cheyenne royalty," Carrie said, glancing over her shoulder. "That's what Greta told me. We've been here since the beginning of the town, or very nearly so. We are a founding family. As such, we are important. Add to that, Papa is chief of police and Michael's father runs the finest boys' school in the entire territory, and there's no possibility of us escaping the day to be alone."

"I was a Pinkerton, and I know a lot of ways to disappear." He put his arm around her and pulled her close. "If you change your mind and want to escape, I'll figure out a plan."

Carrie laughed and snuggled closer against him. "Life will always be an adventure with you. Here I thought I'd always be focused on my work, but with you I find reason to step away and enjoy other things in life."

"Like a moment to love and be loved?" he whispered before placing a kiss on her neck.

She shivered with delight and straightened in her seat to wave to a group of people gathered near the opera house. "I hope there shall be a great many moments. A lifetime, in fact."

The carriage came to a stop, and Spencer jumped up from his seat and down to the ground before the driver could assist them. He reached up to lift Carrie from the carriage and put his arm around her waist as he released her.

"I promise you a lifetime, my love."

Their gazes met, and Carrie saw the love reflected in her husband's eyes. She whispered a prayer of thanksgiving, then drew a deep breath. "Let it begin."

Epilogue

July 10, 1890, President Benjamin Harrison wired a telegram from Washington, DC, announcing that he had signed Wyoming into statehood. The newspaper criers called out up and down the streets, and the citizens of Cheyenne began to celebrate in grand style.

At Edward Vogel's house, the celebration was focused on something entirely different.

"Are you absolutely certain?" Mama questioned.

Rosie and Robert nodded in unison. "Carrie said we're definitely going to have a baby," Rosie replied.

"I'm going to be an uncle," Daniel Vogel said, reaching out to shake his brother's hand. "Congratulations."

Robert looked as proud as any father-to-be. "It's going to be our Christmas gift to the entire family. Carrie thinks she'll deliver around Christmas."

Mama's eyes filled with tears as Papa put his arm around her shoulders. "We're going to be grandparents. Isn't that wonderful?" he said in a calm and collected manner. The smile that seemed to spread from ear to ear betrayed his true feelings.

"We're really excited," Rosie interjected. "We want to have a lot of children."

Everyone laughed and agreed that would be a wonderful thing. A houseful of grandchildren seemed to suit Carrie's parents perfectly. The conversation broke into questions about names and whether they wanted a boy or a girl. Carrie made her way to the kitchen to help herself to a cup of tea. She wasn't surprised that Spencer followed her.

"Do you want a cup of coffee or tea?" she asked, reaching for the teapot of water.

"Nope, I just want my beautiful wife in my arms." He swung her away before she could take hold of the teapot.

Carrie laughed and wrapped her arms around his neck. "Did you and Al get anywhere with finding him a proper home?"

"We did. He's going to rent our house."

"Excuse me?"

Spencer shrugged. "I spoke with Colton today. Everything has been released, and the money is ours. I figure we can use a small amount to buy ourselves a house. I know we haven't really talked about it, but I felt almost certain you'd like my idea."

Carrie's brow raised in curious interest. "Do tell."

"Well, I know you and Bruce settled on the land for your research clinic. I don't know if you realized it, but just a block away there's a large home for sale."

"A large home? Do you mean the Brenner mansion?"

"It's not really a mansion. It's just a very large house." He grinned. "And reasonably priced, for a very large house. Not like those twenty- and fifty-thousand-dollar monstrosities over on Ferguson."

"Still, I would imagine the house you're speaking of is at least five thousand dollars. It's a lovely place, but selfishly, I'd rather put more money into the clinic."

"They're only asking three thousand, after I did some negotiations. And besides, the Pinkertons are giving me a nice check for my work on the Astor case. They received the reward from the Union Pacific and a contract for future jobs, so they are quite pleased."

"You're getting a bonus for your work?" She hugged him tightly. "Congratulations. Why didn't you say so?"

"Because I wanted to surprise you with the house. We can go and look at it, but since it will be very close to the clinic, I thought it would be nice if you didn't have to drive or walk very far to get to work. And it really is a quality place."

"It is. I've been inside more than once. I love that house. I always have. And it's only a few blocks from the family."

"Exactly. So does that mean you'll forgive me for telling them we'd take it?" He gave her what she called his best pleading-child look.

Laughing, Carrie nodded. "I forgive you. When will the place be ours?"

"In two weeks."

She kissed his cheek. "You are quite amazing. Thank you." She paused and grew serious. "For everything. For saving me from marrying Oswald. For tricking me into marrying you."

"I did not trick you into marrying me," he said, sounding offended. "I needed you." He softened his gaze. "I still do. I love you, Carrie. I always have, and I always will."

"I love you too, Spencer. I'm so grateful God brought you into my life." Spencer kissed her long and lovingly, just as Carrie had hoped he would.

If you enjoyed *A Moment to Love*, keep reading for a sneak peek of the first book in Tracie Peterson's new series

Available spring of 2026

Prologue

AUGUST, 1866
PHILADELPHIA, PA

It is important to remember that your gifts will be used to change the lives of those who cannot do so for themselves. Their numbers are high, especially since the war has left a great many women widowed and children orphaned. Remember, no matter your donation, it will be a blessing," the speaker declared to thunderous applause.

Judith Ashton Stanford was among those in the approving audience. She clapped and rose to her feet. The long, hot afternoon of lectures had come to an end, and she was frankly rather anxious to return home.

"I was quite impressed with the speakers," the bearded man standing next to her said, as if they'd been in previous conversation. He was a handsome man with a hint of mischief in his smile. His dark eyes searched her face as if for answers to some unspoken question. "I'm Dr. Roman Turner."

"Judith Stanford." She extended her gloved hand. "I agree, the speakers were wonderful. I've long desired to help the poor in whatever ways possible."

Her passion for widows and orphans had come about partly due to her own situation. She and her husband, Alden Stanford, had married June third in 1862, and the next day Judith had watched and waved with the other wives and daughters as their men marched off to fight for the North. She had never seen him again. He perished in the war during the Battle of Gettysburg in July 1863.

At twenty-two, Judith had been naïve about the risks. Now twenty-six, she felt as though she'd gained far more knowledge than she ever wanted. Losing her husband had only been the start—her mother and father had died the very next year. Her entire life had been altered.

Had it not been for her charity work and taking over her father's steamboat service, Judith might have despaired. Other women certainly had. Every day she learned of widows who had given up, sinking deeper into their loneliness and seemingly impossible circumstances.

"There's so much to be done. In my own town, we are dealing with a growing number of widows and orphans," Dr. Turner said.

"We have so many due to the war that it has become the focus of many charities."

"I can well imagine. I served on the battlefield as a surgeon and saw many a good man breath his last."

Judith had seen so many families devastated by the loss of their men. Sorrow alone was enough to cause hopelessness but add poverty to this and they were helpless to fight back. Rarely did a woman have any means of supporting herself. Losing their men to fight left an immediate financial void that was difficult, if not impossible, to overcome. Families did what they could to watch out for one another, and good men sent home money from their pay. But as the fighting dragged on and battlefront postal services became less available, the needs of those women and their children mounted.

Judith and her mother had gotten involved in helping as a means of healing from their own personal losses. There were multiple agencies striving to create assistance for the widows and orphans of war. Judith and her mother had also seen the need to help those whose husbands and fathers were still living, still fighting. They had created a charity to provide food and clothes for these families. Even after her mother died, Judith continued the good work, urging local churches to care for their own as a service unto God.

"I find that helping those less fortunate has done much to bless me." Judith's necklace seemed to tighten as the heat grew more unbearable. "Women are at a great disadvantage to earn their own living, even more so while taking care of a family. If we do not show compassion on them, I feel they will never be able to make their way to thriving, rather than merely surviving."

"You speak quite eloquently. We have some wonderful folks in Minneapolis but could certainly use someone with your beauty and grace to stir their hearts to action."

"We need women like Judith to stir the hearts of people everywhere, Dr. Turner." This came from an older woman Judith had known for many years. Harriet Silverman was a formidable fund raiser with all sorts of creative ideas for bettering the plight of the poor. "I am doing what I can to convince her to take on larger, more important roles in our various charities. She has impressed me with her attention to detail."

"You are too, kind." Judith smiled at the older woman. Mrs. Silverman had been working quite feverishly to entice her to join a committee overseeing housing for widows with children.

"Mrs. Silverman, I was encouraged by your speech. Thank you for inviting me. There is a definite need to better the living conditions of the poor. Getting the animals off the streets alone will greatly improve health conditions amongst the people," Dr. Turner said.

"I've said as much for years, Dr. Turner. And I will continue to advocate cleanliness. However, it is difficult to choose soap over soup when your child is hungry."

It was true. Hunger was a nagging need.

The older woman tapped Judith on the arm. "If you'll excuse me." Mrs. Silverman was distracted by a couple of wealthy looking men and left Judith and Roman to continue their conversation.

"You mentioned Minneapolis. Is that where you're from?" Judith asked, wishing the temperatures would abate.

"For the last few years, yes. Prior to that, my family was in Maryland."

"And the war sent you west?" She drew her fan and began to use it.

"Not at all. My father inherited property in Minnesota. I remained in Baltimore to finish my education and training, but before I could return to my family, the war broke out and doctors were very much needed in the army."

"I can well imagine. The numbers of wounded must have been difficult to deal with. My own husband was lost at Gettysburg."

"I'm sorry to hear that." His expression changed to one of concern. "I thought I heard it mentioned that you had lost your parents recently."

She continued to wave the fan. "Two years ago. My father owned a steamboat service on the river, transporting goods and people. They were on a trip, and the boiler blew up. Their cabin was just above, and they were killed instantly."

"Was it sabotage?"

"No. At least, those who investigated said there were no indications of such. My father had expressed concerns about the boiler days before the accident. He thought he'd dealt with the problem, but obviously he was mistaken." She reattached the fan's cord to a button on her waistband. The lacy piece hadn't helped cool her at all, and in fact, she thought it might be possible that waving it about had only served to make her hotter.

"Your losses have been great. My father also passed away during the war."

"In battle?" she asked.

He shook his head. "It's a long story, but he died in Minnesota." Dr. Turner glanced past her into the crowd behind them. "It was one of those senseless and unnecessary things."

"I'm so sorry." She couldn't help but notice something about his expression that suggested his grief was still strong, but she didn't feel the situation warranted the intimacy of her questioning him.

"I realize it's quite forward of me, but I wonder if you might consider having dinner with me tonight? Mrs. Silverman has known me for years and can vouch for my character."

The idea of attending supper with the dashing stranger enticed Judith. In normal circumstances, she would probably not even consider it. However, before she could answer, Mrs. Silverman put an end to any romantic notions.

"Judith! Judith!" Mrs. Silverman called.

Judith glanced up and noticed the woman motioning her to come. "If you'll excuse me, I believe I'm needed elsewhere. It was a pleasure to meet you, Dr. Turner."

"For me as well, and if you come to Minneapolis, please be certain to look me up."

She nodded and gave him a smile. "I'd like that."

Roman watched the young woman move through the throng of people. She was as graceful as a swan swimming among the reeds. He found himself mesmerized for a long while. She was beautiful, there was certainly no doubt about that. Her voluminous brown hair had been carefully pinned into place, held by ebony lacquered combs. Her gown, although trimmed in black, was not that of mourning. The dark green suited her complexion, and the lightweight material was sensible for an extremely warm day.

But there was something more to her—something that attracted him in a way he'd not felt before. Judith Stanford had a heart for the very things he did. She cared about those around her who were suffering and in need, and she put others first.

His mother and sister were always after him to find a wife and settle down, but until this moment, he'd never met a woman with whom he could imagine himself married. Judith Stanford, however, was easily a match for the bride he had imagined. She was soft-spoken, yet firm in her opinions and confident in doing the right thing. Just the fact that she was here spending her free time listening to lectures on helping the destitute spoke volumes about her character.

But even as he thought these things, Roman chided himself. He didn't really know anything about Judith Stanford. Certainly not enough to think favorably toward a lifetime together. No doubt it was just the heat.

Sweat trickled down the side of his neck. The temperatures were almost unbearable, and Roman felt he'd had more than enough of crowds and lectures. He made his way toward the back of the room where the exit doors would lead him outside into the hopefully night air. As he drew near to where Judith stood listening to Mrs. Silverman, he sensed there might be a problem. Judith seemed strangely silent, almost distracted.

As he came abreast of her and the others, Judith turned.

The look on her face was one he'd seen on the battlefield just before men lost consciousness. Reaching out, he caught her just as she fainted.

"Oh dear! Oh my!" Mrs. Silverman waved her gloved hands in exclamation. "What has happened!"

"I believe the heat has overcome the poor woman," one of the men declared.

Roman lifted Judith into his arms. "Let's get her outside. The open air will be better. Mrs. Silverman, please find us a way through the crowd."

Outside the air was cooler, but heavy with humidity. Roman stood holding Judith in his arms and wondering what he should do next.

"I believe there is a marble bench to the side, just over there." Mrs. Silverman pointed.

Roman caught sight of the bench and nodded. He crossed the portico and wondered whether to seat Judith on the bench or continue holding her. She was light enough he could have held her forever, or so he told himself, but propriety was important. He gently lowered her to bench and, while still holding on to her, grabbed the fan attached to her waistband. He didn't see how it was fastened and gave a hard yank. The button holding it danced across the stone floor.

Roman opened the fan while balancing Judith and began to use it quite vigorously. "If someone could get her a glass of water, that would help," he said, not even bothering to look up.

She started to rally as he continued to fan her face. When she opened her eyes and met his gaze, she smiled. For a moment, Roman was certain she had no idea of where she was. He smiled back.

Then at once, his nearness seemed to alarm her. She jerked

and sat up straight, pulling herself out of Roman's arms with surprising strength.

"Oh goodness. What happened?"

"You fainted, my dear," Mrs. Silverman announced. "The heat was positively abominable. Thank God for Dr. Turner. He just happened to be passing by and caught you as you fell."

Judith looked into Roman's eyes. For a moment, he lost the ability to reason. He had never met a woman who so completely captured his thoughts. He'd long prayed for a wife, but could it really be this easy? Could she be the one?

"Thank you for helping me, Dr. Turner." She reached over and took the fan.

"I'm afraid I pulled rather hard and send a button flying across the way." He motioned with his head but refused to look away from the glance that kept him spellbound.

She smiled. "It's of no concern, given the service you rendered me." She fanned herself a few times. "It's usually not so hot in the evening, but the room seemed quite confining."

"Yes, there were simply too many people in one small space," Mrs. Silverman agreed. "I will call for my carriage and see you safely home."

Roman thought to offer that himself but knew it would be inappropriate. However, accompanying them would be completely fitting.

"I could go with you," he offered.

"Nonsense. I have my driver and two footmen. We'll be just fine, Dr. Turner. Please return to the fund raiser. I know it was important for you to meet with several of our larger donors."

The wonder of the moment ended with that. He straightened and stood. "I hope you'll be feeling better soon, Mrs. Stanford."

"Again, thank you for your help." She drew in a deep breath. "I am much revived and quite myself again."

Roman smiled and gave a bow. He certainly wasn't exactly himself. The encounter had left him more than a little shaken. Something important had happened, but exactly what, he couldn't say.

Tracie Peterson is the award-winning author of over one hundred novels, both historical and contemporary. She has won the ACFW Lifetime Achievement Award and the Romantic Times Career Achievement Award. She is often referred to as the "Queen of Historical Christian Fiction," and her avid research resonates in her stories, as seen in her bestselling HEIRS OF MONTANA and ALASKAN QUEST series. Tracie considers her writing a ministry for God to share the Gospel and biblical application. She and her family make their home in Montana. Visit her website at TraciePeterson.com or on Facebook at Facebook.com/AuthorTraciePeterson.

Sign Up for Tracie's Newsletter

Keep up to date with Tracie's latest news on book releases and events by signing up for her email list at the link below.

TraciePeterson.com

FOLLOW TRACIE ON SOCIAL MEDIA

Tracie Peterson   @AuthorTraciePeterson

Be the first to hear about new books from Bethany House!

Stay up to date with our authors and books by signing up for our newsletters at

BethanyHouse.com/SignUp

FOLLOW US ON SOCIAL MEDIA

   @BethanyHouseFiction